Black Church Blues

Leander Jackie Grogan

Publishing Services Worldwide

First Edition

Copyright © 2011 by Leander Jackie Grogan

All rights reserved.

For information on permissions, email:
permissions@groganbooks.com.

Visit website at: www.groganbooks.com

Printed in the United States of America
Fourth Printing: February, 2012
ISBN-978-1-61364-034-0

BOOKS BY LEANDER JACKIE GROGAN

Orange FingerTips

Exorcism At Midnight

Baby, Put That Gun Down

Layoff Skullduggery: The Official Humor Guide

King Juba's Chest [Not yet released]

Black Church Blues

Help! The Bible Gobbled Up My Big Sister [Not yet released]

What's Wrong With Your Small Business Team? [Nonfiction Bestseller]

About the Author

Leander Jackie Grogan's excellence in writing extends over a multiplicity of genres. His six novels have been distributed in eleven countries and five different languages. His second short novel, *Exorcism At Midnight*, has become a leading seller with e-book distributors in the US and Canada. He has won numerous local and national awards in creative writing for radio, print and the web.

Besides having authored a number of nonfiction articles in such national magazines as AdWeek and Jet, and a business best-seller, *What's Wrong With Your Small Business Team?*, Grogan serves as a guest blogger for the national crime/suspense writer's website, Murder by 4, has written and produced three local spiritual comedies, and some years ago, had a work of fiction published in Hustler Magazine.

Grogan's favorite writer, and most preponderant upon his current style, is the late Sidney Sheldon. Specific works such as *Polar Shift* by Clive Cussler, *Dead Zone* by Stephen King, *Deep Cover* by Michael Tolkin and *The Rainmaker* by John Grisham have also had a great influence on his commitment to rich, multi-layered characterization and intricately crafted plots.

Dedication

This book is dedicated to my mother and father who first introduced me to Jesus Christ, Pastor Sylvester Duckens, Jr. who preached the sermon that saved my grown-up soul, Pastor Walter K. Berry, Sr. who shepherded my family and young children into maturity, Pastor Carlos Jones who taught me the true essence of the institution of the Church and Pastor J. Amos Jones who showed me what agape love was all about.

During this extraordinary four year journey to get the book to market, my original thought was to call the book Cover-up Christians. I had seen too much hypocrisy, too much restating of the truth to fit a distorted public image of Christians walking around in a state of bliss with hands stretched toward heaven. I felt the image was counter-productive to saving souls because when people came into the church and actually saw members with their masks removed, they felt deceived, even resentful that throughout the "holy" sanctuary, imperfection prevailed. I wanted to debunk the myth before unsuspecting recruits came through the doors, and explain to them why imperfection will be with us until Jesus comes back.

Black Church Blues accomplishes this goal and so much more. If there is one thing I can guarantee, it is once you've read this book, your perspective of the Church, and more profoundly, your journey through the Kingdom will never be the same.

TABLE OF CONTENTS

PROLOGUE

They were all standing around my hospital bed with reverent faces. Seven people in the room and not a mumbling word from any of them, not even the white-coated Indian doctor who lingered in the back, seemingly uncertain whether or not to intervene. A lone crocodile tear trickled down my daughter's high-boned cheek. My beloved Pastor shook his balding, gray head, as if denying an inevitable truth.

They were acting as though I were already dead. Sick, maybe, for quite a long time, from a stomach cancer more stubborn than any of the doctors had expected. But dead? No me. Not Kizzy Marie Sheppard Myles. Not like Mr. Myles or Aunt Twigg or Reverend Coleman or some of the other ethereal figures around my bedside, the figures that no one else seemed to notice. The plasticity of my mind stretched back to the last time I had read the obituary page. I didn't see my name listed in big bold print, which meant I had a few more waning hours on God's green earth to put my business to rest.

If I'd had my favorite walking cane, the one with the wood grain handle and metal tip, I would've popped somebody's thick noggin; the same way I did that crack head when he stole the ring off Buster's corpse. But I had already turned the cane over to the church deacons who had enshrined it in a glass case and hung it on the wall for future generations to see. They called it the miracle cane in reference to the events surrounding that June night back in 1993. They couldn't have picked a more fitting title. After all, it did save our lives.

That's why Mr. Bernstein had come all the way from New York City. A rabbi/historian and representative from the American-Israeli Cooperative Enterprise, he wanted to know the truth. Everybody he contacted had said, "Talk to Mama Kizzy. She was there. She can tell you the whole truth."

An old bearded white man with a steamy red face and bad heart, I wasn't sure he could handle the whole truth. I could tell him why silver coins kept mysteriously appearing next to the Shewbread when the church was a Jewish Synagogue; or the reason an eccentric oilman had built the old ghostly Silver Dollar Hotel directly across the street. But the miracles that happened during the hurricane or how we escaped the ball of liquid fire; I mean, reliving those tense moments might overload his feeble ticker. I didn't want the Jewish community coming after me for pushing the poor man into heaven before time.

He was sitting there, next to my bed, mum, like the rest of them, rocking his head back and forth. I finally asked, "Are you sure you're ready to hear the story? Can you really stomach this nerve-racking journey back in time?"

He didn't say anything. He just kept rocking. I took that to mean he could. If not, what better place to have a heart attack than at M D Anderson Hospital in Houston, Texas? With world renowned cardiovascular expert, Dr. Michael DeBakey, and all his little protégée heart surgeons, running around the Medical Center, surely someone in the bunch would pull him through.

And so, I pushed up on my pillow and steadied my emotions for one last run. I chronicled the events that had led to our fall from grace and how our lives had been torn asunder. I relived the desperate moments during the hurricane and how the miracles imprinted our souls forever.

I reached deep into the dormant cavities of my mind and brushed off the cobwebs of time. And then I said to him, "This is the whole truth."

Chapter One

*M*arch 21, 1993 was a day of three's. Bayboy confirmed it when he leaped up from his third row pew like a bee-stung Brahman bull, and stampeded down the middle aisle.

After teaching math and science for over 45 years, I had come to understand that each day had an identity; a numerical stamp that governed the events of that 24-hour period. Most people knew about the Wisconsin baby, born on the 5th floor at 5:55 am on 5/05/55 weighing 5 pounds, 5 ounces. But they didn't know how to translate the juicy scraps of data into a meaningful hypothesis. I did. Before I retired, I wrote a famous paper about it and then sent it out like a stick-in-the-throat capsule for the entire world to digest.

Of course, the closed-mined Neanderthals at the national trade magazines turned it down, forcing me to launch my own brand of pontification which I affectionately called the *Gray Matter Journal* to match the color of my hair. With the help of the Good Lord and my neighbor's defunct Heidelberg press, I published *The Scholium of Numeric Prediction.* Scholium is a big word I borrowed from Sir Isaac Newton who used it when people attacked his theory on universal gravitation. Sometimes we scientists do that, you know, borrow from each other. The privilege comes with the territory.

The next thing I knew, I had won the Galbraith Award for innovative thinking. They gave me a check for $10,000.

I was tickled pink to make a copy of that check and send it out to all those great guardians of scientific intellect throughout the nation, the ones that saw no value in my Scholium postulation. I told them this was a day of one's ... one last chance to kiss my old wrinkled, but now famous behind.

I know they didn't expect such a lewd invitation from a saved, sanctified, Holy Ghost-filled Christian woman like me. But we Christians do that sometimes, you know, get folks straight. The privilege comes with the territory.

After that, I shut my journal down quite abruptly, like they did the W. T. Grant Department Store downtown; never published another word. But when I tell you that third Sunday in March, 1993 was a day of three's, you're hearing it from the expert, Kizzy Marie Sheppard Myles, the wise old school teacher/scientist/innovator who wrote the book ... at least the journal. That day, three's were everywhere at First Reunion Baptist Church.

I could see it all from my wheelchair, perched high on a stand near the back of the sanctuary. In honor of our many years of service to the church, and as a tribute to my husband's untimely passing, the deacons had built that platform just for me; a nicely crafted trapezoid from sturdy oak, a green matted rubber floor with silver wheel docking locks and a light coat of varnish around the sides.

Each Sunday, two or three of the younger deacons, the strong-armed, well-dressed, Mandingo types, lifted me up those twelve steep concrete steps in front of our red brick cathedral and rolled me inside. My personal processional advanced like palace royalty beneath the old bell tower, pass the foyer's stain glass windows, through the dark mahogany doors, over the faded maroon carpet, to my little bird nest in the sky.

I told them to stop making such a fuss. After all, I was just sixty-seven years old. If I took my medicine and used my walking cane I could still manage a nifty step or two.

But they wouldn't sign on to my declaration of independence, not for a minute. Instead, they listened to Lizzy, my loud-mouthed, over-protective daughter who told them how I groaned at night when that old rheumatism flared up in both knees. I suppose, during those times, I was glad to have a wheelchair, a special platform and a daughter with a loud mouth. That Sunday in March was one of those times.

I sat there observing Thelma Mason, the church's perennial announcing clerk. Squinting through my fancy new seamless sliver-rimmed specs, I could see every detail of her powdered brown face and fleshy, dark rolls, bulging out of that familiar blue poke-dot dress. She leaned against the portable cherry wood podium, temporarily stationed on the floor in front of the choir stand, and began to read the weekly activities. Then, without warning, her whole body contorted. Her big moon eyes flooded with tears.

"For all of y'all who hadn't heard the news, my daughter, Martha Marie, gave birth to triplets this morning at 3:30 am."

As the whole church began to cheer, I tried to convince myself she was shedding tears of joy. But most of us knew how Martha Marie's husband had run around on her during her pregnancy. Rumor had it some Road Runner Inns gave him a discount for his weekly volume. I wondered if Thelma was really lamenting over the thought of Martha Marie and those babies coming home to her house.

Thelma already had problems trying to adjust to her new husband, Theo "Backwater" Mason. He liked to be called Backwater because of his long history with the Backwater Gospel Singers of Tennessee. Besides his great friendship with Jack Daniels, Backwater expected to be waited on hand-and-foot. He considered it her duty. After all, he was the one constantly wiring emergency funds to her during her frequent trips to the horse races in Louisiana. He was the one who bailed out her overdrawn NationsBank checking account each month.

After a rocky ten months of bickering, badgering and biting each other's heads off, all they needed was a triple dose of diapers and milk bottles to complicate the love nest. Maybe Thelma was up there in front of the church crying in advance, poor baby ... a little cry before the divorce papers arrived.

Following her announcements, the Pastor asked the visitors to stand. Three got up. I recognized one as that cocky, obnoxious black real estate developer, Horace Womack. I suppose, after avoiding so many close calls with the penitentiary, he had a right to be cocky.

I was surprised to see he had even given in to the constant hounding by his feeble mother to pry those shiny grill teeth out of his mouth. It was certainly an improvement. Nevertheless, with that lingering potbelly, thin goatee and razor eyes, he remained the epitome of sleaze.

The sixty-four thousand dollar question was: *Why was he at church in the first place?* He spent most of his Sunday mornings sleeping off a hangover on his big sixty foot lime green party boat down in Galveston Bay. I wondered. Had all of the Dowling Street hookers gone on vacation? Had an approaching hurricane closed down the Gulf?

"It's indeed a pleasure to be present in this great tabernackka', fellahshippin' with my brothers and suuusters." He announced it with a straight face. But in my gut, I knew there was nothing straight about his visit to First Reunion. He had something cooking; something the FBI or Crime Stoppers or Better Business Bureau would surely be interested in hearing.

At the end of services, three young college girls, all glitzed up in spiked heels and nightclub dresses, joined the church. But that happened after the sermon, after the big commotion, and after they broke up the fight.

The choir had just begun the third song of the morning: *I Am A Living Testimony*. That's when Bayboy jumped up from his pew and ran down the aisle, squealing like a pig.

I didn't know why they still called him Bayboy, short for baby boy, seeing he wasn't much of either. Sporting those shiny tight green pants and conked Barry White red hair, he was a prickly pear of sorts to the Williams family. We had seen the early symptoms, his wearing makeup and slipping around in his mama's dresses and playing with Chatty Kathy dolls. I tried to convince his mother and very close friend, Cora Williams, not to let him go to California. But she didn't listen.

Now he was back, packing that new HIV virus. Charging down the aisle toward the foyer like a runaway train, no one was going to get in his way.

In the Bible, the Holy Spirit directed the disciples in the way they should go. But Bayboy didn't get any direction. With eyes closed and arms, flailing, he slammed into the backside of the red brick wall. The whole church shook when he hit the floor.

For a while, three ushers stood over him, pondering what to do. They finally dragged him into the foyer, where Mildred, the head usher, a former army nurse, starting slapping him in the face.

Mildred was a big woman with gigantic hands to match. Even though the choir was singing, loudly, I could still hear the volley of licks, plastering Bayboy's puffy jaws. Despite the fact that he quickly came to his senses, Mildred continued to work him over. At some point Bayboy began to slap her back. That's when the fight broke out.

Deacon Grubbs, who, for some unknown reason, still wore a bushy 1960's Afro, stood up, then, whispered to another deacon,

"That punk is back there fighting!" I read his lips.

I dreaded the thought of *fighting* demons, slipping out of the belly of hell to invade our congregation. They were like the German Blitzkrieg of WWII. Once they slithered in and took over a church, it was hard to get them out.

It seemed Deacon Grubbs, who had been a former member of Old Pilgrim Rest when *fighting* demons split up the entire church, shared my consternation. He scurried to the back of the sanctuary and let down the blinds over the foyer windows. That's when Cora Williams got up, one finger high in the air, and tiptoed toward the back of the church. That one finger meant, *Excuse me, people, but I need to see what they're doing to my son.* Since her yellow straw hat had two long feathers growing out of the top, right next to her elevated finger, I counted her finger and the two feathers as another group of three's.

She walked with a quick strut, her yellow strapless heels, flapping against the back of her flat feet. The closer she got to the entryway, the faster her heels flapped. We all recognized the waves of motherly instinct, rippling through her strained face. Somebody was going to have to explain to her what was going on.

When she swung open the door to the foyer, everyone in the church saw what was going on. The ushers had called in the security guard from the parking lot and he was beating the tar out of Bayboy with a billy club.

Tiny John, an off-duty Houston police officer with broad shoulders and a thick neck that stretched his sky-blue, brown-patched uniform to the extreme, had been our church security guard for over two years. He seemed quiet and mild-mannered; often helped those deacons carry my wheelchair up the front steps. But on that Sunday, he looked like a man possessed. Los Angeles was his hometown. I wondered whether he was one of those officers who had stopped

Rodney King.

There's a word that describes people like him. I think it's ... homophobic. But Bayboy, we found out later, had brought the wrath of homophobia on himself when he tried to spit in Tiny John's face. One of the ushers had shouted, "He's got AIDS!" That's when Tiny John's stick began traveling at the speed of light.

It's not clear how Cora Williams collected the huge purple knot on the side of her head. Some say she fell. Others say she threw herself into the fray to protect her son. Still, others say Big Mildred used some kind of military maneuver to trip her up, sending her flying, headfirst, into the beating pile.

The ambulance finally hauled Cora and Bayboy away. Deacon Grubbs took a picture of the spit on Tiny John's uniform, just in case Bayboy tried to sue. Tiny John then headed to the hospital to get himself checked for open cuts and bruises. They all cleared out just before the Pastor got up to preach. By then, everybody in the church was desperate for some preaching. Even the chairs, lights and red brick wall cried out for a comforting word from on high.

Chapter Two

I was just a little nappy-headed farm girl down in Hattiesburg, Louisiana when I first learned how preaching is supposed to work.

After long hours of herding his old rickety tractor across endless rows of cotton and corn, my sun-baked father used to sit on the front steps of our four room shanty, discussing the issues of our time. Each day some neighbor, relative, or group of friends would navigate their way down the long, pothole-infested driveway, through the barb wired gate, past the iron graveyard of old pickups and tractor parts, between the twin vegetable gardens, over the chicken manure and cow dung and onto our little wooden porch to enjoy a cold glass of my mother's sweet lemonade. In the process, they soaked in the simplistic words of my father's wise commentary and marveled at his self-taught abilities to read, write and understand meanings between the lines.

Just behind them, peering through the tattered front window screen, lurked another group of soakers: Mattie, Estelle and me; three little fast-tail sisters, eager to gobble up as much grown folks business as our budding pea brains could absorb.

Mattie was the oldest, a thin, fragile carbon copy of my soft-spoken mother. Estelle was the youngest, a bow-legged diaper baby who held on to her milk bottle far beyond the appointed time. And then there was me: a stocky, tomboyish, smart-mouthed back-talker who got more whippings than anyone in the house. Together, we carried out our youthful espionage, listening with desperation and awe to every voice inflection, every outburst of laughter, every juicy addition to the local rumor mill, anticipating the moment when the watered down lemonade would be overrun by Jim Beam and Johnnie Walker Red.

With no television or video games or chat rooms, that ragged screen window was our training ground, our gateway to the world. We learned the essence of humanity, politics and religion. We saw life in its purest form, through the eyes of the underclass, the survivors of a society that harvested the seeds of prosperity far on the other side of the track.

In those days life was too hard, too weighted down with tribulations to live only in the here-and-now. Not able to vote or own much or have a say-so in the societal decisions that affected their lives, my father's generation needed the promise of the hereafter. That's how we learned about God. And that's how we learned the way preaching was supposed to work.

According to our window screen teachings, God was a Spirit that had separated himself into three different Spirits. There was God the Father, God the Son and God the Holy Ghost. It was the Holy Ghost who was supposed to tell the preacher what to preach.

As I grew older, however, I began to recognize a problem with the system. Some preachers had fallen out with the Holy Ghost and in with the Human Ghost. My father's only sister, Aunt Twigg, secretary for the National Black Baptist Convention, referred with great authority to all preachers as lying scoundrels. "How do you know when they're lying? When you see them moving their lips, that's how."

I suspected her opinion flowed out of a string of broken promises certain scoundrels had made to her during those annual conventions, away from their wife and kids. A New Orleans psychic had told her she was going to marry a preacher. I suppose that's why she kept on waiting for the right scoundrel to come along. He never did. Aunt Twigg died of Lupus ... a cynical old maid.

Still, that cynical old maid, with her sharp mind, long stalking legs and defiant arched face, meant a lot to me. In 1940, when our mother died of pneumonia, it was Aunt Twigg who convinced my father to let me come to Houston to live with my older sister, Mattie.

"The girl is fourteen and smart as a whip." I overheard her telling him during their session on the porch. "There's no need to let her waste away on this God-forsaken farm."

A week later she pulled up, loaded my cardboard suitcase into the trunk of her '38 Buick Slantback and drove me to Houston.

Though Mattie and her husband lived outside of the main school district, Aunt Twigg pulled strings to get me into Jack Yates High, at that time, the best black high school in the city. When I graduated from Yates with straight A's in math, she helped me land a scholarship at her Alma Mata, Southern University in Baton Rouge. In 1948, when I graduated from Southern with a double degree in math and science, she called the Deputy Director of Schools in Nashville who happened to have a friend in the Houston Independent School District. The next thing I knew, I had a contract to teach at Douglass Elementary in the prestigious heart of Third Ward.

Aunt Twigg was my mentor, advisor and second mother. She did things for me my real mother could never have done. But Aunt Twigg had her own distorted notions about the spiritual threads of life, many with which I did not agree.

Frankly, I never swallowed the notion that all preachers were scoundrels. In math, *all* is a hard statistic to achieve. So it is in life.

Not all white folks are racists. Not all black folks steal. And not all preachers are scoundrels. But some are. Some are scoundrels, indeed. That's where the preaching system breaks down.

I remember the Pastor of a church in a little town not far from Hattiesburg. His gospel stated that the congregation should buy him a new Cadillac each year. His reasoning was very simple. The members didn't expect to hear the same old sermons. He didn't expect to drive the same old car.

Another preacher from Fort Worth, Texas cut his early ties with the Holy Ghost in exchange for the opportunity to dazzle big crowds with his Hallelujah Road Show. Because of his running leaps across pulpit banisters throughout the South, he earned the name: The Fort Worth Flyer. He managed these circus-like maneuvers while holding the microphone with one hand and waving a white handkerchief with the other. Eventually, he'd work himself into such a hip-shaking, head-barbing frenzy, he'd fall out on the floor. That's when his deacons rushed in to revive him with smelling sauce.

It was the ultimate in showmanship, a wonderful distraction to hide his sketchy acquaintance with the Bible. During the early 1950's, when the boob tube boredom of Ozzie and Harriet drove Negro audiences to the brink of insanity, you had to pay good money to see a more electrifying performance than the Flyer. That meant going down to the Houston Coliseum and standing in line to buy tickets to see The Drifters or James Brown and the Famous Flames. Otherwise, the Fort Worth Flyer, with his deep growls, circus leaps and rhythmical babbling, was the best show in town.

I remember his last grand appearance in Houston in August of '53. He performed to a packed house at Antioch Baptist Church downtown. I went because they were honoring the historic legacy of John Henry Yates, the church's first pastor and former slave after whom my high school had been named. Mattie went because her truck-driver husband was on the road again. She didn't like staying home alone.

After the Flyers' electrifying performance, we were so worked up, we decided to stop by the Palladium Ballroom to do some dancing of our own. That was where I first encountered Mr. Myles, my handsome, broad-shouldered husband-to-be. I laughed and flirted and shook my fanny until the wee hours of the morning. Mattie and I didn't get home until 3:00 am.

It wasn't until the next day we learned the Flyer's small plane had crashed in a rice patty outside of Dallas. The black gospel stations were suddenly ablaze with farewell callers, lining up to mourn his greatness. What I remembered most about that day, however, was one pastor's stirring comments that flowed in a contrary direction from the sad mourner's parade.

He said to the radio host, "No one can see a man's heart. All we can go by is the quality of his deeds. Quality, according to the Bible, is based on how close we come to doing things God's way. Did the man we called the Fort Worth Flyer do things God's way? I suspect only God knows for sure."

"Who was that man that just called in?" I remembered asking Mattie.

She smiled, insightfully. "That was Pastor Coleman from First Reunion. Sounds a lot like Daddy, doesn't he?"

"Let's visit his church this Sunday."

And so we did. We visited the little white storefront, strip center location on Almeda Road for almost a month before we officially joined. That was the beginning of my lifelong affiliation with First Reunion Baptist Church.

In 1965, the church moved from its cramped quarters in the little strip center to a beautiful Jewish Synagogue just south of downtown. Nestled on a five acre lot near the rustling waters of Braes

Bayou and surrounded by a small grove of golden green weeping willows, the old red brick structure, with its gigantic bronze steeple, three-story bell tower and Tiffany green leaf stained glass windows, was an icon of ethno-religious innovation. It was an intriguing piece of the city's history, a safe haven for blacks during the riots, a Red Cross shelter during the floods, a spiritual cornerstone of Judaism that had withstood the test of time.

It even had an aura of mystery and intrigue surrounding its past. Stories persisted about unexplained noises coming from the basement and silver dollars that appeared out of thin air. Of course, these were all Jewish accounts. When we moved our small congregation into the legendary edifice, the silver dollar factory had apparently shut down its assembly lines.

It didn't matter. We were ecstatic just to move in. As Pastor Coleman had so eloquently stated, "God done orchestrated a deal in heaven that confounded all the property experts here on earth. All we need to do now is just praise his holy name ... and pay the note."

The last part didn't turn out to be as easy as we thought. Because the turbulent '60's had sent local Jews, fleeing to the suburbs, the First Reunion congregation had bought the Synagogue for a third of its value. Little did we know thirty years later we'd be facing the same suburban flight.

But God knew. That's why he had sent us Reverend Fordham. That's why, on that third Sunday in March, 1993, on that precarious day of three's, he was the man of God standing in the pulpit to rescue us from the big rope-a-dope, slap-a-conk, Rodney King melee-in-the-foyer. That's why our hearts opened up to a message untainted by the Human Ghost, a message we knew would be directed by the hand of God.

Chapter Three

Reverend James T. Fordham, young, tall, fair-skinned, with deep-set gray eyes and a likable baby smile, had come to First Reunion Baptist Church in the spring of '88. I remember because that was the year Reverend Jesse Jackson was running for President of the United States. It seemed that every time Reverend Jackson came to Houston, Pastor Fordham invited him over to speak. As far as I was concerned, religion and politics didn't mix.

But Pastor Fordham explained to us that they did mix.

He said, "There's no high place or low place, no crook or cranny, no organization or institution where God shouldn't be, including politics. And if we have a choice between two imperfect men, why not choose the man who is not ashamed of the gospel of Truth?"

Lord knows at that time Reverend Jackson was wearing the veil of imperfection. His organization was full of shysters. And family matters were in disarray. But Pastor Fordham had a point. I believe that was the beginning of my acceptance of his new, hands-on religion. Gradually, his simple, pragmatic convictions won us over.

What people outside of the church didn't understand was the difference in each church is really the difference in each pastor. Unless you're a Jehovah Witness, the Bible stays the same. Unless you're a mega-buck congregation, building multiple cash-cow locations all over the city, the building stays the same. But as each new pastor is installed by way of death, promotion, or scandal, the church changes in accordance with the idiosyncrasies of the new pastor.

Sometimes the changes are good; other times, not so good. But this is what the Bible means by free will. If you don't like the pastor and his new ideas, you are free to go somewhere else. If enough people go somewhere else, the pastor is left pushing his new ideas off on the empty pews.

It's not to say I didn't miss Pastor Coleman. From that first day I heard his stout voice over the radio just after the plane crash, I knew he was a good man. He had faithfully presided over the First Reunion congregation, nurturing and protecting us, baptizing our children and preaching the funerals of our love ones. But a constant diet of fried chicken and butter biscuits had sent the good Reverend's 380-pound frame home to Glory. After a yearlong search, the committee had chosen Pastor Fordham to take his place.

Pastor Fordham had proven to be just the man for the job. With the community in transition, many families were moving to the suburbs, just as the Jews had done decades earlier. Liquor stores, pawn shops and peep shows were springing up on every corner. Crime was up. Collections were down. Most of the deacon meetings in 1989 were dominated by a single question: Should First Reunion relocate or close down?

In another of his great sermons to the church, Pastor Fordham had answered that worrisome question with a soul-searching mandate from heaven. Here's what he said:

"There comes a time when you've done all that you can do. You've run the last mile and sung the last song and cried the last tear. At that point, if it were left up to me, I'd say that's enough. Hang

*up your harps on the willow trees and find some quiet bed of relief.
But what does God say? He says when you've done all that you can
do, then, stand. Don't cut and run. Don't abandon your post. Stand,
because the hour of impossibility is when God can do his best work.*

*"But, as members of First Reunion Baptist Church, we have
NOT done all that we can do. We haven't reached the point where we
simply stand.*

*"We see the decay in our community; the liquor stores and
nightclubs pushing in on us. But what have we done to stop them. We
see the homeless roaming the streets in front of the building. But what
have we done to give them shelter. We see the young boys selling
drugs on the corner. But have we approached them about getting
training for a real job?*

*"If you decide to leave, then I can't stop you. Church atten-
dance is voluntary. But as for me and my house, I'm going to stay
here and fight. I'm going to do all that I can do and then I'm going
to stand."*

He said that in 1990. But I remember it like it was yesterday.
That was the year First Reunion turned around.

By 1992, the church had re-energized. Community outreach
and evangelism were in high gear. Membership had doubled.
Prostitution and drug activity had diminished. And thanks to a legal
maneuver by J. "Grits" Macklin, our ambulance-chasing attorney,
most of the beer joints in the McGregor quadrant had lost their
licenses and been forced to shut down.

There was a shinning history behind the man who stood
before us on that Sunday of three's in 1993. If anyone could wipe
away the stain of embarrassment and incivility that Bayboy and his
supporting cast had brought on the congregation, Pastor Fordham
could.

Standing at the oversized glass podium, clutching the gold-plated angel wings that extended from both sides, he neither opened his Bible nor glanced at his prepared notes.

He began to talk about peace; not the peace that surpasses all understanding, but the peace that follows a treaty. Stretching out his long arms from beneath the sleeves of his glistening white coat, he said, *"We were all once enemies of God. We came out of the womb at war, not only with God, but with our own members. Our legs wanted to go left, but our feet went right. Our mind said no. But the lust of our heart said yes. That which we didn't want to do, we did anyway. Oh wretched creatures were we.*

"But by accepting Jesus Christ as our savior, we signed an everlasting peace treaty with the entire Godhead. We are no longer enemies. He has taken us into his kingdom and called us Sons and Daughters of the Most High God.

"So why do we continue to war against each other? Why do we continue to condemn one sin and justify another? Outwardly you appear righteous unto men, but inwardly, you are full of hypocrisy. It's because we are holding on to our old status as self-reliant, self-serving, narrowly focused creatures of instinct. We want what we want, no matter who it hurts.

"I'm admonishing you today to put away the old battering ram. Accept your newness in Christ. You'll look at your hands and your hands will look new. You'll look at your feet and they will too...."

Pastor Fordham began a rhythmic journey through the human anatomy. Pretty soon the choir was singing; the whole church, shouting and crying. I was fine until he got to the part about new knees. That's when I began to bellow like a country cow.

Old things....

He was right. We hold on to old things ... like Mr. Myles' lunch kit and gate pass. My husband, Jeremiah Luther Myles, my dancing prince from the early days at the Palladium Ballroom, had passed away seven years earlier: January 29, 1986. Nevertheless, I still kept his stuffed lunch kit on the top shelf of my bedroom closet.

And how could I forget my best friend, Charlotte Lueese Cooper, whose phone number was scotch-taped to my large oval dresser mirror? Though, she had gone missing during a hair stylist convention in Portland, Oregon back in '79, I still called that number a few times each year. Thirteen years of calling had forced the various owners to request a new number. Finally, after five different owners, the telephone company had retired it altogether. As far as I was concerned, that number belonged to the Charlotte Lueese. No one was going to take it away until ... well ... until we knew she didn't need it anymore.

The lunch kit reminded me of those twenty-four years I had gotten up at 4:30 am each morning to fix Mr. Myles a hot breakfast, then, lovingly stuff his little scratched up tin container with a double pork chop sandwich or meatloaf or a mess of greens and cornbread. He was the first black man to work inside the Monsanto Chemical Plant in Texas City, Texas. They knew he worked there. But they would never let him inside the gate without his pass. It was their way of reminding him he didn't belong.

They did other things, down-right nasty, degrading things, to make him feel less than a man. But he was a man, a good man. So, in order to remind him of that critical fact, I started calling him Mr. Myles. I figured they had him only eight hours a day; eight hours to get in their licks for Jim Crow. That gave me the rest of the time to soothe his unspoken anger and salvage his fragile self-esteem.

The process worked well until late at night, when I found myself smothered in his big strong arms. That's when I lost my focus and inadvertently mixed in "Mr." with a lot of other names. He never said it, but I suspected those names played as much a role in liberating him from Jim Crow as did the formal title of Mr. Myles.

Of course, Pastor Fordham wasn't just taking about lunch kits and phone numbers. He was talking about actions, like Big Mildred slapping poor Bayboy into a mild coma. I, too, was guilty of clinging to old methods. That day, I prayed the Lord would change my heart.

Following his sermon, just before the benediction, Pastor Fordham reminded us of the church's quarterly business meeting scheduled for 7:30 pm Wednesday night. I found it strange Pastor was proceeding with the meeting. Everyone knew a few days earlier, Buster Williams' big truck had run off a bridge near Oklahoma City. His wake was scheduled for Wednesday night at 7:00 pm.

Deacon Grubbs stood up with a confused expression. "Excuse me, Pastor. There may be a conflict with the Williams family wake."

Pastor Fordham covered his face with embarrassment. "Oh my God, that's right. That's right. To any family members present, I do apologize. Why don't we move it to 8:30 pm? Is that okay?"

Most members of the congregation shook their heads in agreement.

He continued, "We have some very important issues to address." And then he glanced at Deacon Poe.

Everybody knew Deacon Samuel A. Poe was Pastor Fordham's right-hand man. Mr. Myles had often referred to him as a "back-stab-bing, slick-headed devil who would sell you out at the drop of a hat". My husband's persistent warning made it all the more perplexing that Pastor Fordham would allow a devil to run the show.

Back in 1988, when the Moderator of our Association submitted Pastor Fordham's name as a candidate for Pastorship, Poe was the head deacon and most influential member of the search committee. He had the chance to sabotage the nomination and bring in his own money-hungry nephew from Washington DC. But to everyone's surprise, Poe supported Pastor Fordham. Perhaps, that was the reason Pastor kept him in charge.

Whatever the reason, Poe and his little band of cronies had veto power over every aspect of the church's business. Nothing came in or went out without their stamp of approval.

When the service was over, I watched Poe walk Horace Womack outside to his big white Escalade, illegally parked against the red brick sidewalk. As they passed my platform, Womack inquired, "Is everything in place?"

Poe flashed a sly grin. "It will be by Wednesday night."

I didn't hear the rest of their conversation. Before I knew it, the deacons were on me like a professional wrecking crew, unlocking my wheels and rolling me backward down the small incline, into a circle of smiling faces.

"How you doing Mama Kizzy? How's them knees holding up? Don't forget. You're coming home with us for Sunday dinner..."

The Glover family was always asking me to have dinner with them. Although the barbecue ribs and crawfish etouffee were usually too spicy for my old stomach, going through endless stacks of pictures of their little chimpanzee baby was even harder to endure.

I suspected they showered me with the proud photos because I paid the hospital bill when the little darling was born. They needed help, so I helped them. Didn't know I was signing on to a partnership for life.

The Williams family always came over to the platform to see me. Even though Cora had left with Bayboy in the ambulance, her two teenage daughters gave me a big hug.

"Take a look at my report card," said the older one with the pony tail. The younger one handed me her track medal. They knew I'd slip them $10 or so when no one was looking.

Katherine Baker and her family of seven sat a handsome wooden box in my lap. "We brought you something special back from the Holy Land."

I opened it to find some Jewish beads, a fancy Bible and a bottle of holy water, according to the label, taken from a secret well where Jesus once drank. I couldn't help wondering what would happen if I splashed the light purplish liquid on Deacon Poe's bald head. Maybe he would find true religion, or better still, go up in a puff of smoke like honorable vampires were supposed to do.

With over thirty-five hundred members on the books, it was hard for me to match all of the names with the faces; not to say all thirty-five hundred had time for me. But those who didn't take up time with me, took it up with somebody else. Families all over the building laughed and hugged and exchanged words of encouragement. Children ran down the aisle with parents chasing behind them. Deacons huddled in a corner, passing out assignments. Choir members hummed a few broken tunes, polishing up for the services to come.

This was our Sunday tradition, our own brand of church held high on a hill, steeped in the sunlight. Had I looked toward the horizon, maybe I would've noticed the dark clouds moving in.

But I didn't notice. Nobody did ... not until it was too late.

Chapter Four

At 6:50 pm that following Wednesday night, about fifty friends and family members had assembled inside the church sanctuary. They had come to pay their last respects to Buster Williams, whose big silver Peterbilt eighteen-wheeler had plunged over a bridge, into a deep ravine just outside of Oklahoma City. Although details were still sketchy, the people from the Highway Patrol suspected he had fallen asleep behind the wheel. Whatever the cause, Buster had left his mangled body behind, releasing his spirit to be with the Lord.

Unfortunately, Buster had left something else behind as well ... debt; lots of it. Although he had made good money as a truck driver, he had made bad choices as an investor. He had fallen victim to countless land deals, franchise startups and get-rich-quick pyramid schemes. The $30,000 he squandered at the Las Vegas blackjack tables in '82 had finally sent his wife, Mary Bell, and kids packing. Their departure only spurred him on, prompting more fool-hearted investments with the same disastrous results. By the time he died in March of '93, he had no money set aside for his own funeral.

Because of Cora Williams' years of dedication to First Reunion, I felt the church should pay for her brother's funeral. But

Poe and the other deacons refused. After several phone calls, ruffling the feathers of everyone on the finance committee, they finally revealed that Buster had borrowed $12,000 from the church and never paid it back. As far as they were concerned, the unpaid loan was his funeral money. That was as far as they were willing to go.

I gave my friend, Cora, a check for $1000. Some of the other members pitched in too. I had planned to give more until I found out who was handling the funeral arrangements. If they were going to use old man Reedy, then they were on their own.

Reedy & Sons Mortuary was the sleaziest funeral parlor in town. Located in the heart of the notorious Fifth Ward, just north of downtown, Clarence Reedy had built his thirty-year-old business by providing cheap funerals for the poor, ignorant and unclaimed. Poor people were desperate and needed a good price. Ignorant people never bothered to read the fine print in the contract which allowed him to bury bodies on top of other bodies. Unclaimed people, such as murdered dope dealers and prostitutes, posed a problem for the City of Houston's international, oil-rich image and were expediently buried using City funds. Reedy always gave a hefty contribution to the local politicians. Thus, Reedy & Sons was the City's undertaker of choice.

Though Clarence Reedy had gotten too old to manage the daily operations, his jailbird son had stepped in to keep the business afloat. Lurking beneath his polished white smile and pink tinted lenses was a new generation of cunning. Rumor had it young Joe Reedy's latest endeavor involved selling watered down embalming fluid over some kind of wire hookup called the World Wide Web. He held back the pure stuff to sell to neighborhood amp-heads who smoked it along with their marijuana treats.

I often wondered why old Clarence had changed the name from Reedy to Reedy & Sons. Mr. Myles had finally explained that old man Reedy had a bastard child in Mississippi whom he hoped would one day join him and the younger boy in the business. Of course, that never happened. The elder son owned a small fleet of ice cream trucks in Biloxi and wanted nothing to do with either the old man or the dead.

That night, riding a plume of thick, white smoke, Reedy's beat-up black Cadillac hearse sputtered up to the front of the church, forty minutes late. An empty gray limo followed closely behind. The limo was supposed to carry family members. But none of the Williams were willing to take a chance.

Reedy's home pickups were infamously legendary: Too many breakdowns on the highway; too many sweat-box limos with no air conditioning; too many occasions when the family ended up at the wrong gravesite; and too many doped-up drivers that never showed up at all.

The Williams family was afraid to depend on Reedy. Instead, they rented two white passenger vans so everyone would get there on time.

Inside the church, familiar faces began to fill up the pews. The Hendersons were there, wearing their matching neck braces from an accident with a City of Houston METRO bus. They tried to look sad for the occasion, but couldn't stop smiling, knowing their big settlement was on the way. The Crumps were also in attendance, obese, sunburned, and all hugged-up together. After a reconciliation trip to Honolulu, they wanted everyone to know their marriage was off the rocks and back on the "lovey-dovey" train. The Bakers were there too. I waved from my bird nest to let them know how much I appreciated my Jerusalem trinkets. I had the holy water in my purse right then and there, just in case I got a clear shot at Deacon Poe's bald head.

Most noticeable among the distinguished, well-dressed

attendees were Josh and Sally Howard, the elitist of the elite crowd. They sat stiff-necked in the middle of the pew, away from everyone else. Josh took out a small brush and began to stroke his thick mustache, while Sally repositioned the large white straw hat on her prim head. Josh had oil property in Beaumont, home of the great Spindletop fields a few hundred miles away. Sally had once been a runner-up beauty queen at Texas Southern University. I didn't know why she was so proud of her title. One of my former students told me she had earned her votes the hard way, going through half of TSU's football team in the process.

The only reason the Howards had come out was to soothe their consciences after convincing Buster to invest in a lumber deal that had gone belly up. I suspected if Buster could've come back to haunt somebody, the Howards would've been at the top of his list.

I was glad to see Frogman rush into the sanctuary to sit directly behind them. Even more amusing was the double meat cheeseburger he intermittently gobbled on whenever he thought no one was looking.

Everyone knew Frogman. A thirty year old sack of bones with matted black hair, a sunken face and yellowish pumpkin smile, he was ... well ... not all there. He'd go from humming a song to whispering a chant to holding a full conversation with himself. Between his morning job at Schepps Milk Dairy and his night job at Prince's Hamburger Stand, Frogman, in his faded blue jeans and white tennis shoes, might walk fifteen miles to the north side of town just to see his equally challenged young sister, and eccentric aunt and uncle who cared for her.

Originally from the backwoods of Arkansas, some people speculated his family was guilty of inbreeding. But it was only speculation; people throwing out hypotheses without the slightest body of evidence to back up their claims.

Christians did it all the time.

You'd say, "My house burned down."

They'd say, "The Lord is testing you to see if you'll stay faithful to him when all your possessions are taken away."

You're thinking:

No, what really happened was, against my better judgment, I took in my troubled nephew who didn't have a place to stay. While I was gone, he had a Richard Pryor moment, started freebasing that cocaine, turned over that pipe stand contraption and set the whole house on fire.

You'd say, "I prayed to the Lord that my husband and I would grow old together. But I just got a call that he had a massive heart attack and died."

They'd say, "His time was up. He had finished his course and the Lord called him home to his reward."

No, what really happened was he was just like Pastor Coleman ... overweight and couldn't stay away from that fried chicken and butter biscuits. And for the record, he still had plenty to do.

Christians had a way of filling in the blanks and explaining away all of the unknowns using tidy little spiritual algorithms that found broad acceptance over time. If you were a Christian, you could publicly proclaim, "It's easy if the Lord is in it", knowing that every day was a knockdown, drag-out struggle, or "I've never seen the righteous begging for bread", knowing you just left the soup line headed for the food stamp office. Some well-intentioned prognosticators sought to offer comfort and sanity in an insane world. Others sought to elevate themselves as spiritual gurus who knew what God was thinking based on the oversized Bible they carried under their arm.

Whatever their motivation, everyone had a hypothesis. When it came to Frogman, the smart money was on branches of incest springing forth from his family tree.

Still, nobody bothered the Frogman. He was part of the First Reunion family. Even when one of the deacons spotted his mouth-watering indiscretion, he took his time getting there, allowing Frogman a chance to finish his greasy feast. He was a harmless, demented soul, placed under our watchful care. At that moment, he was also Josh and Sally Howard's loud-smacking, onion-breathe tormenter from hell.

Outside of the sanctuary, the old hearse trembled, backfired, and then clunked into silence. A young pudgy, flee-footed Joe Reedy jumped out in his typical panic-stricken mode. He and his crack head helpers unloaded the big, bronze casket and staggered up the steps.

"Peaches! Come on, stop draggin'!" He shouted to his broken down strip club dancer/funeral coordinator who turtled up the steps carrying two bouquets of withered yellow lilies. As she made her slow ascent, clumps of dead pebbles rained on her tight blue skirt and matching platform heels. Passing her up with a long, steady stride was the black-suited, ex-University of Houston basketball player they called GeeNet.

Larry "GeeNet" Willis was everyone's favorite all-American until his sophomore year when he missed two free throws at the end of the games during the Final Four playoffs in New Orleans. That's when depression set in and his little dope habit turned into a hungry monster that not even the deep-pocketed university boosters could feed. Now, there he was with all his talent, lugging around a big blue and white sign for the sleaze balls of the earth. It read:

REEDY & SONS MORTUARY CARES FOR YOU.

In a way it was appropriate for him to carry around a big printed lie. It went along with all of the invisible lies he carried in his heart; lies that people had told him all of his life: *"Don't sweat the grades, just keep filling up the net; Don't worry, this stuff is not addictive;*

Them coaches ain't crazy; They know you the man; They know they can't go nowhere without you."

It took young Reedy's operation to help him capture the true essence of his worth. He was GeeNet, a drug-addicted flunky who hauled around "dead people" signs to keep himself high.

GeeNet and Peaches made their way into the sanctuary to finish setting up. Young Reedy and crew slammed the big casket onto a silver pallbearer's carriage and rolled into the foyer.

"Who's in charge here?" Young Reedy demanded.

Deacon Grubbs walked over, scratching his wooly head. "Y'all running kinda late, aren't you?"

"Not our fault. The family gave some bad directions," complained young Reedy.

Overhearing his contemptuous reply, Mildred, the head usher, lumbered over to them. With one fist noticeably clenched, and her bulky arms, pressing out the seams of her standard navy blue usher's uniform, she grimaced. "Look, that's no excuse to keep these people waiting like this. Everybody in town knows how to find First Reunion Baptist Church."

Young Reedy eyeballed her thick frame and angry brow. He finally broke into a chest cat grin. "You right, Ma'am. You'd be surprised, though, how many churches we go to with a similar name. There's First Baptist, New Reunion, First Union, and Union Baptist, all in this area. Sometimes we get mixed up."

"That's understandable," she relented, seemingly charmed by his attentive smile. "You will apologize to the family?"

"I will, Ma'am. I'll do it right after the service."

As she walked away, one of the crack heads leaned over and whispered in his ear. "Damn, boss man! Who's the muscle?"

Young Reedy chuckled. "Make sure we pay our due respect

after this thing is over so that Cyclops don't gobble us alive."

Deacon Grubbs glanced at his watch, then, interrupted their whispering voices. "Are you ready?"

Young Reedy peeped into the sanctuary through the stained glass window. As soon as Peaches gave him the nod, he turned to Deacon Grubbs. "We're ready."

Deacon Grubbs waved at Anita, the bright-faced, frizzy haired church organist who sat high in the back of the choir stand clutching the white keys of our old but prestigious Hammond double-decker pipe organ. One final thin finger pushed against her black cat-eyed glasses, and the processional music began.

"None but the righteous...." Anita bellowed in a shrill, country voice. The whole church joined in. *"None but the righteous. None but the righteous shall see God."*

The doors swung open. Like soldiers returning from a hard-fought battle, young Reedy and his somber-faced crew marched, gingerly, down the aisle. There were two crack heads in the front; two in the back. Young Reedy stayed in the middle, his hand draped over the casket, dropping white flower peddles as it rolled.

Cora Williams' dark, owl face shriveled with sorrow as she and some of her East Texas cousins began to cry. Cora's oldest daughter, the tall one with the pony tail and good grades, bolted from the sanctuary and into the foyer, a large white handkerchief over her face. "Uncle Buster!!!"

Two ushers followed in hot pursue.

Despite the singing and crying and running, I heard something very odd. It was a faint screeching sound, barely discernible at first. But as the casket rolled a bit closer, the sound grew louder and more distinctive. It reminded me of crickets on a summer night in my home town of Hattiesburg. Except crickets never squealed that loudly.

And then I realized it was the carriage. One of the front

wheels on the pallbearer's carriage was wobbling and squealing and pleading for relief.

The oversized casket was designed for a heavy duty, steel carriage with six pneumatic wheels. Reedy's little four-wheeler was made of some kind of brass tubing with no secondary support. Even an old retired school teacher/scientist like me with a minimal knowledge of synergistic integration and stress points realized this big casket didn't go with the little baby cart.

As the procession reached the row next to Josh and Sally Howard, the screeching wheel popped off. The front of the casket dipped, and then slammed into the floor. The top half of the casket door flew open and Buster's decapitated burnt arm skidded across the carpet.

No one had given us the details surrounding the accident. It was only later we learned the construction pipes Buster had been hauling shifted forward into the cab, severing his arms and head. A small fire had also erupted, charcoaling Buster's body beyond recognition.

The half-cooked, orange and black skin, bloated fingers and protruding shoulder bone was more than Frogman could take. He stood up and unloaded every onion, pickle, tomato and chunk of ground meat in his belly onto the top of Sally's new white hat.

As the multi-colored slime ran down her neck and into the back of her white cotton dress, she began to scream. At least, I think she screamed. There were so many family members scrambling, fainting and bellowing, it was hard to distinguish Sally's scream from everyone else's.

In science, we measure sound by decibels. But that night I found myself measuring it by Mary Bells. Mary Bell Williams, Buster's ex-wife, not only screamed louder than anyone else, but leaped from her prime spot on the front pew next to Cora, ran down the aisle and stood over the arm. With unbridled scorn, she pointed at the ring on

Buster's burnt fingers. "You thieving bastard! You stole daddy's ring!"

She shouted at the lone body part as though it understood. And since Buster was much too dead to defend himself, we presumed she was telling the truth.

Mary Bell's father's diamond ring had been missing since she left Buster in '82. It was a three generation heirloom of sorts, a secret gift from First Lady Eleanor Roosevelt to members of the black Tuskegee Airmen squadron. Buster, we found out later, had pawned the ring for some emergency cash, then, retrieved it with winnings from the Florida dog races. Bitter and embarrassed by the divorce, however, he had never given it back. Buster felt abandoned by his family and used that as justification to keep the ring for himself. At least, that was my official spiritual algorithm.

Mary Bell looked at young Reedy with a nonverbal plea, hoping he would pry the ring off Buster's barbecued hand. I, however, looked at him with a jaundiced eye of condemnation, knowing he hadn't made the slightest attempt to embalm the body. Otherwise, the ring would have already been re-stolen from Buster ... Reedy style."

Sadly, Young Reedy didn't have time to look back at either of us. He was too busy planning his own funeral as Big Mildred headed his way. He had already disrespected the family's wishes to start on time. Now, he had violated their request to keep the casket closed.

Ironically, Mildred walked right past young Reedy and over to Josh and Sally Howard's row. With all the commotion I had missed Sally's mean-spirited act of retaliation. She had turned around and hit the Frogman in the mouth.

As Frogman hid beneath the pew, whimpering, chanting and nursing his lip, Mildred stepped over and nailed Sally with a tremendous backhand Knuckle-Knocker. I had seen it on television. Gorgeous George and Terry Funk had used it almost every Friday night on Paul Boesch's wrestle hour. But I had never seen it in person and never by a woman.

Sally's thick coat of Cover Girl makeup was expensive and of the highest quality. But it was never designed to buffer a lick like that. Sally slithered through the puddle of reddish green vomit, across the pew and onto the floor. When Josh tried to come to Sally's rescue, Mildred slammed her elbow into his nose, sending him in the same direction as his wife. In a split second, Frogman, Sally and Josh were all hiding under the same pew.

Mildred turned toward young Reedy, but it was too late. The corn-fed, county girl pump-and-stump East Texas cousins had already mounted a vigorous assault. Using high heel shoes, metal walkers and pistol-heavy purses the size of roaster pans, the angry battalion began pounding young Reedy's brains out. Their high flying hand bags scattered an awkward array of cash, bracelets, earrings, cigarettes pocketknives, tampons, and lottery tickets across the carpet. But no one seemed to care.

Mary Bell grabbed some tissue, took a deep breath and jerked the ring off of Buster's middle finger. As she examined it, however, two panic-stricken crack heads barreled into her, knocking both her and the ring to the floor. The taller man with the beard stopped, picked up the ring and scamper toward the exit. That's when I got into the fray.

I grabbed my sturdy, wood grain walking cane. As they ran past my platform, I took a Jackie Robinson swing. The bearded one, clutching the ring, ducked. But the other big-eared, bat-faced one, I christened in the name of Jesus.

He fell to the floor holding his mouth, a bloody tooth perturbing between his scrawny, black fingers. But like some kind of juiced-up zombie, he jumped right back up and scrambled for the foyer. Milliseconds later, I heard the old hearse cranking up.

At that moment, the side door next to the choir stand, leading to the Pastor's Study area, swung open. Pastor Fordham led a procession of smartly dressed associate ministers and deacons down the wooden steps and into the sanctuary. Anita, seemingly spellbound by the overturned casket, had never stopped playing the organ. It appeared the music had become her refuse from the horror of Buster's body parts all over the floor.

When Pastor Fordham observed the church-wide brawl in progress, he froze in his tracks. I thought about Moses, coming down from the mountain, finding the Israelites drinking and partying. But this was no party. The *fighting* demons had come out of the walls and gotten into the cousins from East Texas. They had transformed into *Children of the Corn* look-a likes, beating the tar out of young Reedy and his crew.

Pastor Fordham shouted, "People! No! No! Not in the house of the Lord! I'm begging you, stop this! Stop this right now!"

There was something about his voice. Whether preaching or praying or just talking, it had a calming effect. Aunt Twigg use to say it was the mark of the Holy Ghost when the sound of the shepherd's voice ushered in peace and tranquility.

In all fairness, the Human Ghost had made its mark too ... big red ones, up and down the side of young Reedy's face.

The East Texas cousins finally released the young carpet-crawler. GeeNet grabbed him by the arm and staggered toward the door.

Young Reedy glanced behind him with a disoriented squint. "My glasses!"

But a wild-eyed blue blur of bicycling heels, formerly known as Peaches, had no mind to accommodate his request. Somebody had already stumped out the lenses and bent up the frames, leaving a trail of pink glass chips strewed across the carpet.

Observing their frantic departure from my bird nest in the sky, it appeared they were on a slope in Colorado, skiing down the front steps. With the hearse long gone, they jumped into the remaining limo and sped away.

Inside, Pastor Fordham took stock of the damage. He called everyone up to the altar to pray. Ububee, my shiny-faced Nigerian son-in-law, removed me from my bird nest and rolled me to the front.

I had never seen the Pastor weep so intensely. It wasn't long before everyone was immersed in a shameful lake of tears. Well, almost everyone. Horace Womack, the sleazy real estate developer, stood in a corner clutching a bunch of blueprints and drawings. That's when I suddenly remembered the church's business meeting, scheduled for later that night.

Pastor Fordham grabbed the microphone. "I need to make an announcement."

But we could barely hear him. Anita was still pounding away at the organ.

Deacon Grubbs made his way into the choir stand and gently removed her spellbound fingers from the keyboard. Slowly, she began to sob, her head buried in his chest.

Pastor Fordham waited a while, then continued, "We're going to reschedule the business meeting for next week. Hopefully then, we'll all be in a better frame of mind. Amen?"

Most of the congregation responded in agreement. Horace Womack, however, dropped his head with disgust.

After posting a cancellation sign in the foyer, Deacon Poe called one of his contacts in the funeral business. Shortly, thereafter, an ambulance arrived to take the body away.

Poe walked over and put his arm around Cora. "Don't worry. You can still have the funeral tomorrow. We'll take care of everything."

I thought to myself, *What a kind gesture. But isn't that what*

I'd been asking for all along?

Suddenly, it was his idea to come to her rescue, and his moment to play the hero. He knew how to play the hero. He played it well.

As Poe stood in the middle of the family, basking in his superficial glory, I could hear Mr. Myles' voice: *Poe is a back-stabbing, slick-headed devil who would sell you out at the drop of a hat.* Now, he had teamed up an even bigger devil to sell the church some bill of goods. I had seen the blueprints and charts only from a distance. But I already knew the whole thing was wrong.

That night, the Lord had used Buster's deep fried arm to shield us from evil. But who would he use next week when Buster was in the ground?

At that moment, as I sat a few feet from the altar, someone touched me on the shoulder. It was a warm, gentle touch.

I whirled around in my wheelchair, but no one was there. Frogman slouched on the front pew closest to me, dabbing Vaseline on his bruised lip.

"Did you see who touched me?" I asked.

He nodded, affirmatively.

"Who was it?"

Frogman continued to stroke his mouth with the gauze and jelly.

Thinking one of my many mischievous play children had run off to hide, I reassured him, "It's okay. You won't get anyone in trouble, I promise. Just tell Mama Kizzy who it was."

Glaring through those dark, innocent eyes, he grinned, coyly. "It was the Spirit of God."

Chapter Five

Friday morning after Buster's funeral, I sat in my favorite lavender upholstered wing chair, listening to my daughter, Lizzy, run her big mouth. She couldn't wait to tell my younger sister, Estelle, about the Wednesday night melee and how Big Mildred had introduced the Howards to the far-reaching hand of God.

Every subject was fair game at the Sew-and-Grow ministry meeting she hosted each Friday morning. With knitting looms twirling and Singer sewing machines humming, a small group of women prognosticators passed judgment on every critical issue that plagued the universe, from the utter uselessness of men to the indispensable nature of women, and everything in between.

I didn't sew; didn't really want to be there. My cozy little three bedroom wood frame home with its stately blue awnings, immaculate green lawn and white picket fence was more than enough company for me. But since I spent most weekends at my daughter's house, she made it a point to pick me up early so I could be a part of their highly opinionated women-only rejuvenation/rectification and occasional sewing sessions. In my opinion, the only thing we were rectifying was the source of the gossip as it moved from one side of the church to the other. But back then, that's what sewing, baking, knitting, crafting and garden clubs did. The privilege came with the territory.

Lizzy's two-story white brick Perry home with its marble fireplace, custom hardwood floors and interior glass garden sewing room, was a fancy step up from the group's original meeting place in that dusty storage closet in the back of the church. It was no secret First Reunion needed more classrooms, not to mention the cantankerous, old air-conditioning system, rotten interior wood panels and leaky ceiling pipes. Mr. Myles had informed me several of those ceiling pipes transported natural gas to the boiler room. During his stint on the Deacon Board, he had insisted on regular maintenance and inspections to avoid any danger to the congregation.

Deacon Poe claimed the same vigilance in matters of upkeep and repair. But we all knew better.

Poe and his tightwad henchmen held on to the church's money like survivors of the Great Depression. For them, it was all about the cushion in the bank, the bottom line figures that served as indisputable proof of God's favor. Now that First Reunion was back on its feet, they were determined not to let the need for improvements push them into another scary episode of walking by faith.

I was proud to see the meeting move to Lizzy's home in the exclusive new Palm Center Edition of Southeast Houston. The huge 12 x 12 sewing room with its sun-baked vaulted ceiling, glass interior and hanging ivory plants was more than just a meeting place for the sewing chatterboxes of the earth. It was a symbol of progress, a ray of hope for a new generation looking for a better life. That one room was almost as large as the efficiency apartment into which Mr. Miles and I had moved during the early years of our marriage. The sewing room said that we, as a people, were going somewhere. And we didn't have to wait on a government handout to get there.

Ububee was a draftsman who made a good living drawing triangles and squares. Lizzy worked part-time as a hospital billing and coding administrator, only because she wanted to keep busy and only because they agreed to give her Fridays off.

I often wondered why she had gone to school to become a nurse, but didn't do any nursing. She always answered the same way. "I'm your nurse, Mama. That's enough for me."

If she and Ububee were happy with the arrangement, I had no right to complain ... although I will admit it had taken me a while to reach such a complicit state of mind. Frankly, I didn't know why my daughter had married that African in the first place, or whether he was holding her back from her true profession to keep her under control. He seemed sneaky to me; always flashing a wide grin and constantly batting those big white eyes. I suspected he was grinning about all that money his family had stolen when they fled their heathen country. But that's another story.

That Friday morning five of us had gathered in the sewing room, mouths racing, and tongues, lapping in some kind of exotic milk coffee. One of the ladies had brought samples back from California. According to the west coast experts, this mocha cappuccino stuff was going to be the wave of the future. That's what they said.

To me, it was nothing more than warmed up ice cream. Who in their right mind wanted their ice cream warm? And who was going to pay that much to warm it?

"What do you think of the latte, Mama Kizzy?" Olivia Boudreaux, the mistress of a prominent city councilman, wanted to know.

I took a few polite sips. "So, so."

"Drink it slowly, Mama, if you want the full flavor. Let the foam melt in your mouth," Lizzy instructed.

I managed a few more swallows.

"Now, what do you think?"

I could feel the little soldiers marching in my stomach. I set the cup and saucer down on the red oak coffee table next to my fashionable wing chair. "I think all this yarn and material in the middle of the floor needs to be picked up soon and very soon."

Lizzy appeared puzzled. "Why?"

"Because I don't want anything in my way as I reacquaint myself with that hallway toilet."

They all started laughing. They were still laughing when I returned from the bathroom. It seemed to be a morning of laughter, especially when Lizzy offered her detailed account of young Reedy's frantic departure from the church premises.

After hearing the whole story, Estelle shook her head with disgust. "It's a shame and a disgrace. Y'all inside the holy tabernacle of God, fighting like heathens."

I gazed at her little round face and sleepy eyes, and for a moment, considered her tendency to criticize any church that wasn't of the "Holiness" persuasion. No other denomination met her strict ethical standards, especially the notorious, backsliding Baptists. The small truth she seemed to have conveniently overlooked was that her pure-in-heart Holiness bunch had done some backsliding of their own.

And so I pondered aloud. "You know I'm old and forgetful. But if my memory serves me correctly, the Sheriff's Department was just over to Greater Pilgrim Holiness Tabernacle a few months ago, loading members of your most illustrious congregation into the back of a patty wagon."

"It's not the same," she argued. "Those saints were defending our sacred church grounds. They never should've been arrested."

Katherine Baker, plump mother of five, whose family had brought back the holy water and set up my impending purification of Deacon Poe, looked up from her new black and silver Quantum

Quilter. "I think we were on our way to Israel then. I never got the full story."

The whole mess had started back in February when Estelle's lunatic Pastor, Bishop Ebenezer, dragged two giant speakers out on the church's front porch and began piping loud praise music and sermonettes into the surrounding neighborhood. This was his Sunday morning revelry designed to arouse the hungover sinners who failed to honor God's official day of worship.

"These here people are sleeping in on God's day. They need to rise and shine and give God the glory," he had declared to his guileless followers.

As seriously as he had taken his neighborhood wake-up calls, the Jamaicans in the apartments across the street cherished their hung-over drowsing with equal voracity. One week they warned him. The next week they came across the street with a semi-automatic and shot up the speakers.

Most sane people, spiritual or otherwise, would've run for cover. Instead, several hardcore Holiness fanatics rushed out of the church and threw themselves over the speakers, trying to protect the airborne Word of God. Meanwhile, a group of Elders, inspecting a hole in the cyclone fence that surrounded the church, ran up behind the Jamaicans and began to evangelize them with shovels and fence posts diggers. The Sheriff's Department eventually loaded the brawlers into two patty wagons and took them to jail.

"Fighting is fighting," I reminded Estelle, with no expectation she would agree. The only one who could convince her that birds flew south or the sun set in the west was Bishop Ebenezer. Her infatuation with him was the very reason her first husband had run off to Florida with another woman; a woman who, at least, pretended to listen to what he had to say without asking for Bishop Ebenezer's stamp of approval.

Still, she insisted, "They were fighting for Jehovah, praise God. You Baptists wouldn't understand that kind of dedication."

"Hey, Auntee Stell. Maybe Mama can get a better understanding about it when we come to visit your church this Sunday." Lizzy's voice carried a hint of sarcasm.

I pondered for a moment, not having a clue. "What in the world are you talking about, child?"

"This Sunday, remember? It's the celebration of 100 Women in Red."

I rolled my eyes. "I'm not going anywhere near Estelle's church. Those folks are crazy over there. They're crazy in red, blue, white, and any other color."

Estelle waved her hand as though she were holding a magic wand. "I rebuke that, Kizzy. I rebuke it in the name of the Lord."

Lizzy garnered a more serious tone. "Now Mama, we all agreed."

"What? What did we agree? To spend a day at the insane asylum?"

She reminded me. "We all agreed last year at Thanksgiving dinner. Each member of our family could choose one event. The rest of the family would support them."

Estelle concurred. "Yeah, I went to your dedication last year at that little hole-in-the-wall schoolhouse down in Hempstead, Texas; the one where they named the science wing after you? Praise God my new Camry was still in the parking lot when we got out."

"Nobody begged you to come to my ceremony. Plenty of my friends were in attendance without your honored presence."

"Plenty? Since when does Cora Williams and her two daughters add up to plenty?" asked Estelle.

Lizzy intervened. "That's not the point, anyway, Mama."

Estelle clarified. "No, the point is when my event came up last year, you were under the weather ... all of a sudden under the weather, you know what I'm saying? Reminded me of when we were growing up and you were all of sudden under the weather with your menstrual cycle; all of a sudden too sick to go collect the eggs from the hen house. So daddy made me go."

Lizzy offered a blank stare. "Why were you going to this hen house? Why didn't you just go to the store?"

Estelle and I couldn't help laughing. What did the new generation know about hen houses? Everything was prepackaged and microwavable. They never thought past the label on a package of bacon. They didn't know somewhere out there in the gritty, squealing slaughterhouses of the world, a pig had to die.

I finally gathered by thoughts. "I remember last year quite well. It wasn't all of a sudden. In fact, leading up to that event, if you want to call washing the stinking feet of old Holiness sisters an event, I told you my knees had been bothering me. I told you all week long."

Estelle grunted. "Come on, Kizzy. You can walk whenever you get ready. A few minutes ago you broke the New York Marathon record going down that hallway."

They all started laughing again.

Katherine Baker came to my rescue. "Y'all leave Mama Kizzy alone. You know how unpredictable pain is. I have the same problem with my back. It's on again, then off again and there's nothing I can do."

"That is soooo convenient. Oh, it hurts. Oh it doesn't hurt." Estelle looked toward the sun-drenched ceiling. "Oh God, forgive Yee the Baptists as they continue to slip and slide."

"Mama, you always taught me to keep my word," said Lizzy. "Now what are *you* going to do?"

At that moment, Lizzy's husband, Ububee, walked into the room. Clad in a white shirt and blue striped tie, he carried a black briefcase in one hand and drafting books in the other. He spoke in a cheery baritone voice. "Oh, de sound of women laughing; that is never good for de man. We know you are planning something behind our backs."

Lizzy flashed an approving smile. "What are you doing home so early?"

"Oh de computer go down. We all come home ... with pay, of course."

"I'm cooking you some Bobotie and soup. But it's not ready yet."

"No problem. I have some special reading to do." He held the books against his forehead.

"Sure you don't want to join us?" Estelle offered in jest. "I've got an extra machine in my trunk."

"I think not," he blushed. "But I will make you a proposition."

"What's your proposition?" she asked.

"If you good ladies will knit me a sweater for my trip back to de Motherland, I will wish a special blessing on you right now."

Lizzy sniggled. "Come on, U." She never called him by his full name. "It's not cold in Africa."

Ububee shook his head, hopelessly. "Oh how dis woman of mine come to be such a mugu? The mountains of Lesotho are covered with de snow all de time. This will be de place of our family reunion."

"Well, I'm sorry. But we mugus never saw Tarzan or Cheetah all bundled up, skiing off some mountain top in Lesotho."

He frowned. "Tarzan?! You see how de man has poisoned her monkey brain."

We all laughed in unison.

"Monkey brain, huh? So much for your Bobotie and soup." She quickly announced his punishment.

"Okay, okay, now what about this blessing?" Estelle pressed.

"Is it a spiritual blessing?"

"It is indeed; from de great Sangoma ancestors who were touched by de spirit of God."

"Like Moses and Abraham?"

"You might say," he confirmed.

"Then, I'm in," she naively declared. "What color sweater do you want?"

"De brightest of reds and greens. I will leave de rest to you."

Her round face glimmered with excitement. "Consider it done, praise God."

Ububee stacked his books and briefcase into a nearby chair. As he raised both hands to the ceiling, a hush fell over the room.

I was trying to keep a straight face. Many years ago, while attending Southern University for a summer refresher course, I had done scientific research on the compounds found in herbs and intelezis used in natural or alternative healing. The Sangoma tribesmen in Africa were recognized as experts of herbal healing. They were also famous witch doctors who spent a lot of time casting spells and tossing around old voodoo goat bones.

In a best case scenario, Ububee would wave his hands and say a few words. A mysterious spell would manifest itself and Estelle would suddenly succumb to a temporary case of lock jaw. In a worst case scenario, Ububee would raise his arms too high and remind us of his ongoing cultural feud with deodorant.

He finally spoke. "May de roar of de great Sarengette lion, de thunder of de mighty Blue Wildebeest, and de laughter of de Striped Hyena protect you and your family forever."

Looking up from her new pearl Kenmore super stitcher, Olivia Boudreaux flung her long, straight black hair to one side. "What if you don't have a family?"

"Then, may de great mother bird of fertility fly unto you with fullness and grace."

She smiled. "Ladies, I believe Ububee is trying to get me pregnant."

We should've laughed. It had been a morning full of laughter. Instead, the whole room fell into an eerie silence. The lion had suddenly killed the wildebeest, and the hyena was eating the caucus.

****

It weren't as though Olivia couldn't get pregnant. Since running away from her abusive home in Lake Charles, Louisiana at the tender age of sixteen, she had experienced her fair share of pregnancies; two by an old, powerful, opportunistic city councilman named Lee McGoan. Twelve years earlier, Councilman McGoan had snapped her up from the cold streets, set her up with a lavish lifestyle and knocked her up as a symbol of defiance in the face of his failing manhood.

Interestingly enough, his social-climbing wife had gone along with his scandalous indiscretions. The rumor of a young girl across town served as her bargaining chip for a newer Mercedes or a bigger diamond ring around her meaty fingers. But the prospect of some little high yellow Louisiana slut having her husband's baby was a different matter, altogether.

Her ultimatum had been very simple: Lose the baby or lose everything else, including the upcoming election.

Olivia's three year stint with the good life made her decision about the baby as simple as the ultimatum. At nineteen, she had plenty of time to have children. But how long would it take to find a meal ticket like Lee McGoan?

Her second abortion was at twenty-four, just before McGoan died of kidney failure. A mix-up with the new birth control pills had put her in a squeeze, trying to figure out whether it was McGoan's baby or the results of her fling with a pilot for Southwest Airlines. She found out later the pilot had had a vasectomy. Old McGoan had struck again.

A year after his death, Lee McGoan's oldest son, Anthony, approached her. "I knew about you and my father. I have this fantasy about you."

It wasn't long before young Anthony had dumped his live-in girlfriend and picked up the tab to Olivia townhouse, credit cards and BMW payment.

At that time, just after Congressman Mickey Leland's fatal plane crash in Africa, Houston's political climate was shifting like quicksand. In a twist of events, the local political bosses asked Anthony to run for his father's old office. Olivia suddenly found herself promoted from mistress of an old city councilman to official girlfriend of an up-and-coming star. She was out of the shadows and into the light. In '93 she held high hopes that he would soon ask her to be his wife.

At twenty-nine, she was still unusually beautiful, dripping with sensuality and polished in the business of man-pleasing. She was a frequent fixture at the city's best salons and nail shops. And her exotic perfume was the real, one-of-a-kind French bouquet, ordered from a fancy import shop in the Galleria.

Most women hated her. Watching their husbands and boyfriends gawk whenever she came around made the average female squirm in her seat. But Lizzy didn't seem to care. Shortly after Olivia joined First Reunion, Lizzy had invited her into the sewing group with open arms. Whether driven by some great revelation or foolish naiveté, Lizzy was secure in her marriage and considered herself to be just as attractive as anyone else.

Lizzy was honey brown and shapely with dark sparkling eyes, high cheek bones and wavy, shoulder-length hair. Mr. Miles often referred to her as a tweener ... his way of saying she was attractive enough for rich, important men to reach down; and hard-working, everyday Joe's to reach up.

There was, however, a danger for young girls treading the middle ground, in that, their self-image was based on volume. The more they were told they were beautiful and valuable, the more they believed it. More they were told they were a Plain-Jane and just another cog in the wheel, the more they believed it.

I had worked hard to instill confidence into Lizzy. As an only child, with no sibling comparisons, she seemed to be in constant need of reassurance. In my effort to respond to her special needs, I often wondered if I had gone too far.

In her proud, confident, alluring mind, the only difference between her and Olivia was their ability to conceive. She and Ububee had been trying to have a baby for over four years. Olivia, on the other hand, was just waiting for Councilman Anthony to give her the green light.

There was another reason why Olivia's sarcastic remark had clogged up the stratosphere. Rumor had it that some months earlier, Ububee had approached Olivia on the sexual side of the street. Of course, the rumor was unconfirmed. That's why my walking cane was still lying quietly by my chair and Ububee was still alive.

A woman at church with a reputation for starting mess had told Katherine Baker that Ububee had hit on Olivia; the kind of virile proposition that had nothing to do with hyenas and lions. This encounter had allegedly taken place in the kitchen after one of the sewing meetings. Olivia had graciously declined and that was supposedly the end of that ... except, she told a friend and the friend told the messy woman and the messy woman told Katherine Baker. Thank God, no one had told Lizzy.

Still, words have the power to create visual symbols in our minds. Olivia's words had triggered a landslide of visuals that poisoned our imaginations and ushered into an awkward moment of resolve.

At that very instant, I could see Ububee trying to get Olivia pregnant; tearing at her undergarments and pushing hard and clumsily against her delicate frame. Ironically, Katherine Baker told me later, she had envisioned the same thing.

Lizzy, on the other hand, envisioned Olivia being cast into a blissful state of incubation by the great mother bird of fertility, stomach bulging with new life, and people crowded around, fussing over her every move.

When is your baby due? Will it be a natural birth? Have you chosen a name? What are you hoping for, a boy or girl?

These were the maternal images that stampeded through Lizzy's mind. Olivia was suddenly basking in the magnificent sunlight of motherhood, while Lizzy stood on the sidelines, watching the baby-train go rolling by.

Lizzy never told me what she was thinking at that moment. She didn't have to. I already knew. I knew because I had succumbed to the same thoughts before Lizzy was born.

Mr. Myles and I had tried for years to have a child. But nothing seemed to work ... neither the home remedies nor special diets nor tranquilizing shots nor intestinal cleaners nor prayer clothes nor laying on of hands seemed to make a difference. It was Aunt Twigg who finally relieved us of our misery.

"God controls the womb," she prophetically revealed. "You keep thinking you're having a baby for you. But that's selfish thinking. You're having a baby for Him to use in His kingdom. You need to get on His time and wait for Him to unlock the baby door."

For a young Christian couple whose fragile beliefs were slowly fading into resentment and disbelief, her words were eternally liberating. We stopped thinking about the task of having a baby and started praising God for the gift we were going to receive when He was ready.

Somehow our new mindset stirred up a frenzy of cooperation between my eggs and Mr. Myles' sperm. Fifteen months from that day, we found ourselves sitting in the old St. Elizabeth Negro Hospital, proud parents of a beautiful baby girl.

I had tried to pass on the same liberating philosophy to Lizzy and Ububee. But being part of a new, highly analytical generation, she still had questions.

If God needed more workers in the kingdom, why didn't he just send more workers through her? Why was he sending five or six workers through one family and none through another? And why was he allowing neighborhood whores and prostitutes, who didn't want children, to keep getting pregnant and keep having abortions?

I sent her and Ububee to Pastor Fordham. But all he did was remind them of how long Abraham and Sara had to wait. Still struggling with the English language, Ububee went off on the Pastor because he thought Pastor Fordham was telling them they had to wait ninety more years.

That morning, one asinine witch doctor blessing had sent us all into a depressing tailspin. I could think of only one way to pull us out.

I looked straight at Ububee's shiny black face and smiled. "When you gave your blessing and Olivia mentioned getting pregnant, I thought about one person."

Ububee pondered. "Who might dat be?"

"Bishop Ebenezer. Last time I saw him, his big belly looked

like it was in the third trimester."

In an instance, they were all laughing again, a soothing, sterilizing laughter that purged the entire room. Even Estelle managed a waning smile.

Lizzy quickly intervened. "So, Mama. Are you going to see the good Bishop this Sunday?"

I paused a long while. "If that's our deal and I made that foolish Thanksgiving blunder in the presence of a bunch of nagging family members."

"You certainly did, as God is my witness, you did." Estelle insisted.

"Then I guess I'll have to go".

Rising quickly to her feet, Estelle shouted, "Praise God!" And then she began her little hip-hop Holiness dance.

Chapter Six

S unday afternoon came so quickly I wondered if the vernal equinox had miscommunicated with the perpendicular tilt of Earth's axis and skipped over Saturday altogether. Before I could read the weekend obituaries or water my rose garden or wash out my comfortable girdle, we were crowded into Ububee's silver and blue custom van, cruising across Greater Pilgrim Holiness Tabernacle's newly paved asphalt parking lot.

There wouldn't have been a crowding problem had Ububee's two musician uncles elected not to come. But hearing about one hundred black women in one place, they couldn't resist the thought that a couple of lonely hearts might be desperate enough to take them in. With their visas quickly running out, what better way to stay in the United States than to find an American bride with romance problems, low self-esteem and a place of her own?

With their night club attire still smelling of smoke and liquor, they had piled into the van with all kinds of foreign instruments. A very skinny Vunju played the guitar while Tiki, the tall one with the banana chin, sang some kind of Congolese ballets. They strummed and hollered and grunted all the way to the church. The only thing that silenced their noisy serenade was the sight of several big women in red, rumbling across the parking lot. At 3:50 pm and counting, the winded stragglers were scrambling to get inside the church before the choir director locked the back door.

Vunju pointed through his tinted backseat window to the frantic twist of one woman's balloon hips. "Hold on, my brother. I believe we have reached de Promise Land." And then he began to play a song of celebration.

At 3:59 pm we walked onto the white, wood framed porch. Yes, we all walked, though I felt a bit guilty for slowing everyone down. I had intentionally left my wheelchair in the van so Estelle and her holy-roller friends would know that God was very capable of blessing the Baptists too. My old knees were percolating quite well, thank you. And between Ububee's strong shoulder and my sturdy wood grain walking cane, the New York marathon record was in jeopardy all over again.

Several official greeters dressed in white uniforms and matching cranberry and white tams, shook our hands and gave us programs. Then, one of them noticed the bundle of foreign instruments Vunju and Tiki had pack-muled up to the door.

"Are y'all on program?" she asked.

Vunju smiled, exposing the large gap in his teeth. "We always on program for de Almighty."

She swung open the double glass doors. "You'd better get a move on then. They're about to get started and Bishop don't like no latecomers."

They hurried in ahead of us, their boyish faces aglow. Though some members of the congregation seemed amused by the primitive noisemakers strapped to their backs, I was more amused by the clueless adolescence hidden in their hearts. No one had invited them. They were there for the wrong reasons. And if the collection plate stayed in their vicinity too long, my guess was Africa would receive a surprise donation whether the good Bishop authorized it or not.

The white wood framed building was a box the size of ten 7-Eleven Stores smooshed together under a sharp cone steeple with a front porch attached. Unlike our Synagogue, there was no entrance hall or foyer. As soon as we walked through the glass doors, we found ourselves inside the sanctuary, pushing against a cheap brass hand rail and elbowing all of the nappy heads on the back row.

We wanted to move forward but there was nowhere to go. The pews were packed. The ushers were like worker bees on steroids, scrambling to find more folding chairs. Someone had decided that three hundred people could fit into a building designed for a hundred and fifty at best.

If only some safety-minded, conscientious, God-fearing retiree could've gotten to a phone booth and called the Fire Marshall; that retiree could've been back home in little or no time, finishing up the Houston Chronicle's obituaries and pulling freshly ripened figs from her tree.

Lizzy peeped around Ububee's shoulder and frowned. "It's burning up in here!"

She had barely gotten her words out when two usher ran up to us; one with a stack of colorfully designed accordion hand fans; the other, with a hand-written note.

"Kizzy Lizzy?" The chubby note-bearer inquired.

"I'm Kizzy. She's Lizzy." I pointed to my prune-faced daughter who was fanning like a sow in heat.

"Sister Estelle requested seats for y'all. Please follow me."

As we began our long trek down the center aisle, I could see Estelle, all dressed in red, waving from the choir stand, pointing to our precious seats that had been held in reserve. We finally landed on the second pew from the front, right next to one of the small window units. The stream of cool air was a godsend to Lizzy. The knee-relieving, hardwood benches offered a similar sense of rescue for me.

Ububee, however, seemed oblivious to both the priceless chilled air and VIP seating. His moon eyes scanned the building in search of his renegade uncles. He finally spotted them talking to the organist at the far end of the stage. They had joined up with some kind of makeshift floor orchestra which served as an accompaniment to the choir the entire afternoon.

Ububee hunched Lizzy, a proud expression on his face, then, pointed to his uncles' junk pile of instruments. "You see that? De djembes, de berimbaus and de shakere are de only credentials they need."

She glared at him, indignantly. "U, don't push your luck. Next time we're leaving those idiots at home."

At that moment, a young teenage boy banged, loudly, on a brass cymbal, hanging on the front wall. The tall, stern-faced choir director grabbed the microphone and began to yell to the top of his voice. "Let us stand and usher the Almighty Jehovah into this place!"

Two women in white gowns rushed out from behind the velvet maroon curtains and began to speak in tongues. The organist began to play some ear-piercing treble notes as the floor orchestra joined in. A high-pitched soprano grabbed another microphone and began to sing *hallelujah*, over and over again. The rest of the choir joined in with more thunderous praises.

The combined sound was deafening. I thought to myself, *Houston we have lift-off. We also have an old retired school teacher's head caught up in the thrusters.*

The whole building trembled with singing, dancing and the incessant pounding of a hundred tambourines. This was just the first five minutes and already I realized before the service was over, I'd be pronounced dead at the scene from an overdose of acoustic shock waves.

Like the nuclear arms race of the 50's, there had been a sound race in black churches in the late 80's. New technology had ushered in an era of unlimited electronics. Churches, the size of an outdoor toilet, were bringing in microphones and amplifiers and speakers designed for Carnegie Hall. Since few churches could afford a real sound engineer, the fiddlers took over.

Each church had a fiddler, a deacon or elder or trustee who declared himself the expert solution finder for any problems that arose. If the church lawn mower broke down, he would fiddle with it until it started working again, or until his ineptness condemned the remaining parts to a permanent resting place in the lawn mower cemetery. If the church van broke down, he knew the best auto mechanic in town. If the church needed painting or the parking lot needed repaving, he knew the only acceptable contractor that could get the job done at the right price. Thus, when the church needed to upgrade its sound system, he declared himself the master "sound configurator", capable of carrying out the highly technical task.

Before my older sister, Mattie, passed away with breast cancer in '66, her neighbor told us about a gun play at Calvary Baptist in the ship channel district of Fidelity Manor. While finishing up a sewage project in the church parking lot, one fiddler had run over another fiddler's foot with a tractor, aggravating a long standing feud for power over the church's affairs. Both fiddlers had large families with unsaved, pistol-toting problem-solvers among them; some originating from New Orleans and Baton Rouge. Before the day was over, a gun battle ensued along the Houston Ship Channel feeder, forcing one fiddler's pickup truck over a high embankment, into the dark, swirling forty-foot waters of the Channel. A passing tugboat captain fished the first fiddler out of the water. But the feud didn't stop until a few months later when the second fiddler's job moved him to Albuquerque. The *fighting* demons, apparently surmising a greater future in New Mexico, left with him.

The pastor spent weeks trying to cover up the incident. Finally, he admitted to the congregation that "a rare leaven of sin had crept into the body". After years of watching the bitterness between the two men escalate without the slightest attempt to intervene, that was his take, his official spiritual algorithm to set everyone's mind at ease.

What a sorry excuse for a pastor, only concerned with the cover-up. Aunt Twigg would've tongue-lashed him into a coma.

Hearing the story from Mattie's disheartened neighbor, I added my own spiritual algorithm that captured the essence of all congregations large and small. At any given church, there was room for only one fiddler. Otherwise, you were looking for a fist fight, gunplay, or an unauthorized baptism in a nearby channel.

Deacon Poe was our fiddler. He kept his hand in every aspect of the church's business in order to maintain control. Like all other fiddlers, his exclusive claim to enlightenment was self-endowed hogwash. He was nothing more than an experimenter, feeling his way through the ambiguities of life and hoping for the best.

With sound fiddlers, there seemed to be a consensus of approach: *When in doubt, get the biggest speakers you can buy and turn the volume up as loud as it will go.* The speakers that Bishop Ebenezer had used to arouse the neighborhood looked like grown men with no feet. Whoever the fiddler was at Greater Pilgrim Holiness Tabernacle, he had taken the word "volume" to a whole new level.

There was a third component to the sound race over which fiddlers had no control. That was the tendency of most black evangelical preachers to swallow the entire microphone. They didn't just speak into it. They consumed it as though it were a juicy red Popsicle on a hot summer day. They placed their whole mouth around it and yelled into it as though they were calling hogs back on the farm in

North Carolina. Apparently, the louder the Word went out, the more people would be saved, or so they speculated.

I often wondered if the giant speakers were turned back on the pulpit and the preachers were forced to hear their own ear-splitting performances, how long it would take for them to adjust their volume and begin to speak in normal tones.

Of course, that wasn't going to happen at Greater Pilgrim Holiness Tabernacle's sound chamber of death. For them, volume was a prerequisite to praise. And with the praise ship already launched, there was no turning back.

We stood for about ten minutes, torturing ourselves with thunderous decibels of destruction. Just when I thought I was going to pass out, a door opened behind the choir stand. Dressed in white suits and red ties, Bishop Ebenezer and his entourage came marching out. A Bible bearer, holding a silver tray and large black Bible, led the Bishop, seven elders and one tall, ruddy-faced white woman into the pulpit. As they took their seats, the music subsided and the congregation was finally allowed to sit down.

The music had stopped, but Vunju kept going. He grabbed a pair of poke dot shakers from his instrument junk yard and began to shake and jump on the floor in front of the stage. Someone from the congregation shouted, "The Spirit is on him!"

Hearing that, the organist began to play, the drummer began to beat, and the orchestra cranked up all over again.

Ububee turned to Lizzy to flash an amused grin. "You see him go now. He is de master of de Kpoko-Kpoko rattles!"

Lizzy sank down into her seat and covered her face with both hands.

Vunju's performance lasted several minutes, long enough for a few lonely hearts to take notice of his tight silver pants. Then, he danced his way back to his original spot in the orchestra where Tiki tossed him a Holiday Inn bath towel to wipe his sweaty face.

As the congregation cheered, approvingly, Bishop Ebenezer, a beefy, broad-shouldered man with a stumped neck, dark, reddish eyes and premature gray strains, receding from his ringed forehead, stepped up to the podium.

"Praise God!" He shouted in a raspy, baritone voice.

"Praise God." The audience answered back.

"Praise God!!!" He repeated, dissatisfied with their level of enthusiasm.

"Praise God!!!" They responded in a much louder tone.

"I know it's hot in here." He wiped his soggy forehead with a gigantic red handkerchief. "But it's gonna be a whole lot hotter in hell, Amen?"

The members pounded their tambourines with approval.

"The Lord said if you ashamed of me down here, I'm gonna...."

Before he could finish his statement, one of the seven elders finished it for him. She was the only female elder; a stocky, makeup-free woman with sagging cheekbones, a short afro and deep brown eye. She quickly chimed in, "... be ashamed of you up there."

"That's right, Elder Vicky." He quickly acknowledged her. "Let's praise him while we still have breath, Amen?"

"Amen." They all replied.

He looked back at the choir. "What about these beautiful ladies? Ain't they a sight for sore eyes?"

Vunju began clapping, wildly. The congregation joined in.

"They gonna bless us today. The Lord done already showed me. Oh essie, lassie, mcgollah heluuhya...." The Bishop began speaking in tongues.

I looked around for an interpreter, but there was none. In First Corinthians, the Apostle Paul said an interpreter needed to be present so the church would be edified. But Estelle explained that the Bishop held classes on Thursday nights to teach his members how to speak in tongues. As far as he was concerned, it was a holy language and ordinary people didn't need to know what it meant.

He finally resumed speaking in his former, Ebonics-ridden English. "Before this choir bless us with they gifts, we have some very important business to take care of." He looked toward the back. "Brang forth God's chullin right now."

An usher rolled a woman in a wheelchair down the aisle. She looked to be in her late 40's with dark skin, thick glasses, a silky black wig, and a white bandage covering the side of her face. Like the end of a short train, a bony, unshaven man on crutches, assisted by two deacons, limped, gingerly behind the wheelchair. When they reached the front, Bishop Ebenezer grabbed a microphone and stepped off the stage to greet them.

He handed the microphone to the woman. "Tell us your story."

As it turned out, she had been in a car accident and couldn't walk. The doctors claimed there was no medical reason she couldn't walk and had canceled her disability. She was in a destitute state and needed help from the church.

The man's story was similar. He had gotten hurt on his job. He could still walk, but only with the help of crutches. Company doctors felt the extent of his injuries was minor. They had ordered him back to work.

The Bishop gazed at both of them a long time before speaking.

Finally, he asked, "Do you believe in the Almighty God and His great powers?"

They both nodded, affirmatively.

"Then I'm gonna pose a question to you. It's the same question Jesus posed to the man by the pool of Bethesda. He asked the man at the pool, Will thou be...."

"Made whole?" Elder Vicky finished it off.

They both nodded again.

One of the elders walked over to the edge of the stage and handed the Bishop a bottle of cherry colored oil. He poured a generous amount into his hands and began rubbing the woman's forehead, then arms, then knees, then feet. Without warning, he slapped the woman on her jaw, a hard slap like she had eaten the last pork chop. Then he snatched her from her chair.

"Rise, take up thy bed, and walk!"

A bit startled and dazes, the woman stumbled forward, then fell face down on the hardwood floor. When she lifted her head, we could see a small bloody gash across her top lip. One of the deacons gave her a white handkerchief and tried to help her up. But Bishop Ebenezer shook his head, vigorously.

"Leave her be," he declared. "This is between her and God."

The stunned woman finally managed to get to her knees, then her feet. She lurched forward with small, wobbly steps at first, steadying herself as she progressed.

I thought to myself, *What a show. This is almost as good as the Fort Worth Flyer.*

But as the woman drew closer to our side of the stage, I noticed the wild, schizophrenic look on her face. Her pupils had dilated. She had begun to cry, uncontrollably. And the red stuff was not ketchup as I had suspected. She was bleeding real blood. Either she had Adie's syndrome or nerve damage or she was hyped up on some kind of drugs. Or....

The "*Or*" exploded in my mind like tiny balls of light.

She suddenly began to jump; an awkward lunging motion, as though she were trying to get something off the top shelf. Three or four jumps and her glasses fell to the floor. Another few jumps and her wig came off too. Before anyone could get to the glasses, she had smashed the lenses under her wobbly feet. That's when I became thoroughly confused.

Who, in their right mind, would sign up for a scam that required them to be slapped in the face, smashed into a hardwood floor, cut on the lip and temporarily blinded as their thick prescription glasses were trampled under foot? I knew how I felt about my fancy, ultra-modern seamless specs. Young Reedy felt the same way. These weren't Walgreen specials on which she was dancing. These were thick black bifocal liberators that freed her from a blurry, incoherent world.

Things weren't adding up.

It was my duty as a scientist and disciple of inductive reasoning to consider all possibilities. But sitting there, up close and personal, observing every tear that splattered from her reddened eyes, the possibility that seemed most plausible was churning my insides and shaking my old retired frame at the core. What if this elaborate theatrical charade was not a charade at all?

I knew a little about the Holiness Church. Estelle had made sure of that. Its origin was rooted in John Westley's Methodist doctrines. But the driving force behind the Holiness movement was Christian perfection: living clean and overcoming the temptation of bodily sin. Since the Holy Spirit would not dwell in an unclean temple, the objective was to stay clean, at least long enough for the Spirit to manifest itself in one's life.

If you talked to ten Holiness believers ... God forbid you would have to endure such an ordeal ... nine of them would spend their time emphasizing the thrill of seeing the Spirit in the natural realm. This manifestation usually occurred in the form of tongues, prophecy and faith healing. But the Spirit's arsenal of miracles was certainly not limited to the big three.

Once, as a young child back in Hattiesburg, the Fuller Brush man stood up in our little country church and began to speak in tongues. His strange voice scared me and I began to cry. To my surprise, the grownups around me were crying too. My mother took me outside and explained the man was speaking from heaven. He had prophesied that a miracle was about to take place at our church that would sweep away the sinful doubts we hid in our hearts.

Doubts? I didn't understand. I was too young to have doubts. I believed what they taught us in Sunday school and BYPU and on my father's porch. God was as real as they said he was.

As we stood outside talking, a car drove up. Uncle Benny got out ... the same Uncle Benny who had been killed in the war. As it turned out, the Army had made a mistake. The Benny Johnson that had gotten killed in Germany was a different Benny Johnson. Our Benny Johnson was still alive.

I'll never forget that day. I can still see the whole church, rushing out to greet him with hysterical cries of joy. Of course, the Fuller Brush man never did anything like that again. No one in that little church ever did.

Still, one scary encounter was enough for me. I knew the Holy Spirit was real. What I couldn't understand was why the all-knowing third person of the Godhead would want to get tangled up with an addlebrained shyster like Bishop Ebenezer. If the Bishop was really doing miracle healing at Greater Pilgrim Holiness Tabernacle, that was a bad sign. It could only mean that willing vessels for the Lord's work had fallen into very short supply.

Experienced scientists like me understand that empirical evidence is more accurate with increase observation. That's a fancy way of saying the more times you look at an event, the more you can gather from it. There was another healing waiting in the wings. If the good Bishop could pull off two in a row, it would be time for me to buy a brand new tambourine and sign up for Thursday night tongue classes.

They finally calmed the woman down and reattached the wig to her head. She was prancing back and forth in front of the stage, a big smile on her face. They tried to transport her to the back of the church in the wheelchair, but she refused. She insisted on walking, but not before she gave the Bishop a big hug.

"We ain't through with you yet, daughter." The Bishop proudly announced. "There gonna be a cash envelope for you at the end of this service, Amen?"

The whole congregation let out a roar of approval.

He looked at the man on the wooden crutches. "You see what God can do?"

The man shook his head, acknowledgingly.

"Then why don't you give me them crutches?"

The man's eyes bucked. "I, ah...."

The Bishop took the bottle of oil and poured it over the man's wooly head. The oil ran down his beard.

"It's like the precious ointment upon the head that ran down upon the beard, even...."

"Aaron's beard!" Elder Vicky barged in from her seat on stage.

As the oil dripped off the man's chin and to the floor, Bishop reached out and snatched both crutches. "These two crutches is what's got you in jail. It's time to be free, Amen? Go forth and walk!"

The man took one step and fell to the floor. And then he began to cry.

The two deacons allowed him to squirm around on the floor before they stood him up again.

The Bishop placed his hand on the man's shoulder. "You heeled, you hear me. But you must believe in order to receive."

The man began to tremble, afraid he would fall again.

The Bishop handed him the two crutches. "It's left up to you, my son. The heeling is upon you. Go now and sin no mo."

They led the man to a seat in the back.

The Bishop stopped at the podium and shook his head. "Oh Lord, deliver us from the sin of unbelief. Oh, ahla sola mukukool sisilah ...." He went on for a few seconds more.

Finally, he turned to the choir. "We ready for y'all. Sang us a song from the celestial hymn books. Let the praises go up as a sweet aroma to our Lord and Savior, Amen?"

As the one hundred women in red stood and began their deafening recital, I found myself more confused than ever before. In order to fool the people, the good Bishop needed both healings to be a success. Arranging that neatly contrived ending should've been an easy task. All he needed to do was go out and hire two actors or two street people or two unknowns to play their role. So, why would the bearded man refuse to play his role and make himself a payday?

The answer kept coming back the same: *Because he hadn't been hired.*

So why hire one and not the other? I asked myself. The answer kept coming back the same: *You wouldn't hire one and not the other.*

A chill ran down my spine.

I was captive in a ridiculous setting. There were African hunters, prowling for wives, giant speakers emitting decibels of death and a babbling idiot trying to call down tongues from heaven. Would God stop by a place like this to perform a miracle?

When I emerged from my mental exercises, the choir had already sung two songs. The Mission's president and vice president were standing at the microphone, reading a long list. One by one they called the names of the one hundred women in red. One by one each woman stood up to announce her individual offering.

They would say, "Sister Erma Jean Wallace."

She would stand and say, "Sister Wallace: $200."

Each woman walked from the choir stand, down to the offering table in front of the stage to deposit her red envelope. It was peer pressure at its best ... or worst, depending on how you looked at it.

It took two women announcing their offering of $200. That's when I realized it was a day of two's. The two uncles, the two ushers with the fans and the note, the two candidates for healing, the two deacons that assisted the man with the two crutches; It was all coming back to me now. I thought about the principles in my *Scholium of Numeric Prediction.*

I took out a pen and wrote down a number. I handed the paper to Lizzy who then showed Ububee.

What is dis?" he asked.

"You'll see," I whispered.

When all of the ladies had given their offering, the two Mission officers announced the tally. They had raised a grand total of $22,112. The paper I had given to Lizzy had $22,222.

Lizzy, realizing what the numbers meant, whispered into my ear. "Mama, that's amazing. You came so close!"

At that moment, a woman in an expensive designer red suite stood up a few rows behind us. "Excuse me. Sister Lillie Brock couldn't make it today. But she did send her offering. It's $110.00."

The woman walked to the front of the church to drop it into one of the shiny silver offering plates.

The president took a minute to recalculate. "With that addition, out grand total is $22,222."

The congregation followed with thunderous applause.

Lizzy's mouth flew open. Ububee grabbed the note and looked

at it again. Immediately, he stood up. "May I have your strictest attention please?"

The church fell into an abrupt silence.

"I must tell you all something. Dis woman, who is my mother-in-law, has prophesied what would happen in dis church. You can see de number on this paper. It is de exact amount you raised. De thing is she handed me de paper before you raised it. I can truly say de Spirit of God is upon her right now. Praise Him! Praise His Holy Name!"

A hundred tambourines began to beat. The organist began to play. Tiki broke out in a song of praise.

Estelle's face contorted into a big grapefruit. "What?!!!"

I smiled and gloated, as though I were an accomplished student of Deacon Poe's class on hogging the spotlight. Seeing Estelle's utter contempt made the whole trip worthwhile.

A few minutes later, the tall white woman stood at the podium. "I am here to make a special presentation. As you know, Bishop Ebenezer has been away for the last two weeks. No, he hasn't been goofing off. He's been on a sacred retreat with us in the Appalachian Mountains."

Us turned out to be the National Holiness CampMeeting. Bishop Ebenezer had gone through a rigorous test of fire to become an exalted leader and spiritualist in the national organization.

"He's no longer Bishop Ebenezer," she solemnly declared. "He is now Grand Bishop Ebenezer."

The congregation rose to its feet in celebration.

She handed him a golden plaque and placed some kind of red ribbon around his neck. Taking her seat, the Bishop was left at the podium to make his acceptance speech.

"Dis here is a great honor for me." He acknowledged with

tearful humility. "The last two weeks I spent with Reverend Debbie, here, and the other members of the Council have renewed my strength in the Lord. I'll go so far as to say it's changed my life. When I came back from the mountain tops of the Appalacheees, I lookdid at my hands and my hands lookdid new. I lookdid at my feets...."

"And they did too." Elder Vicky finished it off.

"I never thought I could go any higher in the kingdom of the Almighty. But time and time again the Lord done showed me he can't be boxed in. He can do whatever he want to do, with whoever he want to do it with, Amen?"

Another chill ran down my spine. At that moment in time, I found myself believing the good Bishop, not for who he was, but for what he was saying. The words were searing my conscious, reminding me of how many times I had belittled Estelle about her little group of religious fanatics. But what if God had declared them to be legitimate cohorts in the expansion of the kingdom? He did it with the Gentiles. Why not with these Holiness fanatics? He could do whatever he wanted to do, with whoever he wanted to do it with.

I tried to remember the last time God had stopped by First Reunion to perform a miracle. The closest thing I could recall was Fannie Grubbs' hair growing back after her alcoholic hair dresser burnt it out with some kind of off-brand relaxer. But that was no comparison to making the lame walk again.

I was still struggling with my hypothesis when the good Bishop dropped his final bombshell.

"I have received the second blessing of God," he boldly declared.

Even on a day of two's, Bishop Ebenezer's reference to the second blessing was mind-boggling. In 1993, there may have been fifty black people in all of Houston who knew about the second blessing of God. According to the good Bishop, he not only knew about it, but possessed it in its fullness.

John Wesley and some of his Methodist disciples first introduced the concept of the second blessing back in the 1700's. But it was the Holiness movement a century later that had made it popular. I knew because my best friend, Charlotte Lueese, had done some research on it before she ... disappeared. She was considering becoming a Methodist minister and had read an assortment of books on the church's history and guiding principles.

According to respected theologians, the second blessing was a special baptism by the Holy Spirit after a person was saved. In accepting Christ, a believer automatically received the gift of the Holy Spirit. Ephesians called it a seal or mark that let the demons and angels in the Spirit world know that a person had been converted and that certain rules applied. For instance, no demon could possess a person with the seal, and no action could be taken against that person without first getting permission from God.

The second blessing was a super charged dosage of the Holy Spirit that allowed one to live a life of perfection, entirely devoted to the Christian calling. People who received the second blessing were gifted with certain powers, like Mother Teresa, to do the work of the ministry. These powers often manifested themselves in prophecy and miracle healings.

Bishop Ebenezer stood before us declaring that he had received the second blessing. The woman with the broken eyeglasses stood in the back, waving her hands, declaring she had been healed. What was an old, retired school teacher/scientist to believe? All the empirical data seemed to confirm the Bishop's claim. What I really needed was a sign from the good Lord to let me know these people were not really crazy and that the new Grand Bishop Ebenezer was on the up and up.

As the Bishop continued to describe his new found relationship with the Spirit, Reverend Debbie left the sage and went into the offices behind the choir stand. She returned with a small, black leather suitcase and set it at the Bishop's feet. I noticed that the case made a noise when she set it down. It reminded me of broken glass, sliding around on the inside.

The Bishop looked back at his elders. "Do you want to move to the next level in kingdom building?"

They all shouted, "Amen!"

"Do you want to mount up on wings like eagles; run and not get weary; walk...."

"And not faint," Elder Vicky chimed in. The others responded with an enthusiastic Hallelujah.

Like a nimble legged Santa Claus, sharing his bag of goodies, Bishop Ebenezer stooped down, unzipped the suitcase, gently reached in and pulled out a five foot long diamondback rattlesnake.

"Are you ready to walk by faith?! He shouted to the top of his voice.

"Oh hell no!" Elder Vicky shouted back. Those were the last discernible words I heard before the stampede began.

Elder Vicky leaped from her chair, off the stage and onto the offering table. The weight of her stocky body caused the table legs to collapse, sending her and the stack of silver trays, crashing to the floor.

She lay in the treasure trove of offering trays, stuffed envelopes and splintered wood for about three seconds. That's when she spotted the second rattlesnake slithering out of the case.

Newton's Third Law states that an object cannot "bootstrap" itself into motion with purely internal forces. In other words, to achieve acceleration, it must interact with an external object, disconnected from itself. Elder Vicky, however, was apparently unfamiliar with the laws of the universe. Catapulting herself off the floor at the speed of light, she broke the sound barrier and defied all gravitational pull.

She streaked down the middle aisle and out the front door. A cluster of white-suited co-laborers followed closely behind. I couldn't tell whether the other elders were running to get away from the snakes or from the onslaught of choir members, barreling out of the choir stand. Whatever the reason, the leadership was leading at a pace much faster than anyone could follow.

Like a scene from Rawhide, the congregation suddenly turned into a wild herd of cattle, pushing, shelving and stampeding through the glass doors. Seeing the utter pandemonium at the front entrance, a group of terrified choir members scrambled toward the back.

They quickly realized the choir director had locked the deadbolt and run off with the key.

One of the sopranos screamed. "We're trapped!" That's when the woman with the balloon hips rounded the corner with a full head of steam. She crashed into the door, tearing it from its hinges and opening up a gaping hole that made her full-figured comrades shout for joy.

Vunju did not see his bride-to-be transform the small, wood framed building into the Dome Stadium. During the commotion, he had conveniently fallen into the pile of red envelopes and was now helplessly thrashing around. Ironically, Tiki had gone down near the same spot.

Ububee stood up, a frantic look on his face. "We must depart from dis place."

"We can't leave my Mama!" Lizzy whined, hysterically.

"Would I do such a thing?" Ububee scolded her.

Before she could answer, Estelle yelled from the rear of the stage. "This way, Y'all!" She pointed to the jagged opening that had once been the back door.

Ububee finally noticed the lame woman's wheelchair. The deacons had left it parked next to our row.

He picked me up like a China Doll and lowered me into the seat ... a cheap, hard seat, made for a person with a meaty rear end. Had I known the Barnum and Bailey Snake Circus was coming to town, I would've brought my own chair.

Sitting in the middle aisle, I was no more than ten feet away from Bishop Ebenezer. I could see his every expression; hear his babbling repertoire of heavenly phrases. As he stood there with out-stretched arms, holding the rattler a few inches from his face, he appeared to be mesmerized, locked in some kind of transcendental state. I couldn't be sure whether it was the sunlight coming in from the makeshift hole in the back wall or the angle of the podium beneath the flood lights in the ceiling. But there was an aura about his countenance, a delicate glow around his burly frame. Something was going on, some abnormality that my scientific observation could not yet explain.

I needed more time to observe the unusual phenomenon. But Ububee had already begun our lightning departure past the stage and choir stand, headed toward the door. The wheels on the old chair spun so rapidly, they began to screech, like the wheels on Buster's casket. I gripped my purse, tightly, just in case I was the next body part to tumble into the aisle.

Fortunately, the chair proved to be more resilient than I had expected. We arrived at the back door with all the shoddy mechanisms intact.

"I can walk now." I tried to reassure Ububee. But before I could get up, he had lifted the whole chair onto the parking lot and resumed our frantic retreat.

I looked back in search of Lizzy and Estelle.

They had just stepped out of the building when a wobbly, disoriented figure stumbled through the door behind them. In heedless desperation, he almost knocked them to the ground. He blistered past my chair so quickly, I barely caught a glimpse of his bearded face. It was the lame man, still spotted up with oil, and carrying one crutch over his shoulder.

The good Bishop had told him he was healed. But it was left up to him to believe. I guess believing came a lot easier with rattlesnakes crawling around the sanctuary.

In chemistry we call it a catalyst, the thing that makes other things do what they normally wouldn't do. An asinine witch doctor blessing had prompted me to attend a church run by fanatics. A snake induced stampede had set the lame man free. Now, as we fled from Greater Pilgrim Holiness Tabernacle like rats from a burning building, I wondered what the whole ordeal would do to Estelle's faith.

And then it hit me that I was avoiding a more pressing question: *What was it doing to mine?*

As we climbed into Ububee's van, Estelle jumped in after us and closed the door. "Just take me home. I'll get my car later."

Knowing how much Estelle cherished her Camry, Lizzy whirled around from the front seat. "Are you sure?"

Estelle shook her head. "Right now I just want to get as far away from here as I can."

As Ububee pulled off, I spotted Vunju and Tiki, running behind the van.

"Your uncles are trying to flag you." I pointed through the back window.

Ububee sped out of the parking lot and onto the street. "I suspect they have more than enough money for de taxi."

Ububee was right. Glancing back, I noticed Vunju had

suspended his chase and swooped down to retrieve two red envelopes which had fallen out of his pocket.

Except for an occasional sniffle, the drive to Estelle's house
was cloaked in silence. A few blocks from her Sunnyside neighborhood,
she turned and stared at me. "Go ahead and say it. You were right.
Bishop is a fool."

After years of debating about denominations, religious
doctrine and biblical interpretations, I was finally sitting in the
cat-bird's seat. The good Bishop had thoroughly embarrassed her. The
membership had nearly trampled each other. The great life of purity
and moral perfection had come crashing down like the Greater Pilgrim
Holiness Tabernacle's back door. All I needed to do was remind her of
the many warnings I had given her about throwing in with a bunch of
fanatics. All I needed to do was shake my finger like an all-knowing
big sister and say, "I told you so".

But I didn't feel like shaking my finger. I didn't feel like I
was the great sibling authority who knew it all. If anything, after seeing
Bishop Ebenezer's face in its radiated glory, I felt that I was the one,
struggling to understand the infinite unknowns and unpredictable
nature of life, itself.

I had reached into my innermost vault and pulled out some
worthless preconceptions about the rules of engagement. God wasn't
supposed to get his hands dirty with fanatics and misfits. But there
he was, performing miracles at Greater Pilgrim Holiness Tabernacle.
I wasn't supposed to listen to a preacher who butchered the English
language and referred to the complex structure of mortise and tendons
below his ankles as *feets*. But there I was, agreeing with the Bishop's
declaration of God's unlimited, unfathomable, unpredictable power to
do whatever he wanted to do.

The good Bishop was truly misguided. But then so was the
Apostle Paul in his early ministry. Which was worse, holding the

coats of murderers or holding the snakes of mountaintop fanatics? Paul had to be knocked off his donkey to see the light. Maybe God had a donkey ride in store for the good Bishop as well.

He can do whatever he wants to do, with whoever he wants to do it with, Amen?

I looked into her teary eyes, filled with disappointment and betrayal. I finally replied with a soft, consoling voice. "He's a fool. But he's a fool for the Lord. That's the best kind."

She perked up a bit. "Are you saying I should stay?"

"If you still believe in him."

She pondered for a long while. "Anything else?"

"Yes." I nodded, slowly, reflectively, soaking in the boundless possibilities associated with a life in Christ.

"What?"

I wiped the smudged makeup from her cheek and gently patted her shoulder. "Pray for a donkey ride."

Chapter Seven

The following Wednesday night an unexpectedly large crowd assembled at First Reunion Baptist Church to continue the church business meeting that Buster's home-going wake had curtailed. Anita, the organist, who doubled as the church secretary, had called most of the members to remind them of the importance of the meeting. Curiosity, however, seemed to have been equally responsible for the spirited turnout. Rumors swirled that something big was going down, something that would put First Reunion on the map for years to come.

Still recuperating from Estelle's 100 Women in Red fiasco, I had missed our regular 11:00 am Sunday service. I had gotten a call from Cora Williams early Monday morning.

"Do you know any battered women at the church?" she had asked.

You and Bayboy. That was my amusing thought.

Not wanting to hurt her feelings, however, I responded more responsibly. "Not off hand, why?"

"I overheard Deacon Poe ask Deacon Grubbs if he had gotten the battered women figures together for the meeting," she reported. "What do you think that's about?"

"I don't know. Maybe they're trying to start some kind of therapy group."

"Or, maybe Poe is trying to get Grubbs to fess up. You know him and Fannie been fighting again."

I had already heard about the ongoing spat between Deacon Grubbs and his wife. There was a rumor Deacon Grubbs was having an affair with Anita, the organist. But in the larger scheme of church politics, it didn't make sense for Deacon Poe to shine a light on Grubbs' indiscretions. As the church continued to grow, Deacon Poe needed all of his loyal henchmen in place to keep his grip on power.

"That's not it." I told Cora. "Poe is up to something else."

My suspicions led me to call Katherine Baker's oldest daughter, Dottie, who worked as an editorial assistant for the Houston Post Newspaper. A twenty year old community college student with a perpetually serious face and pointy white girl nose, she was the most promising of the Baker's over-active five. She came by the house later that day to drop off a ton of articles on battered women nationwide.

"Here's the information you asked for, Mama Kizzy. I hope you're not planning to open up your home to these people."

"No. Why do you ask?"

"These domestic disputes can get pretty violent," she said. "Sometimes the victims start to have second thoughts about leaving and phone their abusive spouses to let them know where they are. It could put you in harm's way."

"No, no not a chance," I reassured her. "The only harm I'm worried about is what certain underhanded deacons are trying to do to our church. I'm hoping with this information I can quarantine the harm virus in a big test tube ... or maybe, set the whole lab on fire."

****

That night the meeting began with a long prayer by Deacon Moore. A distinguished gray-haired gentleman in his late fifties, who owned a small construction company, Moore was one of the few deacons willing to stand up to Poe. Though Poe tried to control him with small fix-it contracts around the church, Moore remained his own man. That night, his prayer was for discernment and a cooperative spirit within the flock.

When Deacon Grubbs chimed in with a second prayer, his petition was for the congregation to be obedient and for detractors from God's vision to be cut off.

As a scientist, I often thought about the mechanics of prayer. It was a wireless operation with very complicated logistics. First of all, only saved people had a sending unit. Secondly, if a unit was clogged with unconfessed sins, the transmission would shut down. Finally, if a prayer was unsuitable to the Father in Heaven, the Holy Spirit would clean it up or block it, altogether.

Like the splitting of an atom or the reversal of a magnetic field, all of these processes took place in an invisible world. As members of the family of God, all we had to go on were the laws of operation, set forth by the manual we called the Bible, and the belief that all these things were true, according to our faith.

As I listened to Deacon Grubbs, I wondered whether there was a big trash compost deep in the earth in which unacceptable prayers were deposited, or whether they just disintegrated into thin air. Either way, on that night, disobedient detractors had absolutely nothing to worry about. Deacon Grubbs' prayer had been sucked into the big compost the minute it left his mouth.

Not that I considered myself a detractor. I had sat through many business meetings and not said a word. But with Mr. Myles gone on to Glory, I had to speak out, especially on critical issues that affected the entire church. As a tithe-paying member in good standings, the privilege came with the territory.

As soon as Deacon Grubbs finished filling up the compost, the door opened to the Pastor's study. Pastor Fordham and his entourage of deacons and trustees marched down the steps and onto the sanctuary floor. After attending Estelle's church, their bland entrance seemed melodramatic. It didn't help that the old sleaze ball, Horace Womack, was bringing up the rear. Dressed in one of his patented green striped suits, he was loaded down with more posters and diagrams than he had the meeting before.

There were three microphone stands and two flimsy card tables set up on the floor in from of the pulpit. A handful of deacons sat behind the tables while the other church officers filled in the front row pew.

Pastor Fordham stood at the middle microphone in blue dress slacks, a white shirt and blue striped tie. He held a small black leather note pad in his hand.

Finally, he cleared his throat. "I'd like to welcome you all to a very important event in the church's history. The Board has presented me with an ambitious plan to meet the growing needs of this community. And before the night is over, we hope to win your support."

Several deacons grabbed stapled documents from a large cardboard box and began passing them out to the congregation. Deacon Poe sat quietly behind one of the tables, watching the action unfold.

Pastor Fordham continued. "While they're passing those out, I want to congratulate Aisha Baker and Tyrone Willis for their winning essays on *God's Promises To Youth*. They will receive a

$1,000 scholarship to the college of their choice. Let's give them a hand."

The church responded with a round of applause.

"Secondly, our drive to feed 500 homeless during the upcoming Juneteenth Parade has already been realized, thanks to a generous donation from Astro City Cleaners. Can you say Amen?"

The congregations shouted, "Amen!"

"Now, I don't know where you've been taking your clothes to get them cleaned. But, I'm asking you. Between now and June 19th, I want you to take your clothes to Astro. They've got a number of locations around the city. And right is just right, Amen?"

"Amen, amen!" They confirmed his sentiment.

"Finally, I'm proud to announce Deacon Moore had one of his plumbers come over and fix the pipes in the basement. It took some doing to tear away the cement and drywall to get to those old pipes. But I'm told the problem is solved, and at a sizable savings to the church. Let's give Deacon Moore a hand."

The women applauded more enthusiastically. The pipes had created a foul odor in the women's restroom for months.

Pastor Fordham looked at Deacon Moore and smiled. "I tell you what, Deacon Moore. That basement is kind of spooky. It's damp. It's dark. Nobody ever goes down there. I understand the Jewish congregation before us used to hear noises like somebody was filming a horror movie. I don't know whether your plumber went down there with his Bible or his twelve gage shotgun. But I appreciate you getting the job done. Now if we can just get somebody to clean the place up."

The congregation broke into laughter. But there were no volunteers.

As the deacons returned to the front, Pastor Fordham glanced at his copy of the document. "Okay, it looks like everyone has a copy.

I want to call your attention to page two where you'll find an itemized budget. Everything is here in black and white. You'll also notice that the salaries for the total church are listed as a comprehensive number. They're not broken out for each individual because we have some full-time people here. And frankly, they're entitled to the same privacy that you have on your job. I don't think you want everyone at your company to know what you make. Amen?"

A sprinkling of members responded. "Sure don't."

"Now I'm aware that people want to know what the preacher makes. And I don't mind telling you. You are paying me $62,000 a year, plus a small housing allowance. Some say that's too much. Others say it's not enough. So, I guess I'm okay."

Frogman, who appeared to be asleep at first, stood up and waved his hand.

Pastor Fordham recognized him. "Yes sir."

"You, you, you want to know what I make at the diary?" he asked.

The Pastor scratched his head. "Not unless you just want to tell me."

Frogman thought about it for a while. "I don't."

He sat back down.

The whole church erupted.

Pastor Fordham sniggled. "I wish more of you were open like that. Maybe we could get these tithes to match up with your income."

Deacon Poe shook his head with great vigor.

The Pastor continued, "Any questions about the budget?"

Still wearing his neck brace from the accident with a City of Houston METRO bus, Maurice Henderson stood up.

Pastor Fordham spotted him. "Brother Henderson, come on up here to the microphone if you have a question."

Clad in a tan jogging suit and orthopedic shoes, Brother Henderson walked gingerly to the microphone closest to his side of the sanctuary. "I just want to know why we're spending so much on security this year."

Pastor Fordham glanced at the $48,000 figure. Before he could reply, however, Deacon Grubbs stepped up to the other microphone. "If you don't mind, Pastor, I'd like to take that question."

The Pastor nodded, approvingly. "Go ahead."

"Everybody here knows the neighborhood has changed. We had two break-in attempts last year. Five vehicles we know of were either broken into or vandalized. Some of the local drug addicts stole the cooper out of the back air conditioning unit. And from what we hear, somebody robbed Pastor Buford at the Pentecostal church down the street. That's right, armed robbery right there on the church grounds."

Pastor Fordham shook his head with contempt. "What I think you're saying is we have to be proactive about this issue?"

"Exactly, Pastor." Deacon Grubbs confirmed. "By the end of this month we plan to have burglar bars on all the windows, additional security cameras on the inside and outside, motion detectors at the front and back, and an expanded security agreement with Brinks' night patrol. All that cost money. Should've cost more but Deacon Poe found us a deal."

Fiddlers rule, I thought to myself.

"I see," said Brother Henderson. "You gotta do what you gotta do."

He headed back to his pew.

"Any other questions?" Pastor Fordham surveyed the entire church. "If not, let go to the main event."

Deacon Poe sat up in his seat.

Pastor Fordham slipped into his serious preaching face. "As a church we have a spiritual obligation to serve the community in which we live. We can't be everything to everybody. God didn't intend all churches to be the same. When you look in Revelation, you see John writing to the seven churches in Asia with names likes Sardis, Philadelphia, and Laodicea. One thing becomes clear. They all were different. First Reunion is different. And so our calling is different.

"We have been blessed with a congregation that can do more. And to whom much is given...."

Much is required. I toyed with taking up Elder Vicky's legendary role, but kept the audition within the confines of my mind.

"We have a situation in our city where women are being beaten, bullied and besieged; Not by strangers nor callous actors from the outside world. No, these women are being tormented by people they know: husbands, boyfriends, live-ins. We had a woman come by the church a few months ago, just trying to find a place to hide. We called around to six different shelters and barely got her in.

"As God would have it, about the same time, Deacon Poe and the brothers came to me with a bold idea. I kept thinking about that woman's black eyes and bruised face. I felt like God was telling me this is something First Reunion needs to do.

"I'm going to ask Deacon Poe to come now and share the details of our plan. Once he's finished, you'll get a chance to vote up or down on this important initiative. I know it's an ambitious undertaking. I also know with Christ, all things are possible. Come on Deacon Poe."

From my bird nest in the sky, I could see Cora Williams looking back at me. I nodded my head as if to say, "Here we go". And go, we did.

Deacon Poe, tall and slender with a cleft chin and thick mustache, stepped up to the middle microphone with a different set of papers. He glanced at the pages a few seconds, as if allowing the suspense to build. Finally, he spoke.

"Good evening. I want to thank our Pastor for this opportunity. It's hard to find a man like him; a man with an open mind and a dedicated heart for God's work. I know we have the Pastor's Appreciation Services coming up in a few months. But let's just stopped and give him a big hand, just to show our appreciation for him right now."

The whole church stood up and clapped for almost a minute. Poe waited for them to settle down, then, started to read from a prepared script.

"In Houston, Texas, a woman is mentally or physically abused by her husband, boyfriend or live-in every 45 seconds. Battered women shelters turn down about 70% of the requests made for emergency shelter each week. Hospital emergency rooms have observed an overall increase of 30% more women being admitted for treatment from altercations related to domestic violence. Over 42% of murdered women are killed by their intimate partners.

"Brothers and sisters, the trends are clear. Whether we blame it on broken families, higher unemployment, pornography, drugs, or the general pressures of everyday life, the results are still the same. Women are being mistreated and abused. The tendency for this horrible occurrence is on the rise.

"We've put together a bold plan to address this issue in our community. First, we'll provide shelter and protection for those seeking to escape the abuse. Secondly, we'll provide counseling for both the abused and the abuser so they may work together to eliminate any reoccurrence of abuse within the relationship. Finally, we'll provide job training and referrals for victims wanting to start a new life on their own."

Like a balloon with a slow leak, I quietly exhaled. Despite by built-in skepticism, I couldn't help being impressed by his professionalism and thoroughness. According to the articles I had read, Poe was right on target. He had left no stone unturned. Furthermore, there was a real need to do something about the growing abuse within black families. Porno, television, the military and even well intended feminist groups had given women a durable, hard-nosed, unrealistic image; one that exaggerated their physical and emotional endurance. My students played popular rap songs from the rat-infested Fifth Ward projects that suggested "bitches" liked being slapped around. It was supposed to be a sign in the context of street life that the abuser really cared.

Leading up to 1993, there had been a movement afoot to strip the modern woman of her delicacy and grant her equal status in the most barbaric way. That meant having the liberty to slug her with an angry fist or slam her against a wall; whatever merciless acts it took to get her back in line. If it was okay for Charlie's Angels to beat the tar out of a full grown man, then it was okay for a man to beat the tar out of a full grown woman.

After years of power grabbing and self-glorification, Deacon Poe was finally on to something. What I couldn't understand was how sleaze master, Horace Womack, was going to fit in.

Eventually, Poe explained, "Our church is too small to house this kind of operation. Our plan is to buy the Silver Dollar Hotel across the street."

The Silver Dollar Hotel was an anomaly of sorts, a big white elephant left over from the mid 1950's when the Jewish community owned all of the large mansions along nearby Brays Bayou. Named after its eccentric owner, Silver Dollar Jim West, a millionaire oilman who threw silver dollars to strangers from his chauffeur-driven limousine, the sixty room tower was a memorable part of Houston's socialite history. The rich and famous toasted the evening at many private galas in the exquisite Silver Ballroom. It was not unusual for celebrities such as Frank Sinatra, Johnny Cash and Senator Lyndon Baines Johnson to be in attendance.

Of course, back then, blacks were not welcome at such lofty establishments. Only the colored cooks, busboys and maids had access. They were the ones who brought back to the community the tantalizing stories of sloppy drunk governors, cattle ranchers and oil magnates. They were the ones who saw the big, important white folks with their guard down.

Legend had it Silver Dollar Jim had built the hotel out of spite. Late one night he had pulled one of his many blue Cadillac's into the Shamrock Hotel, only to be turned away because of a national publisher's convention. Since Jews owned most of the publishing industry, and since the desk manager who told him there were no more rooms was Jewish, Silver Dollar Jim took it personally. He bought some high profile acreage in the heart of the Jewish community and built his own hotel. He also gave orders to his managers that anyone with a name like Levine or Goldberg or Bernstein should immediately be turned away.

The hotel never made money. So, in 1958, just after Silver Dollar Jim's death, executors of the estate sold the hotel to some foreign businessmen who eventually shut it down. The building was set aside as a possible historical site. But no one on City Council ever followed through. Thus, the old gray and white structure just sat there for thirty years, boarded up, abandoned and rotting to the ground.

Over the years, several murder victims had been found inside the hotel. At one point, crack heads had taken up residence and started selling valuable relics and furniture out of the back door. Though dilapidated and ransacked, in 1993 it was still standing. If Deacon Poe had found a way to bring it back to life and use it for the good of the community, then I was all for it.

That's when Deacon Poe called Horace Womack to the

microphone. "This is our real estate consultant and project manager. He'll explain how the whole thing is going to work."

"How y'all doing tonight?"

With you in our midst, we all have severe finger cramps from holding tight to our wallets.

"Is everybody glad to be in the house of the Lord?"

A few people responded. "Amen."

Womack held up his poster with a blueprint of the building. "I'm gone make this real simple. That hotel needs a lot of work. The total cost to refurbuus the whole thang and bring it up to code is $3.4 million. Using my contacts with the Department of Housing and Urban Development, the government is gone pick up 90%. You only pick up the balance of 10%. That includes all fees. And I guarantee no overruns. Now that's a sweet deal. It don't git no better than that."

Deacon Poe went on to explain that in approximately twenty months, thirty-one dorm rooms would be available for occupancy. Another twenty rooms would come on line six months later. To give hope to the battered women of Houston, all we needed to do was approve the plan and the leadership and Womack would take care of the rest.

"Any questions?" asked Poe.

Several hands went up.

Deacon Poe recognized his wife, Nora.

With a fresh short silky cut from the swankiest beauty shop in Third Ward and meaty brown face loaded with makeup, she stood up in some kind of spotted fox fur jacket. It was totally inappropriate for Houston's weather, but representative of her many trips to the east coast.

Because of her incessant posture of raising both hands and reaching for the sky during praise services, some members referred to her as the Sky Witch. She tried to cultivate the image of a spiritual elitist, walking on clouds and communing with the Holy One.

Yet, everyone knew how quickly the communing ended when you rubbed her the wrong way. Step on her $300 spiked pumps or park your car in her parking spot and you were in for the cursing out of your life.

"Thissss is wonderful, darling." She puckered her proper lips. "I know you've been burning the midnight oil on this project. I want to apologize publicly for nuut being the understanding wife I norrrrmally am. But seeing this plan tonight, you have my full supportttt."

A few members clapped. Most people just sighed, however, trying to stomach her bad acting. The least Poe could've done was written her a script with the same polish as his own.

Another woman, middle-aged and neatly dressed, walked up to the microphone. She was a new member I didn't recognize. "Who will decide who can get in? I mean, I have a daughter who needs this right now."

Poe quickly explained, "We plan to set up an admissions team to screen all applicants. But I can assure you members of this church will get first priority."

Old lady Blake stood up, bony and fragile, with a head full of bluish gray hair. Her purple and white flowered MuuMuu dress resembled an oversized nightgown. With her son's help, she hobbled up to the microphone that had been inadvertently set for shorter people. With Alzheimer's disease knocking hard at her door, no one knew what she was going to say.

"Giving honor to God, to the Pastor, to the officers of this fine church, and to all my brothers and sisters in Christ. I'm so glad to be here tonight to witness this glorious occasion. I praise God for the Pastor and the deacons of this here church. Pastor, you don't know what this means.

He extended a courteous nod, allowing her to continue.

"I remember back in 1938. This was before y'all time; right before the war broke out. My first husband used to git drunk every Friday night. He'd come home and beat me every Friday night." Her voice began to break up as she remembered the pain. "I didn't have nowhere to go. There wasn't no government homes you could run to. That's the reason I shot that bastard. I shot him right between the eyes."

Her son tried to pull her away from the microphone. But she grabbed it and dragged it down the aisle with her. Her small wrinkled hands were like tiny immovable clamps around the microphone's extended base. After a brief struggle, her son finally relented, allowing her to finish.

"Young women you better know who you getting tangled up with before you get all starry-eyed in love and foolish in the head. You can see the signs of a beater right from the start. It don't take long for him to find a reason. Just remember, a leopard don't change his spots and a devil don't change his ways. He stays the same."

As they escorted her to her seat, her profound warning triggered a lonesome thought in the back of my mind.

Mr. Myles had told me Poe was a back-stabbing, slick-headed devil who would sell you out at the drop of a hat. And yet, there I was, trying my best to soak in his rhetoric and overlook his sleazy supporting cast. I wanted so badly for the project to work. I wanted every woman in every corner of the city to find a safe haven from their pain. I wanted the word to get out that First Reunion was making a difference. But old lady Blake had called us out with a hard dose of reality: *A devil don't change his ways.*

Poe waited a while for the sniggling to subside. "If there are no more questions, I believe we're ready to vote."

I did have questions, for me, for Mr. Myles and for the rest of the congregation. I needed to know whether Mr. Myles' assessment of Deacon Poe was absolute. I needed to know whether a devil could change his ways. And for the rest of the congregation, I needed to know whether the project in which they seemed so willing to plunge was powerful enough to overcome the reputations of the people who brought it to them.

When you slice open a frog, the guts fall out. That's when you can really observe the true condition of the animal. The insides tell you whether it was sick or well. The insides tell it all.

I raised my hand and began to slice.

Deacon Poe smiled a crooked smile. "Sister Kizzy, don't worry about coming down from your skybox. We'll send the microphone to you."

Deacon Grubbs walked back to my platform and handed me a portable microphone.

"Before we vote, I'd like to ask a few questions about the plan."

"That's what we're here for, Sister Kizzy." Poe reminded me with a condescending tone.

"As I understand it, the church would be responsible for 10% of the cost of rebuilding the hotel. That comes out to $340,000. Is that right?"

"Approximately. That's correct."

"Do we have $340,000 in the bank, over and above our normal expenses? I know when we wanted to get our bell tower fixed so the bell would ring again on Sunday mornings, we were told there wasn't any money. Same thing when we wanted to send our youth to the National Convention in Atlanta. Same thing when we tried to get a new van for the Sunday pickup. Same thing-"

He interrupted. "If you're asking how we plan to finance the 10%, we've already talked to two local banks that are willing to provide the capital."

"Once we get the loan, who do we pay?"

He frowned. "I'm not sure I understand your question."

"If we vote yes and the loan is approved, who does First Reunion write the check to?"

"The general contractor, of course."

"Who is the general contractor?"

"Well, it's a little early to say right now. Our project manager will handle that."

"The project manager, meaning Mr. Womack?"

"Yes, Sister Kizzy. One in the same."

"Who pays Mr. Womack to find the general contractor?"

Growing more irritated by the minute, Horace Womack grabbed the microphone. "It ain't that hard to understand. The church pays me and I pay the general contractor. That's how it normally works."

I took out a pink Kleenex and dabbed my forehead. "Y'all please bear with me. I've gotten up in age and it takes me a while to understand. I could've sworn I heard Deacon Poe say the church writes a check to the general contractor. Now you're saying the church writes a check to you."

Womack's voice roared. "What difference does it make?"

"No offense to you, Mr. Womack. But I'm just wondering. If we wrote a $340,000 check to you and the hotel somehow didn't get built, from whom would we expect to recover our money?"

"It's gonna to get built. You don't have to worry about that."

Now that the frog was open, I had one last slice to make.

"Mr. Womack, you say the 90% is taken care of by the government?"

"That's what I said."

"Which government entity is providing the funding?"

Poe grabbed the microphone. "I think we already said the Department of Housing and Urban Development."

"Is this a loan, grant, guarantee, what?"

Poe growled. "It's a partnership, Sister Kizzy. This whole initiative is a government/private sector partnership. It may be a bit too complicated for people not in this business to understand."

I smiled, respectfully. "I'm hoping it's not too complicated for you to explain whether it's a loan, grant, guarantee, what?"

Womack snatched the microphone from Poe. "It's a guarantee."

"Do you have a copy of this guarantee with you, something that says the government is committing this money to this project?"

"This is reedikluus!" Womack bellowed. "It's way too early for that."

Poe grabbed the microphone back. "Sister Kizzy, I feel like you're wasting everybody's time, here."

Deacon Moore stood up. "Well now, Deacon Poe, I don't think it's a waste of time. I'm in the business and frankly these are some of the same questions I wanted to ask."

"If you had been at the deacon's meeting, maybe some of these questions would've been answered for you," declared Poe, scolding him publicly.

"That's true. But were these other people invited to the meeting?" He asked in a calm, steady voice. "I'm just saying we owe them an explanation too."

Cora Williams stood up. "I think that's a lot of money to put into something if we don't know all the in's and out's."

Katherine Baker stood up. "I have five children, three still in school. If something like that happened to me, would my children be able to come along too? And if so, would they have to change schools to match the address across the street?"

Pastor Fordham could see that things were getting out of hand. He walked over to another microphone. "I can see we have a lot of questions; some of which we don't have answers. As Deacon Poe mentioned, this is a very complex undertaking."

"But doable, Pastor." Poe tried to reassure him.

"Doable, indeed. But let's take our time and do it right, Amen?"

"Amen." The congregation responded, emphatically.

"I'm going to ask the deacons to set up a question box out in the foyer. Anyone with questions, just write them out and drop them into the box. You don't have to sign your name unless you want to. We'll collect the questions on Sunday, then meet again next Wednesday to see if we can go forward."

Deacon Grubbs stood up. "Pastor, you have those two revivals in Kansas City next week."

"Oh, oh that's right," Pastor Fordham blushed. "Let's make it the last Wednesday in May. Is that okay?"

The members nodded, affirmatively. Horace Womack shook his head, disgustedly, then, wrote the new date in his planner.

As the meeting adjourned and Ububee backed my chair down the small ramp connected to my platform, several members came over.

"Thank you, Mama Kizzy. We didn't know what to ask."

"I'm no expert, child. Just hoping to sort things out."

Ububee leaned over and whispered, "You made dim look like monkey fools."

"Believe me. I wasn't trying to do that," I explained.

"Exactly, what were you trying to do?" A penetrating voice rushed over my back shoulder.

I turned my chair to see Deacon Poe standing a few feet away.

"I beg your pardon?" I responded, politely.

"Do you have something against battered women?" Poe asked.

"No. But I do have something against tainted frog guts."

"Huh?" He squinted.

I took a few seconds to stare at his clueless face. And then I rolled away.

Chapter Eight

The following morning my phone rang off the hook. Members of First Reunion called to thank me for making the deacons more accountable. Deacon Moore called to remind me of Mr. Myles' courageous opposition during his hay-day on the Board.

"Ole deek used to give 'em hell." He remembered, fondly.

With so many people calling, it reminded me of the time I had won the Galbraith Award for innovative thinking. They had published an article in the newspaper and shown my face on the Channel 2 evening news. Ironically, not a single well-wisher had read my hypothesis. Apparently, reading was a bit too much to ask from a Great Depression generation only one step removed from illiteracy. All they cared about was my new-found notoriety and the fact that I had won $10,000.

My best friend, Charlotte Lueese, had read my *Scholium of Numeric Prediction*, though. She had read every word. I guess that's why the rash of phone calls sparked a curious depression deep down inside my stomach. They made me think about my best friend and the similar calling frenzy I had experienced when she disappeared.

I decided to dial her number; the one perpetually taped to my egg-shaped Saxon antique dresser mirror in the bedroom. I hadn't tried it in a long time.

When Southwestern Bell's standard analogue recording came on and said what it usually said, I did what I usually did.

NOT A WORKING NUMBER. The poor excuse for a human tried to pound it into my stubborn, she-devil brain. I slammed the stupid phone down and began to cry.

It was always a good cry ... a cleansing, liberating cry, like passing gas after a big bowl of cornbread and buttermilk. It sustained me for another round of wishing and hoping and longing for her return.

Mr. Myles use to say, "As long as she's not officially dead, she's officially alive."

But that was a lot easier to believe back in '79. By 1993 the official case status had changed from missing to inactive. Inactive was a polite way of saying forgotten. A thousand new crimes had edged out the old unsolvables and no one seemed particularly interested in following the hounds down a cold trail. Every time I called the Portland Police Department some rookie flatfoot stumbled through a new discourse of ignorance and hooted like an owl. "Hoo, hoo, who is that again? And hoo, hoo, who are you? And hoo, hoo, who gives you the right to ask these questions about an ongoing investigation?"

Traces of her blood had been found in a stolen rental car twenty miles from the Portland Marriott. With three hundred hairdressers sashaying in and out of the hotel's fancy swivel glass doors, who would have noticed one squatty little, bright-faced ball of energy, pushing against the crowd? And then again, who wouldn't have noticed her?

A seventy-one year old doorman thought he remembered seeing her, talking to a policeman outside the hotel. But at his age, investigators received his testimony with a grain of salt.

Old people often see things that aren't really there. We

scientists call it mind plasticity. It's a sophisticated mechanism that kicks in to help them cope with the harsh realities of a chaotic life. It dampens the fears and frustrations that accompany memory loss, aching joints, and constipation. It revisits the past and massages painful memories so that the future can salvage some fleeting sense of hope and the present can exist in a self-serving vacuum of peace.

Just before she died, Aunt Twigg confided in me that a man was following her around. But no one ever saw the man; no one but her. I came to realize the man was a figment of her imagination, a composite of all the men who had taken advantage of her wishful heart. In the end, they pursued her from the shadows of her mind. Their collective shame had merged into one spineless suitor, tormented by thoughts of what could've been.

I understood her pain. When Mr. Myles died in '83 of congestive heart failure, not a week went by without my smelling a faint whiff of cigarette smoke, coming through the front porch window. It wasn't just any cigarette smoke, but rather, the strong, eye-watering variety that came from a pack of unfiltered Camels. That was the only brand he smoked.

Since I didn't like him polluting the house, he would take a seat on the old white wooden bench outside of the front door. There, in private meditation, despite my repeated concerns about his health, he would savor each poisonous puff. Sometimes, just for a minute or two, he would hum a quiet tune. It was always the same tune and always the same verse:

Oh when the saints, go marching in
Oh when the saints go marching in
Lord I want to be in that number
Oh, when the saints go marching in....

I guess, in those early weeks of mourning, the plasticity

mechanism that allowed me to smell the Camels through the open window calculated the potential damage to my sanity had I heard him singing too. Thus, the smoke came to me as a silent comforter, a personal reassurance that Mr. Myles was still there by my side.

Maybe the old Marriott doorman was lonely and needed the attention. And so his brain created a false memory to make him the center of attraction. Or maybe, just maybe, he did see Charlotte Lueese talking to someone. Maybe the overworked, under budgeted Portland Police Department had been given a solid lead and simply dropped the ball.

Whatever the case, I intended to keep calling. No one was going to forget my friend until we found out the truth.

At 12:00 noon, the phone rang again. This time it was my daughter, Lizzy, calling from the hospital. "I'm leaving now, Mama. Are you ready?"

With all of the calls coming in, I had forgotten to make out my bills. On every first Monday of the month, Lizzy took me to the light company, phone company, and finally to the Weingarten's Grocery Store courtesy booth to pay my bills. Although it was a Safeway grocery store now, I still called it Weingarten's.

Back in the day when black folks were still Colored, Weingarten's was the only grocery store in town that treated us with respect. They supported the community. They once gave my class a donation to attend the state science fair. I even got a chance to shake hands with old Joe Weingarten's son.

Mr. Myles use to say, "Them some smart Jews. They know how to make the cash register ring."

But they did more than make money. They figured out a way to bring together two cultures at a time when catering to anyone other than whites was a risky business. Everyone in the store shopped shoulder to shoulder and basket to basket. Black and white children laughed and played, while slobbering on the store's legendary thick, double-glazed donuts, baked fresh every day. Meat cutters made every customer, black, white and brown, wait their turn. Cashiers smiled the same smile for me as they did for everyone else in line.

Sure, Kroger's and Randalls and Foodtown were closer and had better prices. But I made Lizzy take me to the last standing Weingarten's twenty miles away. The store brought back fond memories and gave me a chance to say hello to the hand full of old timers still waiting to retire. Safeway was painted on the big sign in front of the old brown brick building. But Weingarten's was still ingrained in the store's heart.

Besides, a feisty old security guard named Jacob smiled and winked at me each time I came in. That bit of amorous attention made the trip worthwhile.

I knew Lizzy didn't like the inconvenience of driving way across town, just like I didn't like the inconvenience of changing her smelly, childhood diapers or cleaning up her puke or hauling her to piano and voice lessons twice a week for God knows how many years. But she was my daughter and I had an enduring love for her, and an obligation to take care of her. Now, I was her mother and she had an obligation to look after me. The privilege to be chauffeured all the way across town came with the territory.

And so I extended to her what Buster Williams used to call a gambler's bluff. I said, "I'm ready. I'm waiting on you."

Immediately, I hung up the phone and scrambled for my bills. I would've had them done and my new Deluxe checks filled out when she arrived, had it not been for my surprise visitor. I looked out of my window to find Bishop Ebenezer, standing on my front porch.

It took him a while to ring the doorbell. I suspected he was having second thoughts about addressing me face to face. Ironically, I felt the same way.

Things were a lot simpler when he was an addlebrained shyster, swindling insurance companies and selling stolen goods in the back alleys of Missouri City. But now, I didn't know exactly what he was ... budding theologian, miracle healer. Willing vessels for the Lord's work had apparently fallen into very short supply.

When I opened the door, I spotted something familiar in his hand. It was my favorite walking cane, the one with the shiny wood grain handle; the one I had lost during the Holiness stampede.

"I believe dis here belong to you." Without a clue of formality or howdy-do, he handed it to me through the screen door.

"Well, thank you." I gripped it tightly, breathing a sigh of relief. It felt curiously warm like a tree limb that had been baking in the midday sun.

As if he could read my thoughts, he explained, "God told me to bless it for you, a mighty blessing."

Surely, he wasn't expecting me to believe that his meager incantations had raised the temperature on my old walking stick.

In the Bible, Elijah had called down fire from heaven. But Bishop Ebenezer was no Elijah. He was more of a street thug turned religious hustler, turned oddball fanatic for Jesus Christ.

Oddly, he was something else too. I could feel it in my spirit, like standing next to someone with a low-level radioactive Geiger counter on. Against my better judgment, I invited him to come in.

He smiled with embarrassment. "Thank you, but no ma'am. The Council don't approve of ministers going into no widow woman's house alone."

The quest for righteous living.

That was no way for an addlebrained shyster to respond.

"What are you now? Really?" I finally asked him, directly.

He pondered a moment. "I'm a traveler, like you, Sister Kizzy.

I'm a traveler on the King's Highway. I done left where I was. But I ain't got to where I'm gone be."

"You're healing people now?"

"I ain't. But God is."

"So what's next?" I asked. "Another snake carnival come-to-town?"

He dropped his head, trying to choose the right words. "Estelle came to see me bout' that. She said you told her to."

"Estelle is a grown woman. She makes her own decisions."

"I pre'shate what you did. It gave me a chance to say what I've been needing to say for a long time."

"Did you apologize for that foolishness? Did y'all get an understanding? Is she still a member of the church?"

"More than that." His eyes sparkled with anticipation. "She's my wife to be."

"What!" My heart pounded like a million kettle drums.

"I love that woman, Sister Kizzy. I asked her to marry me."

"And she said ... yes?"

"Not yet. But God told me it's gone be alright."

Thank you, Jesus. Still time to stop a catastrophe.

And then I heard my favorite German Black Forest cuckoo clock go off in the living room with chimes from Home Sweet Home. "Listen, Bishop. I have to get ready now. My ride is on the way."

"Show-nuff, Sister. You pray for me and I'll pray for you."

"Pray, I will, as hard as an old widow woman can pray. You can count on that."

****

An hour later, Lizzy and I cruised down the crowded Southwest Freeway, headed to Weingarten's.

She glanced over at me. "Why are you so quiet today?"

"Oh, just thinking."

"Thinking about what?"

"I'm thinking about God's lenient admissions policy."

She frowned, "Huh?"

I'm wondering why in the world he'd let an illiterate imbecile into this family."

"Now Mama I resent that. U is not an imbecile. He's a smart man. And he's a good man. Why can't you just accept him for what he is and stop looking at his culture?"

"I wasn't talking about Ububee."

"Well, that would be a first," she snapped.

We rode another five minutes without saying a word. Finally, I broke the ice. "I was talking about your Loony Tune auntie."

"Auntee Stell?"

"Yes. Bishop Ebenezer is trying to marry her."

Lizzy held it as long as she could before bursting into a loud, howling giggle. "She *do* likes her some Bishop."

"It's a shame and a disgrace. I mean, the man says *feets*. Mr. Miles never had a whole lot of schooling. But he never said *feets*."

"You stay out of that, Mama. That's their business."

"Bishop was the one who came to my house and got me into their business."

"Still, you can't pick people's soulmate. What's good for you might not be good for someone else."

"Would you marry the Bishop?" I asked as we pulled into the Weingarten's parking lot.

"Maybe."

I thought about the odds of getting a straight answer out of her. "Why am I asking you? You already have your own imbecile."

Lizzy didn't hear me. She was preoccupied with the two Houston police patrol cars parked directly in front of the red brick veneer main entrance. An old scratched up off-white Harris County ambulance idled nearby, flashing emergency streaks of orange, blue and white.

We pulled into an open parking spot next to a green Dodge Caravan with rowdy, unattended young children throwing paper out of the windows. I told them to stop in my most authoritative teacher's voice. But they just laughed, then, tried out a few newly acquired Spanish cuss-words before diving beneath the tattered leather seats.

"Oh my Lord!" Lizzy was still enthralled by the flashing lights. "Someone must've robbed the place."

We struck out, aimlessly, like a pair of inquisitive country bumpkins, scuttling across the cracked gray concrete and faded white parking stripes, leading to the electronic glass doors. By the time we reached the entrance, a crowd had gathered. I spotted one of the old ruddy-faced meat cutters in a corner, taking his smoking break.

"What in heaven's name is going on?" I asked.

Wiping his thick glasses with his bloodstained apron, he finally replied. "They caught a woman shoplifting. Security had her on camera from the time before."

Lizzy's eyes bucked. "You think she's part of one of those motorcycle gangs that's taking over Houston? I hear the women have to steal something to become a member."

"If it's a motorcycle gang, they've got good taste. She had some of my choice cuts under her dress."

I grimaced. "She was stealing meat?"

"Meat, medicine, perfume. She had it strapped in a net between her ... well, you know, private parts."

"What kind of woman would do that?" I asked.

He pointed toward the entrance. "Maybe you can ask her, yourself?"

The exit doors slid open. Sandwiched between two HPD officers and a store security guard was none other than Thelma Mason, the church's announcing clerk. She had her head down, fiddling with the silver handcuffs around our wrists.

I called to her in my most compassionate voice. "Thelma?"

She finally spotted my anxious face in the crowd.

"He left," she whispered, softly. "Theo just left us." And then she began to cry. One last cry before the divorce papers came.

They lowered her head, pushed her into the back seat of one of the patrol cars, then, slowly drove away.

Lizzy sighed, deeply. "Our black men can be so selfish and irresponsible."

Recalling Thelma's perpetual gambling debts for which Backwater had footed the bill, I reminded her, "There are always two sides to every story."

"The man abandoned his family, Mama. What other side could there be?"

The meat cutter lit up a long cigarette, pushing a toxic white plume of smoke into the air. "There could be the nagging side ... the sneaking-around-while-you-at-work side ... Or the clean-out-your-bank-account side."

"I don't remember asking you for your life story," she snapped.

I grabbed her by the arm. "Come on here, girl, before this man makes your hindquarters the daily special."

Once inside the store, I took a moment to relish the familiar surroundings, the bright fluorescent tube lights, dangling from the vaulted ceiling, the hastily stacked end caps, loaded down with bargain-basement promotions and the dingy black and white checkerboard floor that stretched out with clever optical deception to make the store appear larger than it really was.

I quickly eyeballed the trusty friend with which I needed to collaborate, an old fashioned glass and wood model Western Electric phone booth with an accordion door. I couldn't begin to count the times I had used it to call Mr. Myles to check the cupboard for me. Just gripping the chunky black receiver spark a procession of enduring memories that almost made me cry.

"What are you doing, Mama?" Lizzy inquired.

"I'm calling Pastor Fordham. Somebody needs to know that Thelma's in jail."

Before I could drop my quarters into the slot, a clerk in the bakery department shouted, "It's out of order."

I heard his warning loud and clear. But it was too late to short circuit such a familiar routine. My old fingers released the two coins into the metal receptor and dared the clerk to say another word.

"Why don't y'all have a sign up?" I scolded him.

He pointed to the white sheet of paper under my feet. "You're standing on it."

Lizzy reached into her purse and pulled out her new one-pound, brick-heavy $900 white Motorola car phone. She raised the collapsible antenna. "Here, Mama, just use this."

"Over my dead body."

I wasn't about to use anybody's mobile phone. As a scientist, I knew all about the technology on which mobile phones were based. The radio waves that carried transmissions from one phone to another were full of radiation. That radiation passed directly through the soft tissues of the ear and into the brain.

I had warned Lizzy about the dangers of her new high tech status symbol. But she was part of a new generation that had to be shown. She wasn't going to be satisfied until her whole head turned into a big pumpkin and all her hair fell out.

Lizzy re-deposited the big white log into her bag, then, glanced toward the front of the store. "There's a phone at the courtesy booth, Mama. I'm sure they'll let you use that one."

It was a reasonable alternative. The problem was the phone was out in the open, available for everyone to use, and hear. I didn't want the entire store to know my church member had just shoved a bunch of sirloin steaks between her legs. Why did Thelma have to come to my Weingarten's in the first place?

"I have a better idea."

Jacob, the old security guard who had been flirting with me for years, had a desk and phone at the east end of the store. All I had to do was flash a friendly smile and he would let me use his phone. With the unexpected attention, he might even pull it out of the wall and give it to me to take home.

We made our way through a cluster of baskets and over to the security guard's desk. A young white man with reddish pimples sat at the desk, his dark eyes glued to a small portable computer monitor. He finally looked up. "Can I help you?"

I offered a courteous smile. "Is Jacob around?"

He paused. "Jacob, the old guy?"

"Jacob, the regular store security guard whose seat you're sitting in; Yes."

He shook his head. "Guess you haven't heard."

"Heard what?"

"The old guy dropped dead last week. He was sitting at this

very desk."

Lizzy's mouth flew open. "Oh my Lord, what happened?"

"His old ticker just stopped ticking, I guess. They said it was natural causes."

Lizzy stared at me. "I'm so sorry, Mama. Are you going to be alright?"

For a moment I stood there, mummified. It was not as though I had any romantic feelings for him. Mr. Myles was the only man for me. But to think how quickly things could change; how a kindred soul could be here one day and gone the next.

I read the obituaries each week, not to see who had died, but rather, who was still around. If their name didn't appear on the page, I assumed they were still out there, sucking in their fair share of oxygen, frustrating the masses, passing on bad habits to the next generation and giving some young smart aleck a piece of their mind. Jacob's name never appeared in the obituaries. He should've been sitting there at his desk.

I wondered how many poor, neglected souls had crossed over without receiving their rightful place on the page. If I ever started up another journal, I would devote a full section to people who had been left off. Maybe I would call it *The Overlooked* or *The Forgotten Few*.

As I pondered the best name for the new journal, Lizzy draped her arm around my shoulder. "Are you going to ask him?"

I looked at her, a blank expression on my face.

"The phone," she clarified. "Are you going to ask him about using the phone?"

Before I could respond, a huge eighteen-wheeler flashed on the security screen.

The guard checked his watch. "I'm sorry ladies. You'll have to excuse me. I've got to open the doors for this delivery. Maybe we can finish this conversation when I get back?"

He stood up from his chair, stretched, lethargically, then, walked away.

As I reached for the phone, a loud, intrusive baritone voice cried out from behind me. "Excuse us! Coming through."

I turned to see two medics rolling a heavyset black woman out on a stretcher. With the oxygen mask over her face, I barely recognize her. It was Eddie Maye, one of the old timers from the deli.

"What happened?" I asked another cook who trailed alongside the stretcher.

"She's gonna miss her pension." The young girl tried to explain.

"What do you mean?"

"I caaint say no more. They won't let us talk about it."

"Talk about what?"

The young girl loosened the apron string around her neck, then, followed the stretcher out to the ambulance.

I turned to a young grocery sacker, collecting empty baskets nearby. "Somebody's going to tell me something."

The young blonde headed kid appeared terrified. He chugged off with his basket train, leaving a group of stray carts scattered in the aisle.

That's when I spotted a familiar face a few aisles away. It was old man Weingarten's youngest son, Benjamin. Still lean and handsome, with dark hair and horn rimmed glasses, he stood by the courtesy booth, talking to the store manager.

I hobbled up, abruptly, without the slightest cordiality or howdy-do. "You probably don't remember me. But I remember you. Can you tell me what's going on?"

The store manager, round-faced, with a thick mustache, tried to intervene. "Ma'am, I'll be glad to help you in just a moment."

I repelled him with a harsh glare. "If you don't mind, I was talking to Mr. Weingarten."

"Well, Ma'am-"

"Hold on, Harry." Benjamin Weingarten interrupted. "I'll handle this myself." He looked at me for a brief moment. "I do remember you. You're a school teacher aren't you?"

My face melted into an appreciative smile. "Retired now."

"Has it been that long?"

"Six years, three months. But who's counting?"

"I'm sorry I don't remember your name."

"Kizzy Marie Sheppard Myles."

Mrs. Myles. Yes I recall now. What can I do for you?"

"They just rolled a friend of mine out of here on a stretcher. Nobody can tell me why."

"That would be Eddie ... Eddie Maye Lewis. She's been with the store for a long time."

"What happened?" I pressed.

It seemed an eternity before he finally replied. "Change happened, Mrs. Myles. Change that has a mind of its own."

The store manager walked away.

I stared, blankly. "I don't follow you."

"Have you ever seen a lake dry up?" Before I could answer, he continued, "I have. Two to be exact. One in the back of our house when I was growing up. First, you see mud where water use to be. Then deep, ugly cracks like somebody took a giant razor and carved up the ground. Finally, the weeds take over.

"It's not the lake's fault they've built a new dam upstream. But it's the lake that suffers. It's the lake that dies. It'll take the ducks and frogs and fish with it, unless they move on."

There was a deep sadness in his voice as he pointed to the

busy aisles behind me. "This is the second lake I've watched dry up."

"What do you mean?"

"This store will be closing in thirty days."

I pressed hard on my walking cane, desperately trying to balance my shaking knees. "What? The last Weingarten's ... closing?!"

He shook his head. "It hasn't been Weingarten's for a long time. It's Safeway now, part of a thousand Safeway's nationwide. They've built a new store three miles from here, near Greenway Plaza. They don't need this one anymore."

"Is this why Eddie Maye passed out?"

"They tried to find positions for the employees being displaced. But some didn't make the cut."

"Eddie Maye is the best cook at this store," I reminded him.

"She never finished high school. They discovered the error when they updated the files."

"What does a high school diploma have to do with being able to cook?"

"Safeway's HR department has its rules," he explained.

I pleaded in a soft voice. "Can't you do something?"

"Mrs. Myles, you haven't been listening. This is Safeway, not Weingarten's. We own the land. We own the building. But Safeway owns the store. In thirty days, this is going to be a dried up lake. There is nothing I can do."

At that moment, a professionally dressed Hispanic woman with long black hair walked out of the back office. "I'm sorry to disturb you, but the home office is on the line. They need to speak with you right away."

He gazed at me for a brief second, then, reached into his wallet to pull out a Weingarten's Realty business card. "I'm sorry we had to reacquaint ourselves under these circumstances. If you run across anyone who's interested in a dried up lake, have them give me a call."

He and the woman disappeared through the office door.

I stood there for a moment, soaking in the sorrow of it all. Change was like a great hurricane coming in off the Gulf. It had a mind of its own. All of the ducks and the frogs and the fish were moving to higher ground three miles away. Only me and Eddie Maye and the old Western Electric phone booth were still stuck in the mud.

I wondered what the new store would be like. But deep down inside, I realized I'd never know. For me and her and the old phone booth, the journey was over. The legacy ended here. The sweet memories of a magical era were passing before my eyes.

I took a deep breath and sucked in the moment, the smell of freshly baked bread, basket wheels squealing and cash registers ringing their glorious tune. And then I let go. For the last time I let it all go.

I turned around to find Lizzy standing behind me with a basket full of knickknacks. "Figured I'd pick up a few things while you were holding afternoon detention. Everything okay?"

"Yes," I nodded.

"Then why are you crying, Mama?" She walked over to me with a handful of tissues and dabbed my cheeks.

I paused for a while, trying to muster the words that would convince a member of her generation that all progress was not good. There were no words to capture the pain of those of us still stuck in the mud. And so I whispered, "You wouldn't understand."

"Now, Mama, you know you're going to have to tell me something. What did you find out?"

"I found out I won't be needing you to drive me across town anymore."

"Oh no? Why not?"

I stared at her a long while, a solemn expression on my face. And then I revealed a profound truth that would take her a lifetime to understand.

"The lake has dried up."

And that was all I was able to say.

Chapter Nine

I didn't go to church the following Sunday. The news about the store closing, Eddie Maye's dismissal and the old man's death pushed me into a lingering state of depression. I needed some time alone to gather my thoughts. Besides, Pastor Fordham was still out of town, conducting another revival. That usually meant one of the two associate ministers would have to fill in.

If there was one mystery about the black church, it was the universal incompetence of most associate ministers. Aunt Twigg used to refer to them as little horses, pawing in the valley; and rightfully so. They sat under the teaching of some of the most prolific orators in the country. But when it came time for them to grace the holy podium, they came off as babbling idiots. Some of them tried to sing their way through. Others resorted to the proselytized, doxologized, ecclesiasticism of big words to sound impressive. Still others tried to wear the congregation down with a never-ending series of commands to "look at your neighbor".

Most people didn't come to church to look at their neighbor. They came to hear the word of God. This vital piece of insight seemed to escape the purview of aspiring young messengers of the cloth. They plowed ahead with their own specialized brand of awkwardness and then cried foul when people didn't show up in droves to hear their puzzling report from on high.

Cora Williams called that Sunday afternoon to confirm my prediction. Reverend Abernathy had bellowed and spit and stumbled through a full hour of bad doctrine, this time, on the miracles of Jesus Christ.

"He told us the reason the Jews got angry at Jesus was because he messed up their breakfast," reported Cora, providing me with my first laugh since the store's closing. "He said when Jesus told the demons to go inside the swine, that meant no more bacon, no more poke sausage, and no more pig feet! He said that's the reason the Jews don't like Jesus today."

We cackled like two old chickens, until we were out of breath. Fortunately, the building had been void of any visitors and two thirds of the congregation had taken an on-the-spot sabbatical. It was reassuring to know his buffoonery hadn't pushed some unsuspecting soul through the gates of hell.

There was something else in her report that caught my attention. She said part of the church's front steps were roped off and torn out. Some kind of construction had begun, but no one seemed to know what. With Pastor Fordham out of town for two weeks, I wondered if Deacon Poe had pulled a fast one. Maybe some of his construction buddies needed a little project to tide them over.

I called Deacon Moore to see if I could get more information. To my surprise, he told me he was not at liberty to discuss the matter.

The whole point of the church's business meeting was to let the congregation know what was going on. There had been no mention of capital projects in the budget. And how could they improve security by tearing up the front steps?

Mr. Myles would've surely known about the details had he still been alive. But with him gone on to Glory, and Deacon Moore, biting his tongue, there was nothing I could do. The Pastor would be back in town for the meeting on Wednesday. I would most assuredly ask him about it then.

Later that afternoon, Lizzy and Ububee dropped in to check on me. They had stopped by Alfreda's Soul Food Cafeteria and brought me some oxtails, cabbage and sweet potato pie.

"Y'all know this is going to make my knees swell." I scolded them unmercifully as I took another delicious bite.

"It's not for de knees, it's for de heart." Ububee comforted me.

"Yeah, Mama. You've been a prune all week," added Lizzy. "You've got to stop worrying about things you can't control."

I wiped some of the cornbread crumbs from my lips. "You're right. You're both right. It's just that sometimes it seems like the world is going in the wrong direction."

"It's not so much the world, it's the US of A," declared Ububee. "The Devil is taking over dis county."

"Oh here we go, again," whined Lizzy.

"It's true. That is why I am going back to the motherland. I need to purify my spirit and get my mind in order."

"Admit it, U. You're going back to gloat in front of your relatives. You want them to know what a big man you are America."

I was well respected before I came to America," he insisted. "My whole family was."

"Then why did you come?" Lizzy asked, already knowing the answer.

Oddly enough, I didn't know the answer. In all of their six years of marriage, neither Lizzy nor Ububee had shared the deep secrets surrounding his migration to America. I hadn't pressed the issue. Frankly, I hadn't expected him to stay around long enough for it to matter. But now, as it became more apparent their marriage was going somewhere, I felt I should know.

And so I chimed in. "Yes, my dear son-in-law. Why did you come to this country?"

He stood by the kitchen counter for a long while, staring into space. "I will tell you, but only in the strictest of confidence."

I nodded, slowly. "Agreed."

"As boys, my two brothers and I grew up in a country full of turmoil and strife; religion against religion, tribe against tribe. People used to tell de joke to say Nigeria was like a water faucet. Even de weakest hands could turn it on and off.

"Our father was a government official in the Republic of Biafra under Colonel Ojukwu. He was a good friend of my father. I remembered de man coming to our house a few times just before de war started.

"In the north, a devil named Yakubu Gowon came to power. He attacked de Republic and began killing those who had been loyal to Ojukwu. One night the soldiers came for us. My father hid us in de jungle until we could get to Chad. From there, our uncle took us to London and then de United States."

As Ububee's face tightened, Lizzy intervened. "I know this is hard for you, baby. Maybe you should tell Mama the rest of the story another day."

"No," he insisted. "She should know de truth."

He moved closer, loosening his black church tie and taking a seat at the dining room table across from me. "My father went back to Nigeria."

I frowned. "Why? Weren't they trying to kill him?"

"They were holding my mother and her sister in prison in another town. Do you know what the soldiers did to women in prison back then?"

"No," I answered, softly.

His stern face seemed to grow darker, filled with contempt. "You don't want to know."

"U, please. Just leave it there," Lizzy pleaded.

But he continued. "My father thought he could bribe de officials. He knew of a sum of money. He would tell them for safe passage out of de country for him, my mother, and her sister. De officials agreed. They told him it was a deal. But when they got de money, Gowon's brother went back on his word. They executed all three of them. Of course, de torture came first."

My head dropped with empathy. "I'm sorry. I didn't know."

"De man who did this lives in South Africa now. Hotta Gowon they call him there. As a diamond trader, he lives very well, with fine cars and lots of wives. Do you think God forgot about what he did?"

"Our Bible tells us that God is omniscient. He knows everything and he never forgets," I reminded him.

Ububee shook his head with comfort. "This is good, because I never forget too."

We all fell into silence.

The pain of loss is like a blistering wind on a cold winter's day. Your eyes water and your face cracks. Your ears slowly succumb to the numbness of death. Still, you never see the wind, just the morbid imprints from its relentless assault.

At that moment, Ububee's face looked like my face, the one I would see in the dresser mirror each time the Southwestern Bell recorder reminded me that Charlotte Lueese's number was no longer a working number. Over the year, the pain had prompted me to ask the same question that Ububee asked. "Had God forgotten?"

Lizzy walked over to the cupboard and pulled out an old bottle of cooking wine. "You're depressing me, both of you. I keep saying the same thing."

"Which same thing is that?" Ububee inquired.

Lizzy took a quick gulp from her glass, then, grimaced. "Stop worrying about things you can't control."

Ububee glanced at me and smiled. "This is de thing of humor, Mama Kizzy. She pushes me out of the worry cart so she can have the whole wagon to herself."

"I'm not worried. Do I look worried?" She took another drink.

"What is she worried about?" I asked.

"Wedding bells," he revealed. "We see the good Bishop and Estelle, sitting in de soul food place, holding hands."

"They were NOT holding hands. I keep telling you that."

"Okay, the peach cobbler make their hands stick together," he taunted.

Lizzy huffed out of the kitchen and into the living room.

I marveled at her absent mindedness. "I told you about them the other day."

"Yes, I remember. It was funny then. But now...."

Ububee shook his finger. "She reeed about this forty-six year old woman having a baby. She think maybe the Bishop and Estelle will get married and have babies too."

"And she'd be the only one left out." I finished it off.

Lizzy sighed, disgustedly. "It's possible, isn't it? I mean, I see it every day at my job. Modern medicine has changed everything ... well ... except for me."

"Let me ask you a question, Lizzy ... Lizzy ... Lizzy! I'm talking to you."

She finally raised her head up.

"Come back in here so I can give you a piece of my mind." I

wiped the final traces of greasy crumbs from my mouth.

She got up from my white flowered sofa and flopped down at the far end of the dining room table.

"First of all, Estelle is really fifty-two years old, not forty-six like she tries to pretend. That makes a big difference in Babyland. Secondly, she doesn't want any more children. She has a grown daughter from her first ... encounter."

Lizzy's head popped up. "Auntee Stell has a daughter?"

"Somewhere in Georgia. They don't really keep in touch."

"Why hasn't anyone ever mentioned this?"

"You don't mention a fourteen year-old, moron-headed reee-tard having a baby out of wedlock, especially when it's your younger sister, and the father is the principal of the school."

Lizzy's chin dropped. "A principal raped her?"

"He seduced her. He did it with little gifts, kind words and nail polish money. Imagine a young girl in a small country town getting that kind of attention from a man of his stature."

"You didn't try to stop her?"

"Your Aunt Mattie, God rests her soul, and I had already come to Houston. Estelle was the youngest. Mama had died and Daddy was too old to keep up."

"So what happened?"

"They ran the principal and his family out of town. But he still sent money back to take care of the baby. A few years later, his wife showed up on Daddy's doorstep and asked to raise the child. She promised to care for her like she cared for her other children. Daddy agreed."

"So that's why you're so protective of her. You know Auntee Stell is gullible."

"You would say de proof is in de pudding slop," surmised Ububee.

129

"That's not the point. Just listen, will you?"

"Okay Mama. I'm listening."

"If God wanted to send you a child, would he send it through Estelle?"

She pondered a while. "I don't think so."

"That's right. Even if her ovaries made the comeback of the century, that has nothing to do with you. If God has given you something, and I'm sure he has, you don't have to worry about anyone else taking it away."

"You ... you're right, Mama," she acquiesced.

"Listen. I've told you this before. God controls the womb. You keep thinking you're having a baby for you. And that's selfish thinking. You're having a baby for Him to use in His kingdom. Y'all need to get on His time."

Ububee stood up. "I claimed that blessing. I claim it right now in the name of Jesus."

"Now, why don't y'all go back to your own home, and give Jesus something to work with." I winked at Ububee and he winked back at me.

Lizzy covered her face. "Oh, Mama, you're embarrassing me."

Ububee grabbed her hand. "Then let us take our shame back to de privacy of our own home."

I could already feel my knees throbbing from the oxtails. I pointed to the hallway. "Pass me my walking cane. I'll see you pregnant folks to the door."

Ububee walked over and grabbed the one with the shiny wood grain handle from the rack. He took a few steps, then stopped and turned back toward the hallway. "Have you been running your heater?"

"Of course not." Lizzy answered for me. "Not on a beautiful

spring day like today."

"Why do you ask?" I inquired.

With a curious expression, he stared at the old walking stick. "It feels warm, like de wood next to a cooking fire."

An eerie chill slid down my spine. I hadn't touched the cane since our trip to Weingarten's. When Ububee handed it to me, it felt the same as the day the good Bishop had delivered it to my door.

So much for my pragmatic deductive reasoning about the cane being locked up in the Bishop's hot car. So much for the erratic sensitivity I had assigned to the nerve endings of my feeble hands. The young generation had confirmed what the old generation was unwilling to admit. Something strange was germinating inside the old stick, something none of us understood.

It was dust dark when they finally left. As I stood on the porch, watching Ububee's tail lights fade in the distance, I realized I had prophesied in their lives. According to my race car mouth, God had already given them a child and everything was going to be alright. That's what I had told them. Was that my wishful thinking or had God actually spoken through me?

The Human Ghost was notorious for capitalizing on the strong but misguided desires of mankind. That was the source of many spiritual algorithms that bounced around like baby blocks inside the playpen of Christian infancy. I wanted so much for my daughter to be happy. I was just the right candidate to be misled, just the right vessel to send an unsuspecting young couple down a dark road of dashed hopes and unfulfilled dreams. The Lord is saying this and the Lord is saying that. Those were the sweet tarts that Christians threw out like candy from a Mardi Gras float on Fat Tuesday weekend. But who really understood the mind of God?

My solution in times of uncertainty was always to pray. But after sixty-seven years of navigating the murky waters of life, I had come to understand that prayer was no silver bullet. I prayed for Mr. Myles to stop smoking. But he never did. I prayed for Charlotte Lueese to come back home. But so far, she was still missing. I prayed for First Reunion to get back on track. But Deacon Poe and his cronies were still running the show.

Finally, I had prayed for Lizzy to have a child. But unto this very day....

At this juncture in my life, the Holy Grail was no longer prayer, but trust. I trusted that God was going to make everything alright. There was a contingency, however. He didn't have ninety of those Old Testament, Abraham-and-Sarah years to make it alright. My eyes were failing, my back teeth were falling out, my stomach was bubbling, my urine was occasionally laced with blood and my old knees were crumbling beneath me. If he was going to do something while I was on this side of River Jordan, he needed to do it soon.

As I started back into the house, my nostrils detected a familiar scent. A long time had passed since I relished the unmistakable aroma of an unfiltered Camel. I looked over at the old white bench where Mr. Myles use to sit, and I began to smile.

What more did God need to tell me? He was speaking in a language that only I understood. He had taken time out from his busy schedule of propping up the moon and the stars and keeping the mountains from tilting into the sea, just to let an old feeble-minded widow woman know: Everything was going to be alright.

Chapter Ten

The call came in on Wednesday, May 31st at 10:30 am. I know because I was parked in front of my big 32 inch wood cabinet Panasonic, watching the Channel 13 weatherman. He was tracking a large tropical depression over the Pacific Ocean. If you lived along the Gulf Coast, you paid close attention to anything that had the slightest resemblance to a hurricane. Just a year earlier, hurricane Andrew had slammed into south Florida packing an eighteen foot storm surge and 177 mph winds. It killed a bunch of people and caused $26 billion in damages. It barely missed Texas and only God knew why.

Texas had a history of calamity, from Galveston's great killer storm of 1900 to Hurricane Carla, a Category 5 monster that ravished the Texas coast in 1961. A little atmospheric trough over the coast of Africa could turn into a mild depression over the Atlantic, then blossom into a monster hurricane, headed for the Gulf of Mexico. Once it entered the Gulf, its point of landfall was anybody's guess.

People living along the Texas coast had two choices: evacuate, or ride it out. These were mortal decisions that could mean the difference between life and death. Even those who didn't have a formal understanding of barometric pressure and inverted troughs had their own set of hurricane rules.

As Mr. Myles put it just before hurricane Claudette hit in '79, "I'm gonna watch all three channels. Depending how worried these white folks look, I'm gonna to run like hell."

On that day in May of '93, the tropical depression being tracked by The National Hurricane Center had not yet reached the running stage. And so I took a break from my official observation post on the sofa to answer the phone call.

Anita, the church secretary, was on the line. She had called to notify me the scheduled church business meeting had been cancelled. The tropical depression had created severe weather conditions throughout the Midwest. "Pastor Fordham's return flight had been indefinitely delayed."

It wasn't until Friday morning at Lizzy's sewing club that I found out the full extent of his delay. Sitting there in the glass garden room, chatting with the group, I sensed that something was missing. And then I realized it was the exquisite fragrance of lilies and roses and honey and whatever else they put into Olivia Boudreaux's perfume. The diva of sensuality was conspicuously absent. Yet, no one had said a word. An older, frail faced woman named Stella McGee had taken over her spot.

After listening to Lizzy discuss fertility drugs, Estelle complain about her budding courtship with the Bishop and Katherine Baker reveal that her five children were really aliens from out of space, transported here to suck the life out of her, I finally asked, "Where is Olivia today?"

A sudden hush fell over the room.

Katherine Baker looked up from her machine with a smug face. "You might as well tell her."

"Tell her what? There's nothing to tell!" Lizzy flared.

134

Suddenly, I caught a flash of Ububee pushing clumsily against Olivia's delicate frame. I didn't have my cane. But I did spot a black iron poker near the fireplace in the next room, a wonderful substitute for bludgeoning an African skull.

Katherine Baker cut her eyes at me. "She's in Hawaii."

Ububee was still in Houston, which offered some hope his life would be spared another day.

Gauging Lizzy's agitated response, I continued to query. "Is there something wrong with her going to Hawaii?"

"That depends," said Katherine Baker.

"On what?"

Estelle chimed in. "On whether your sweet-tipping, night-creeping Baptist Pastor is in Hawaii too."

That's when the whole story came out.

Olivia and her fiancé, interim City Councilman Anthony McGoan, had gotten into an argument. With re-election coming up in November, his opponent had dug up some dirt on Olivia and her previous relationship with Anthony's father. The polls showed older, more conservative voters were not comfortable with Anthony's wife-to-be, so campaign consultants had advised him to distance himself from her until the November election was over.

"Baby, all we have to do is tell them the engagement is off," Councilman Anthony had told her. "After the election, we can pick up where we left off."

Olivia was furious. She had stormed out of his condo, packed her suitcase, and caught a plane to the most therapeutic getaway on the planet; at least, that was what the Southwest Airlines pilot had made her believe.

Councilman Anthony thought she was upset about the public embarrassment the break-up would've caused. What he didn't understand was the implications of six little words: *"pick up where we left off"*.

"She's tired of him, stringing her along," growled Lizzy. "She wants to settle down and make things official."

After so many years of being the other woman, Olivia was ready to become *the* woman ... a newspaper bride with a big diamond ring, a public ceremony and some pot bellied minister saying "till death do ye part". Councilman Anthony, on the other hand, was naïvely offering her a continuation of the status quo.

It was a typical boneheaded blunder, committed by the stupid male species over and over, again.

When a detective in the Houston Police Department finally helped Councilman Anthony track her down, she was at the Hyatt Regency Waikiki Beach Resort in Honolulu.

He had tried to reason with her over the phone. "Baby, I told my advisors the whole thing was a bad idea. I'm willing to take my chances with you."

As elegant as it sounded to him, the idiot had still missed the mark. Despite all of his pleading, she refused to come home.

Katherine Baker suspected there was another reason she refused to come home. The messy woman at the church had called to say Pastor Fordham's plane had not arrived in Houston until 11:30 pm Wednesday night. Deacon Grubbs was supposed to pick him up, but had to work the night shift at his job. Instead, he sent his doofus nephew, a want-to-be understudy of TV Detective Columbo. That's how the gossip train had started to roll.

The nephew told his girlfriend the tags on Pastor Fordham's luggage didn't say "Kansas City" like they were supposed to. They said "Hawaii". The girlfriend told the messy woman and she told Katherine Baker.

"I was sick and tired of that gossip hound calling me, lying on everybody," said Katherine Baker. "So I did some calling, myself."

"Who did you call?"

"My babysitter's mother. She works for Hobby Airport security. I ask her to look on the passenger's list for Pastor Fordham's name."

"Was he on there?" I asked with growing suspicion.

She shook her head. "Not on any of the Kansas City flights."

"But he was on a flight," added Estelle. "The one-stop from Honolulu to San Francisco to Houston."

That's why the weather created such a problem for his return flight. He was over the Pacific. I thought to myself.

My heart dropped. "Okay, okay what are you trying to say? Pastor Fordham flew to Hawaii to meet Olivia?"

Katherine Baker rolled her big milky eyes. "I'm just saying you have to be preaching mighty loud for the people in Kansas City to hear you from Hawaii."

"That's ridiculous," declared Lizzy. "Pastor Fordham's not like that, is he, Mama?"

"Of course, not. Pastor Fordham is a man of God." I declared with solemn confidence.

"Jimmy Swaggart was a man of God before they caught him down in Louisiana in that motel with a prostitute," Katherine Baker conveniently recalled.

"That's completely different," I defended.

"Baptist preacher in the room with a harlot. How is that different?" Estelle asked.

"First of all, Jimmy Swaggart was Pentecostal, not Baptist." I felt the need to correct her for whatever it was worth. "Secondly, nobody saw Pastor Fordham go into a room with Olivia."

Lizzy continued, "And thirdly, Olivia is not a harlot. Is

she, Mama?"

My tongue stuck to the roof of my mouth. I was still having flashes of Ububee, tearing at her clothes, and me, reshaping his head with the iron poker in the next room.

"Mama?"

Suddenly, all the machines had stopped and everyone was looking at me.

Plato's theory of human perception states that each person carries around a different sense of reality based on imperfect perceptions and flawed beliefs. I might label someone dishonest because they have a long nose. My perception would be based on the fact that, when I was a little girl, the boy who jumped over the fence and stole my bicycle had a long nose. The teacher who said I cheated on a test had a long nose. The milkman who told my grandmother he'd left three bottles of milk on the porch, when in reality, he'd left only two, had a long nose. President Richard Nixon had a long nose.

In my world, people with long noses were not to be trusted. Whenever Mr. Myles' cousin Lucille came around, I locked up my purse and put my fine silverware away. Whenever I went to my bank, I was careful to avoid that little bossy woman with the red hair. I didn't want her big, long snout poking around in my financial affairs.

And yet, deep down inside, I realized it was ridiculous to believe that honesty was tied to the size of a person's nose. Too many short-nosed people had ripped off society and lied through their teeth. Too many flat-nosed people had gone back on their word.

What my nose meter did, however, was simplify the endless variables in life. It provided a convenient way to protect me from the unknown. It was too burdensome and time-consuming to try to get to know everybody, to separate the wheat from the chaff through observation or trial and error. My nose meter, however, was instantaneous. With one quick measurement, I could spring into action or rest comfortably on my laurels, fortified by the results of my imperfect truths.

Katherine Baker possessed a meter too. Only, hers was shared by every female that had ever competed in the Olympics of Matrimony and watched in agony as some undeserving hussy ran off with the prize.

Driven by the hope of finding a man in the depleted pool of misguided, uninspired eligible mates, women used every trick in the book: beauty, charm, sensuality, cunning, money, accidental pregnancies and so on. The more you had, the more you had the right to flaunt it. Dresses went up. Blouses came down. Mini's became micro-mini's and bikini's became tinny-bikini's. By 1993, the wholesale flesh trade had gotten completely out of hand.

Even before '93, you could see the moral freefall coming.

Aunt Twigg once declared, "Men are getting dumber every year. They no longer have to use their brain to fantasize about the delicacies of a woman's body. All they need to do is stand on the corner. Sooner or later she'll come along and show it to them for free."

Some men were leg and hip men, while other salivated over big breast. The key was to know and show that which enticed your suitor the most.

I knew that Mr. Myles was a big hip man. So every time some floozy came around swinging her small waist and wide haunches, my meter went off. I'd grab Mr. Myles by the arm and steer him to the other side of the room. There was no need to take evasive actions with some humpy-dumpty or thin legged blond. My meter was tied to his preferences. And his preferences determined whether another woman was friend or foe.

The problem with Olivia Boudreaux was that she set off everybody's meter. You couldn't really tell whether it was her silky black hair or hazel eyes or protruding breasts or swaying hips or tantalizing smell or tiny ballerina feet or a combination of all the above. All you knew was that she was a seductive witch, an unfair competitor in the race for companionship and love.

Someone needed to bring her down a peg, dragged her name through the mud and make her human like the rest of us. That's what they were all thinking. Every woman in every setting throughout the city was secretly hoping to witness her demise, even help it along if necessary. All I needed to do was to go along with the verdict, confirm what they had already declared. She was a tramp and a wretch undone. And now she had pulled the man of God out of fellowship.

Or had she?

There was still one person in the room who believed in her, one apparently meterless, clueless optimist whose sense of reality had not been tainted by her instincts to survive. She had invited Olivia into her home, openly exposing her marriage to an unpredictable test of fire. Did she understand the risk she was taking? Did she know something that we didn't know?

They were still staring at me, waiting for their witch to be officially condemned and burned at the stake. I finally answered Lizzy's question with a question. "How much do you know about Olivia's past?"

"Everything," she flatly declared.

"Everything?" asked Katherine Baker, cutting her eyes at me with a smug glint.

"Everything," Lizzy repeated. "Including the proposition that U made to her."

Our jaws dropped like cannon balls.

Katherine Baker stuttered. "Hiiah-How did you know-"

"Because I told him to do it."

Our jaws dropped again. I grabbed the ice tea glass on the

table next to me and took a hearty shot. I told myself it was straight Jack Daniels to calm my nerves.

"I needed to know," said Lizzy. "I had heard so much about her, I just needed to know."

I took another nervous gulp. "So Ububee told you the whole story?"

"Actually she did," revealed Lizzy. "She came to me not knowing that U was part of my little scheme. She was hoping we would be able to fix our marriage before it was too late. I felt so bad."

"That's unbelievable!" said Katherine Baker.

"I know she's done some things in the past. But she's changed now. Since she's been coming to First Reunion, Pastor Fordham has really touched her soul."

Estelle grunted. "You hoping that's all he's touched."

"Come on, Auntee Stell. You still think they slipped off to Hawaii?"

"You still think those tags on his suitcase were a coincidence?"

"Estelle, don't be so quick to condemn the man just because you have a thing against the Baptists. Pastor Fordham is a happily married man." I reminded her.

Katherine Baker shook her head again. "Now, that statement gives me a little trouble. I mean, has anyone seen his wife lately? Where is she?"

Stella McGee, who had been quiet most of the morning, gazed up from her machine. "In therapy."

We all gawked at her, then spoke in unison. "For what?!"

"Nervous breakdown. She snapped about five months ago."

"From what?" I asked.

"Her oldest son committed suicide. The boy was from her first marriage so I guess Pastor Fordham didn't feel the need to publicize it."

"How do you know about all of this?" asked Katherine Baker.

"Pastor Fordham's wife and I have the same doctor. You know how nurses talk."

"No. No I don't," defended Lizzy.

Estelle stood up like a bow-legged, backwoods trial lawyer and started to pace the floor. "Okay, let me see if I can put this whole thing together. While the Baptist preacher's wife is back and forth from the psychiatric ward, his lustful eyes land on a little she-devil sitting in the congregation and he decides to take a trip to the Islands to meet up with her. God sends a mighty wind to blow off the covers, hallelujah, praise his name. Now their little secret rendezvous is not so secret anymore."

"That's totally unfounded, Auntee Stell. And you know it."

"Okay, okay. Then explain to me why your Pastor is coming back three days late. Why is his luggage tagged from Hawaii? Why is it that one of his little tender members just happens to be over there at the same time?"

"I... I can't answer that," Lizzy admitted. "I just know it isn't true."

"How do we find out for sure?" asked Katherine Baker.

"I'll ask him," I finally replied.

Katherine Baker flashed a disbelieving frown. "And you think he's just going to come out and say, 'Oh yeah, me and Miss Pretty Thang were over in Hawaii getting down?' You think he's going to say that?"

"Whatever he says, I'll know the truth."

"How will you know, Mama? I mean really know?"

I smiled, confidently. "I'll know. I'll know because ... besides a nose meter, I've got a lying meter too."

Chapter Eleven

That Sunday morning, June 4th, started out shrouded in a haze of stressful anticipation. All the way to church Lizzy and I made small talk about the brightness of the sun, the birds attacking my fig trees in the backyard, and a swollen dead dog along the side of the highway. Ububee kept bringing up his impending trip to Africa, but nobody was listening.

In the back of our minds, Lizzy and I kept thinking about the question I would ask and the answer Pastor Fordham would give and if my lying meter would be able to decipher the truth. God said a liar shall not tarry in his sight. But he was describing those heathens scheduled for a quick boot to hell on judgment day. Meanwhile, the lying business was booming here on earth. Even for the people with short noses and a record of integrity, the Human Ghost had a way of creeping in and corrupting the soul.

We believed in our Pastor. He had come in and turned our church around. Although Poe and his cronies were still too front-and-center for my good taste, First Reunion had a solid foundation. There was still love and giving and a fellowship that stretched from heart to heart. More importantly, Pastor Fordham was still preaching the uncompromised word of God.

We wanted so much for our Pastor to be immune to the temptations of life, remain a bright and shining star in an ever-darkening world. But the evidence was pointing to a more fallible, susceptible shell of a man, a member of the great masses who had fallen short of God's calling. One or two words were going to clear everything up, or bring everything down. Two generations of trust and belief were hanging in the balance.

When Ububee's custom van pulled into the church's front parking lot, we all gawked at the big blue and white banner, stretched across the brick veneer. It took a few seconds for my weary eyes to get past the dangling yellow ribbons to focus on the bold inscription. But once I did, the tears started to flow.

It read: WE LOVE YOU, MAMMA KIZZY. A crowd of well-wishers stood on both sides of the steps.

"It looks like the whole U.S. of A. has come out to see you," joked an energized Ububee.

He helped me into my wheelchair and rolled me toward the entrance. The closer we got, the more the clapping swelled. Several cameras flashed like opening night at the Academy Awards. Someone flipped on a handheld recorder that played processional music, the kind you'd expect to hear as the Queen of England entered the room.

Finally, Pastor Fordham stepped out from nowhere and pointed to the left edge of the steep concrete steps. A brand new ramp and iron railing, draped in yellow ribbons led to the top of the porch.

So this was the mysterious construction that Cora Williams had talked about, I thought to myself. They were building a wheelchair ramp just for me.

I looked over at Deacon Moore, standing in the corner with a sheepish grin on his face. I shook my fist at him. "You knew about this, didn't you?"

He hunched his broad shoulders with superficial innocence.

"Who me?"

Of course he knew. All of the deacons knew, including Deacon Poe who stood next to the shiny black railing, brandishing his best fake smile.

Pastor Fordham grabbed a portable microphone and cleared his throat. "Sister Kizzy Marie Sheppard Myles, this is your life!" Everyone started to applaud.

Recalling the 1960's television show, he laughed. "I always wanted to say that. Old Ralph Edwards used to bring all your embarrassing relatives out of the woodwork and force you to kiss your mother-in-law."

Everyone started to laugh.

"Don't worry, Sister Kizzy. We don't have a bunch of long lost friends and relatives waiting backstage, ready to embarrass you."

I display a charming smile. "If you did, I'd be concerned. That's a lot of trips to the cemetery."

The crowd roared.

Pastor Fordham finally contained himself. "Although it's not the TV show, it certainly is a tribute to your life and all you've done to make this a better church and a better community. You've given so much to us, and now we just want to give a little back to you."

The crowd echoed a chained reaction of Amens.

"On behalf of the officers and members of First Reunion Baptist Church, we dedicate this ramp to you, praying that as God sees fit to bless those feeble knees of yours, you'll use it less and less. What a spiritual irony ... building something and then praying for its obsolescence."

"Amen!" The crowd answered back.

Deacon Grubbs strolled down the steps to my wheelchair and handed me a large pair of scissors. "Will you do the honors?"

I glanced at the gigantic yellow ribbon draped across the entrance to the ramp. "Of course."

Ububee rolled me over to the ramp, then, helped to position the huge scissors into cutting mode. One hard snip and we were instantly gliding up the incline.

The feeling was unbelievable, as though I was out at the NASA Space Center in Clear Lake, riding the big Challenger shuttle into the clouds.

At the top of the ramp, Pastor Fordham leaned over and gave me a big hug. "We're not finished yet. There's more for you inside."

A procession of deacons, ushers and Mission sisters led the congregation inside the sanctuary. Rolling down the aisle to my familiar bird nest, I immediately noticed the changes. The oak paneling gleamed, brightly, from a new coat of varnish. The tattered green linoleum mat had been replaced with a thick, rich wine colored carpet. A cup holder and small glass cabinet had also been installed, already stocked with bottles of water, mints, a box of Kleenex, and one of those new leather Bibles with the large print. Finally, a battery-powered light bulb protruded from the front of the stand. With the push of a small button I could alert the ushers of my impending request.

Once Ububee had locked my wheels into place, I took a moment to look around the sanctuary. To my surprise, the church was almost full, an unusual phenomenon since most people straggled in after the opening prayer services. Many members considered it a waste of time to sit through the deacon's "ten thousand tongues" prayers week after week. Thus, they timed their arrival for just after the announcements or just before the choir began to sing.

That morning, however, they seemed willing to pay the price. It was as though I had died and they had all come out to pay their respects. Of course, I knew I hadn't died, not with Deacon Poe

146

standing up front, still in one piece. There was no way I was going to leave God's green earth without, at least, jabbing him in his behind with a pitchfork to prepare him for his future home.

Cora William's youngest daughter stepped up to the microphone to read a proclamation. Her sister, the one with the ponytail, recited a beautiful poem. The main attraction, however, was Frogman and his golden horn. He jumped up from the front row pew and began to blow.

Everyone knew about Frogman and his famous saxophone. On any given weekend, you could find him standing in front of the old Foley's Department Store in downtown Houston, serenading the passing crowd. On good days, the generous tips spilled onto the sidewalk from his wide-necked Schepps Dairy milk jug. On bad days, the police declared him a public nuisance and chased him off to another part of town.

In a way, Frogman welcomed their periodic evictions. It helped to build his legacy on the streets. Whenever he spotted the officers approaching, he'd throw on his multi-colored James Brown cape and begin to creep off like a long-necked ostrich, playing, *Please, Please Don't Go*. The Main Street crowd would go wild as police found themselves trapped in his bizarre street show with no recourse but to go along.

An HPD spokesman once commented off the record. "We know how to handle a crazy with a gun. But what if all he's got is a horn? What do you do then?"

No matter what they did, Frogman seemed determined to pursue his musical dreams. He played at weddings, churches, funerals, and at a number of official events to which he had not been invited. No one really knew how he found out about certain functions or what prompted him to show up. All we knew was that he loved to play his horn, and would do so without the slightest provocation.

There was another curious aspect to Frogman's spontaneous serenades. You never knew what he was going to play. He might blow a sad, depressing tune at a crowded wedding or an old spiritual at a drunken party. His brain seemed disconnected to the celebration at hand.

So when he stood up from the first row pew, fully dressed in a red and white Houston Rockets NBA uniform, it didn't surprise me one bit. A few months earlier, the Rockets had almost made it to the Western Conference Finals. Not a day had gone by without Ububee bragging about his great countryman, Hakeem Olajuwon.

"With de dream shake in de middle next year, dey go all de way. Guaranteed!"

Frogman had evidently joined the citywide bandwagon of prognosticators, predicting, in his own strange way, the team's 1994 Championship. In his mind he was a member of that Championship team, eager to play a song of celebration. Before members of the procession could find a seat, he lit up the building with a familiar rendition of *This Little Light Of Mine.*

Anita was already sitting at the organ. And so she joined in. Before we knew it, everyone in the congregation was clapping their hands and stomping their feet to the beat. Then, just as quickly as he had started, he stopped. Anita was still playing and the people were still clapping. But Frogman's horn went cold as ice.

Finally, he reared back and pushed out a long, hard note which turned out to be the first note of another song. It was Whitney Houston's familiar hit, *I'll Always Love You.*

The church was stunned. Lizzy explained later the song had been at the top of the charts since the release of the *Bodyguard* movie in '92. They were still playing the song on all of the Pop and R&B radio stations across the nation. It was on the cassette tape players in everybody's car. Yet, no one expected Frogman to break out in the middle of a church service with such a worldly offering.

Members of the congregation soon found themselves facing a growing dilemma. There were long-standing traditions, taboos and protocols of righteousness heaped into the Sunday morning worship service. How were they supposed to carrying out their roles as pious-faced spiritual sky walkers, disconnected to a sinful world, when the smooth, mesmerizing sound, coming from Frogman's golden horn was riveting their very soul? It didn't help when Lizzy got up from her seat, walked over to the baby grand piano on the far side of the choir stand and began to accompany him.

Her voice rang out like a guest soloist with the Mormon Tabernacle Choir. "*And I ... I'll always love you....*"

It was the perfect complement of voice, piano, horn and finally, organ, as Anita chimed back in. I thought about all of the money Mr. Myles and I had spent hauling her to recitals and piano lessons and summer voice camps. At that moment I realized it had all been worthwhile.

I found myself fighting back a new onslaught of tears, not because of her melodious singing. Rather, it was her extraordinary character that had me all choked up. It took a lot of courage to step into such an awkward situation, to join forces with an unpredictable bedfellow like the Frogman in order to rescue her mother's special day. But that was my Lizzy: a beautiful, virtuous, trusting, loud mouth sentimentalist. She was the reason we still believed in Pastor Fordham. She was the reason we hadn't thrown Olivia Boudreaux to the dogs.

I wished, in my heart of hearts, that Mr. Myles had been around to see the precious fruits of our labor. As a parent you pour your very soul into the little snot-nosed, stained-diapered, measles-infected, disobedient, beautiful, loving, indispensable bundles of pure joy for whom you would gladly give up your own life.

You watch their friends and classmates succumb to drugs and

alcohol and gang rapes and fatal car accidents and mysterious disappearances. You wonder when you'll get the call. When will the police show up at your door?

For twenty years you worry about them and hover over them and drill into their steel-plated heads the dire consequences of entering an evil world without being cautious and well-prepared. You love them and scold them and empower them and mold them. And then suddenly, before you realize it, they're gone. They're all grown up and living on their own. And all you have left are the picture frames, filled with fading memories, and the hope your effort was not in vain.

To see Lizzy in action, reflecting the Christian values that we had poured into her, risking her own reputation for the sake of a cantankerous old soul like me, was more than I could bear. I broke open the new box of Kleenex and boo-hooed to my heart's content.

As the trio finished, the congregation erupted with loud applause. Pastor Fordham rushed to the podium. "Come on y'all! We can do better than that!"

The clapping reached an ear-piercing decibel, like the waves that had flooded Greater Pilgrim Holiness Tabernacle. Then, just as it began to die down, Frogman raised his horn high in the air. "If anybody wants ah autograph, see me in the parking lot after church. And bring fifty cents."

The crowd roared with laughter.

Pastor Fordham nodded his head. "We'll do that, Brother. We'll see you right after church." He looked out at me, with a proud smile. "Sister Kizzy, we love you. May God continue to bless you in every way."

My heart clamored. I waved, graciously, as the crowd managed another round of applause.

Then, the Pastor looked at the deacons. "Let's move into our service, deacons. For this is the day the Lord has made."

****

As we plowed into our Sunday morning routine, I noticed a new face sitting among the deacons. Still obese and sunburned from his trip to Hawaii, Marvin Crump offered the second prayer. It didn't surprise me that he stumbled through every line. As my father used to say to his porch followers, "practice makes perfect", which in Crump's case, no practice made for a disaster.

Crump was too busy telling dirty jokes to pray. That's why I was relieved he was somehow able to get through the prayer without cursing out the entire church.

The Bible asks a question: *Can blessings and curses come from the same mouth?*

Crump had a quick answer, "Hell yes." Add that to his penchant for pornography, and the congregation had a question of its own: *What was he doing up there in the first place?*

I wanted to blame Deacon Poe. But I knew for a fact Poe didn't like him either. Crump was too rough around the edges, too eager to take charge. Suspecting one day Crump might want his job, Poe had worked hard to keep Crump out of the power loop. Nevertheless, there he was, down on both knees, depositing prayers into the giant compost. He was one of the bigwigs now, another cog in First Reunion's spiritual wheel. *"Oh, ahla sola mukukool sisilah ... porn."*

About the time my angry juices reached a boil, prayer meeting was over. That's when the announcing clerks stepped up to the microphone and melted all my troubled thoughts away.

I was so happy to see Thelma Mason out of jail and back at her post. Unable to reach any of the deacons on that faithful Weingarten's day, I had bailed her out and retained the church's lawyer, Grits Macklin, to handle her case. My only stipulation was for her not to tell anyone about my involvement. Giving in secret and receiving rewards from heaven was so much better than a human slap on the back.

But what did she do? The first thing out of her mouth was a public acknowledgement.

"Before I read these announcements, I just want to tell the whole church I'm sorry for all that I've done." Her watery eyes looked up toward me. "I also want to let y'all know that during my time of trouble, Mama Kizzy has been right there by my side."

Didn't I tell her to keep her mouth shut?

Then came another round of broken hand claps, led by Cora Williams and her girls. Deacon Poe looked back at me but didn't join in.

A few minutes later the choir had finished singing. Pastor Fordham took the podium. "First thing I want to say is I'm glad to be home. That beef stew and cornbread in the Midwest is okay. But it just doesn't add up to our good old southern fried chicken."

Katherine Baker looked over at me and worked her lips, slowly. *"What about Hawaiian chicken?"*

I decided to ignore her.

Pastor Fordham continued. "Before I go any further, I want to recognize the newest member to our Deacon Board. Stand up Brother Crump."

While Pastor Fordham extolled the values of having Deacon Crump on the Board, Cora Williams wrote something on a piece of paper and handed it to an usher who brought it to me. It read:

KEEP YOUR DRESS DOWN. OTHERWISE, YOU MIGHT END UP IN ONE OF HIS TRIPLE X SPECIALS.

Cora was one of several people who had seen Marvin Crump's car parked at the big porno shop on the North Freeway. Why Pastor Fordham felt Crump was fit to become a deacon was anybody's guess. I knew Mr. Myles was turning over in his grave.

When Pastor Fordham finally began to preach, it was almost noon. By 12:15 pm I realized for the first time since he had been the Pastor of First Reunion, he had nothing useful to say. Maybe he was all preached out from the Kansas City revivals. Or maybe his conscience had gotten in the way of the message from on high. Whatever the reason, his words had no power. His text seemed disjointed and struggling to find a cause.

And then it occurred to me that maybe it wasn't the preaching at all. Maybe it was the listening. Maybe the tainted reality that swirled around in my head was compromising the message because it came from a compromised messenger. The more I thought about it, the more I realized how critical it was to find out the truth.

At the end of service, Ububee went up front to receive prayer for his upcoming trip to Africa. Lizzy stood by his side. Afterwards, Pastor Fordham reminded us of the Wednesday night business meeting.

"I'm sure you've heard about the proposed shelter for battered women," he said. "Our hope is to move forward with this monumental project. We just need to come together on the details, Amen?"

After the benediction, just before the hordes of well-wishers rushed over to my stand, I flipped on my new light bulb. A few seconds later, Big Mildred walked up. "Having trouble, Mama Kizzy?"

"Not really. I just need to see the Pastor before he retires to his study."

"You got it." She headed toward the front.

Ububee finally came over to unlock my wheels.

"I am under the special protection of the Lord, do you see?" He slowly guided my chair to the floor. "What I do in the motherland will surely be blessed."

Several families were already waiting in the aisle. "Mama Kizzy, we are so happy for you ... you've done so much, you deserve it ... try not to get a speeding ticket going down that ramp." Their adoring voices rang out in unison.

Though I listened and laughed and received their well-wishes with warm humility, I kept my eye on Pastor Fordham. Once he had finished talking to a young couple, he headed my way.

I slipped the young Williams girls ten dollars apiece for their impressive presentations. Then, I gave Lizzy an envelope to give to Thelma Mason.

Lizzy opened the envelope to see the $250 check. "What is this for?"

"For the triplets," I whispered. "Backwater is gone. Thelma's not working. Those babies have to eat."

"Don't you think you've done enough?" The smug expression on her face made me wonder if she had recently joined the Republican Party.

I grabbed her arm and pushed my mouth right up to her ear. 'I'm the mother, Miss BossyAnn. Now take that check over to her before I tell Big Mildred you're disrespecting a helpless old lady."

She glanced at Big Mildred, then flew down the aisle.

Her spirited departure came just in time to free me up for Pastor Fordham. He approached with a warm smile. "I understand you needed to see me? Is everything alright?"

"I was wondering, Pastor. You have time to chauffeur an old

lady out to the parking lot? I needed to ask you something."

Pastor Fordham appeared puzzled. "Suu–Sure. I can do that."

As he grabbed the handles to my chair, Ububee turned around. "Have I been replaced by de big brass?"

"Just this time," I reassured him. "Why don't you meet us outside in about five minutes?"

"Okay, but now I'm confused. My job has been taken. I don't know what to do with myself."

We laughed, causally, as Pastor Fordham rolled me toward the door.

In the foyer, Deacon Grubbs walked over to us and pointed straight up into the hollow bell tower. "Pastor, we've got another leak up there, just behind the support wedges. But like I told Deacon Poe, all our funds are committed to fixing that west wall. It so rotten underneath the window seals, a grasshopper could burst through."

Pastor Fordham nodded. "I understand. I'll see you back in the study. We can talk about it then."

Rolling away he mumbled to me in a low voice. "Wasn't Jesus a carpenter?"

I nodded. "That's what the Bible says."

"Wish he'd send his crew down to fix this place up. The maintenance is killing us."

Little did we know He was listening to every word.

Once outside in the bright sunlight, he chauffeured my chair with guarded precision, down the shiny new ramp. "I'm trying to think of a line from *Driving Miss Daisy*. But nothing comes to mind."

"That's because the movie never showed her with a pastor she loved and worried about," I explained.

"This is beginning to sound more serious than I'd thought."

We rolled across the bumpy parking lot and stopped in a

shady spot at the back of Ububee's custom van. Pastor Fordham walked around my wheelchair and took a seat on the back bumper. "Okay, tell me what this is all about."

"Hawaii," I replied, candidly. "I know about your trip."

He smiled. "When I came to this church back in '88, I was told nothing went on without you knowing about it. I guess it's true."

"Is there a reason you wanted us to think you went to Kansas City to those revivals?"

"Oh, I went to Kansas City. I did both revivals as usual. But then I flew out to Hawaii for some R&R. Even the preacher needs to get away at times."

"But under what circumstances do you ... get away?" I pressed him, gently.

He nodded his head. "I know where you're going with this and you're right. I put myself in a compromising position. Doing the right thing gets harder every day."

I looked over my shoulder to see Ububee and Lizzy headed toward the van. My time was running out.

"What are you going to do now?" I asked.

"It's done. I'm going to live with. I'll try to make sure it doesn't hurt the church in any way." He looked at me with shameful eyes. "I'm not perfect, Mama Kizzy. If you want to see perfection, you'll have to wait until Jesus Christ comes back again."

Noticing Ububee and Lizzy a few yards away, he stood up from the bumper, picked up a small gravel rock off the ground and handed it to me. "I'll say this. I'm sorry if I let you down. But he who is without sin, let him cast the first stone."

A few minutes later, as we cruised down the 610 Loop, Lizzy turned back to look at me. "Did your meter work?"

I nodded, slowly, affirmatively.

"So what's the verdict?"

I gazed out of Ububee's black tinted windows into the sun-drenched sky. If I had been Superwoman I would've burst through the rooftop and found a hiding place in the clouds; anything to avoid her question; anything to spare her from the truth.

Naiveté can be a beautiful thing when it filters out the harsh realities of life. It delays our plunge into a world of cynicism. It allows us to expect the best from our fellow man. Truth, however, is not so beautiful. It's like an errant wind, stirring up the dust and sandblasting our eyes with the bitterness of discovery. It's ruthless in its pursuit of clarity. And quite often, it leaves us with a sour predisposition about things to come.

But what is a child of God without truth. It's a necessary virtue, a mandate handed down by our Savior who came to us in spirit and truth. Whether it crushes us or liberates us or confirms what we already believe, there is no acceptable alternative, no substitute standard to which heaven would comply.

When I finally mustered the courage to look into her eyes, I realized my hesitation had given me away. She already knew. The veil of disappointment and betrayal was draped across her face.

Still, I had to say it. I had to let the ruthless voice of clarity take its toll.

"Guilty as charged." I finally vomited out the verdict.

That was the first time I could remember, my loud mouth daughter had nothing to say.

Chapter Twelve

The following Wednesday morning, I received a call from the church secretary confirming the business meeting scheduled for that night. I didn't need a reminder. All morning long I had been reading over a draft of the proposed remodeling contract for the Silver Dollar Hotel. Deacon Moore had delivered a confidential copy along with some intriguing news.

"They're already at each other's throats," he reported, comically describing the budding rivalry between Deacon Crump and Deacon Poe. "If ever we needed a strong handgun law in this country, we need it now."

As a child of the kingdom, I wasn't supposed to take pleasure in the difficulties of the church. But anybody who gave Poe a hard time was a friend of mine. The Bible said trials and tribulations would come. I just needed the scribes to end the sentence with an arrow pointing toward Poe's name.

One thing I had to acknowledge. Deacon Poe's proposal was well thought out: a precise timetable for completion of hotel repairs, letters of commitment from all the government partners, occupancy limits, insurance and bonding requirements, security installations and volunteer hours from the church. Everything was very impressive, that is, until I looked at it with a spiritual eye.

There was a sleaze factor written in invisible ink ... the lack of oversight and competitive bidding, and the way the funding slithered out of the bank and into Womack's hands.

Before he died, Mr. Myles had helped his brother build a small apartment complex to get money from the Section 8 government program. He had taught me how the system worked.

There were certain red flags that spelled future disaster. The more I read the proposal, the more I found them flapping in the wind. If Poe and his cronies were going to use church money to fund their project, they would have to offer the members more disclosure and more control.

Around noon, I was sitting at the dining room table, still in rollers with a big ugly purple-flowered muumuu dress on. I had just finished finalizing my notes for the meeting when I heard a soft tap at the door. To my surprise, Olivia Boudreaux was standing on the porch. She had a brightly colored red and green sweater in her hand.

I didn't bother to greet her. What was the use of pretending?

"Yes?"

"Mama Kizzy, can I talk to you?"

"About what?"

"About Lizzy?"

"What about Lizzy?"

"I ... I don't know, exactly." Her eyes began to water. "I went by her house to drop off Ububee's sweater. She told me I was no longer welcome there. Then she slammed the door in my face."

"Honey, what do you expect?"

"I guess I expected her to at least tell me what I did."

I could see the tall, hawk-faced postal woman coming up the sidewalk with the morning mail. She was another one with a long

160

nose, and a reputation for getting into everyone's business. Not even a Honolulu hussy like Olivia deserved her incessant scrutiny. I open the door and motioned Olivia to come inside.

Her thin fingers were trembling like strips of paper. Her hazel green eyes were now red and fearful, like a child who'd been sent to the principal's office to await punishment for an unforgivable crime. She sat on my flowered sofa as if a board were pressed against her back. Draping the sweater across her lap, she waited for me to speak.

I eyed her for a hard minute, trying to decide whether slicing frog guts so early in the day was really worthwhile.

I finally throttled up her much-deserved tongue lashing. "You expect me to believe you don't know?"

"Know what? If someone would just tell me," she pleaded.

"Okay, okay I'll tell you. We know about you and Pastor Fordham."

She's stared, blankly. "Me and Pastor?"

"There is no need to deny it. The cat is out of the bag."

She appeared genuinely perplexed. "Did he tell you that me and him...."

"Yes. Yes. In fact he did."

She dropped her head. "I-ah, I don't know what to say."

"You could start with I'm sorry, although the Bible says true confession should come from the heart. Maybe that's not a good place for you to start after all."

She took a deep breath, then started to smile.

"So you think bringing down the man of God is funny?" I scolded.

"I'm sorry, Mama Kizzy."

"You should be!"

"No, no you don't understand."

"What don't I understand?"

She hesitated a moment, carefully choosing her words. "I can't tell you how many times I've been accused of something like this. It makes me feel so good to know that this time, it's not true."

"Are you saying that Pastor Fordham lied?"

"I believe Pastor is a good man. I don't think he would lie about something like that."

"Then, are you saying I didn't hear what I heard?"

"Mama Kizzy, I don't know what you heard. But if it had to do with me and Pastor Fordham, it wasn't true."

"Give me one reason why I should believe you."

"I'll give you two reasons: Anthony and Lizzy. They mean so much to me. I'm going to marry Anthony one day. I just know it."

"And Lizzy?"

Olivia's face brightened. "She's the best friend I've ever had. I wouldn't do anything to let her down."

I was stunned and confused. My lying meter was working overtime. But all I was picking up was ... sincerity. Deep down inside I wanted to dismiss her plea of innocence as a bunch of Louisiana sweet sauce sprinkled inside a seductive harlot sandwich. Instead, my instincts cried out on her behalf.

She continued in a mellow tone. "Listen. I know how people feel about me. But I'm not that person. Actually, I never was that person."

"Olivia, be honest with yourself. You wrecked a woman's home. You stole her husband and her son."

"Lee and his wife had been sleeping in separate bedrooms a long time. Of course, they got together and made these public appearances. But it was all based on a schedule. It was all about satisfying the public's eye."

I deliberated a bit longer. "Ummh. I guess if you and Councilman Anthony ever have problems in your marriage, a little help from the outside would be okay by you? Some pretty young thing to fill in the gaps?"

Her eyes dropped to the floor, searching every thread of my green oriental rug.

After a long silence she admitted, "I'm not proud of what I did. I was a young, stupid, runaway dropout with nowhere to turn. I did what I had to do to survive."

I glanced out at the shiny convertible BMW sitting in the driveway. "I would say you've done more than survive."

"Anthony bought that for me, along with all this other stuff." She massaged the expensive diamond pendant around her neck. "It's where he wants me to be."

I shook my head, pitifully. "You poor, poor thing, you. Burdened down in all that silver and gold."

"I know you don't believe me. But I'd give all of this up for a relationship like the one Lizzy has."

I was suddenly reminded of what my Aunt Twigg use to say: *Everybody wants what everybody else's got.*

Olivia wanted a loving marriage. Lizzy wanted a womb that spit out babies at will. But God had a way of distributing blessing that kept the universe confounded until the day of his return.

He did it deliberately. He said, *"I will bless who I will bless."* And then he hid the underlying threads of logic and comprehension so his blessing machine could never be dismantled or pulled apart. Good living didn't necessarily bring in blessings. Bad living didn't necessarily keep them away. The threads were twisted and torn into incomprehensible patterns of mercy and forgiveness so that not even the angels in heaven understood.

God also had a way of changing people from the inside, out, so that only the vibrancy of his supernatural light shown through.

The more I listened to her, the more I realized she was telling the truth. My slicing and dicing was simply confirming what the good Bishop had already told me in an Ebonics-laced message from on high: *God can do whatever he want to do, with whoever he want to do it with, Amen?*

I picked up the phone and called Lizzy. "Olivia is here. I think you need to hear what she has to say."

"I don't have time for any sob stories," she growled. "I'm trying to help U pack for his trip."

"Okay, then just listen to me. Olivia told me nothing happened between her and Pastor Fordham."

"And you believed her?"

I looked over at Olivia, sitting at the edge of her seat, desperately hoping to be redeemed. "Yes, Lizzy. She's telling the truth."

"Mama, that doesn't make sense. How can both of them be telling the truth?"

I didn't know how to answer her question. In science there's a law of pairwise mutually exclusivity. It means that the occurrence of one event automatically implies the non-occurrence of the other. If a coin flips on heads, it automatically excludes tails. So why was I seeing heads and tails at the same time?

"I'll call you back," I told Lizzy.

Hanging up the phone, I turned to Olivia Boudreaux. "She's not ready to open up to you just yet."

She nodded. "I understand."

"Leave the sweater with me. I'll make sure Ububee gets it tonight."

"Tonight?"

"Yes. They're picking me up for the business meeting."

She pondered a moment. "You think I should come to the-"

"No, no. That wouldn't be a good idea. Give me a chance to work through all of this foolishness. I'll let you know what I find out."

As she backed out of the driveway and headed down the street, I could hear Lizzy's voice in my head.

She's not a harlot, is she, Mama?

My answer was different now. For some unfathomable reason, God had allowed me to look into her soul. She was just like the rest of us ... fragile and afraid, addicted to the familiar tools that promised her the best chance for success. I used my Master's degree, 45 years of teaching, 41 years of marriage and the wisdom of 67 years of walking God's green earth to get to my next destination. All she had was her GED and the curse of incomprehensible beauty to get to hers.

Olivia Boudreaux was a new creature in Christ and that was that. Now, my tired old brain slowly reconfigured itself to unraveling a mystery. How could a coin show heads and tails at the same time?

****

That night, we arrived at the church about 7:25 pm. A modest crowd had already gathered in the sanctuary. Deacon Grubbs and Deacon Crump raced through the prayer service so quickly, I thought the Catholic Diocese had bought us out.

I watched as Frogman tried to enter the church eating a big

Coney Island hot dog. Big Mildred immediately blocked his path. There were still stains on the carpet from his last fiasco with Sally and Josh Howard. She wasn't about to set the stage for a repeat performance.

A more pungent regret was her failure to blocked real estate sleaze-ball, Horace Womack. He sat on the front row, all decked out in one of his gold striped double breasted suits. I recognized the egg headed attorney who sat next to him from mug shots I had seen on the Channel 13 News. It was none other than Westley Westgate, freshly released from federal prison for his role in a nationwide insurance scam. I suppose it didn't matter to Womack that Westgate had been disbarred. The main thing was to keep the best criminal minds united and active in fleecing the church.

Pastor Fordham offered a few words of welcome, then quickly turn the microphone over to Deacon Poe.

"We've got a lot of ground to cover tonight. So let's get right at it." His voice rang out, harshly and unvarnished, as though he were about to auction off some mules.

The deacons passed out a copy of Poe's remodeling contract to each member present. Then he began to explain the ramifications of the Board's proposed decisions, section by section.

About half way through, old lady Blake raised her hand.

Deacon Poe stared with irritation. "If you don't mind, just hold your question until I've gone through the whole document".

He continued to read, first, then explain what he had just read. Once he had reached the end of the document, he looked over at her. "Now, Sister Blake. Would you like to ask your question?"

She stood up, slowly. "Giving honor to God, to the Pastor, to the officers of this fine church, and to all my brothers and sisters in Christ............"

Deacon Poe frowned, curiously, waiting for her to continue.

"Sister Blake...?"

An eternity passed before she finally admitted, "I done forgot what I was gonna say." And then she flopped back down.

The congregation chuckled in a polite tone.

Deacon Grubbs stepped over to the other microphone. "We do have some questions that were dropped into the box out in the foyer."

Poe reasoned, "It may not be necessary to go over those questions if we've already answered them in our opening explanation of what this document is all about."

Deacon Crump stood up. "Well now, Deacon Poe, if the people took the time to put the questions in the box, I think they have a right to hear the answers. Don't you?"

"Deacon Poe turned to him with daggers in his eyes. "Deacon Crump, as you become more familiar with the process, you'll realize that we can avoid certain redundancies by simply exercising a little common sense."

Deacon Crump's filthy mouth had a mind of its own. Before his hair-trigger brain caught up to his fiery temper, half the name he had designated for Poe had already slipped out.

"Son of .... the Almighty God, Jesus Christ," Crump barely recovered. "He is our example. He was always looking out for his flock and we should too, Amen."

Poe hesitated a moment. "Read the questions."

Deacon Grubbs cleared his throat. "Okay, here are the five questions they left in the box. Number 1: Why is it that we can build a hotel, but we can't build any new classrooms for our youth?"

Deacon Poe shook his head with empathy. "That's a good question. First of all you have to understand that we're not building a hotel, we're refurbishing a hotel; something that's already right there, across the street. And we're doing it with government money. If we decided to build new classrooms that would all be on us."

Pastor Fordham looked back at the congregation from his front row pew. "Does that answer your question? If not, you need to let us know."

No one said a word.

Pastor Fordham looked at Deacon Grubbs. "Next question."

"Number 2: How can I apply for a job when the work begins?"

Deacon Poe smiled. "That's an easy one. Mr. Womack's company will be in charge of all of the contracting, subcontracting and direct hiring. I'm sure he'll have a system in place to announce job openings and process applicants. Is that right, Mr. Womack?"

As if they were appearing before some big congressional hearing on Capitol Hill, Horace Womack leaned over and whispered something in his attorney's ear. The attorney whispered something back.

Womack stood up. "I am not at liberdee to answer your incantations at this time, not until we have signed the legal contract." He sat down again, the smirk of accomplishment on his face.

I couldn't help wondering. *How is it that Amos 'n' Andy went off the air without having these imbeciles as special guests?*

Poe tried to keep a straight face as he called for the next question.

"Number 3: Will the Pastor or the deacons make any money off of this project?"

Poe looked at the Pastor. "Would you like to address that?"

Pastor Fordham stood up. "The answer to that question is an unequivocal no. We're not in this for the money. We're in it to help people. If you look at the budget, you'll see that we're not making a dime. I hope that's clear."

He sat back down.

Poe nodded for the next question.

"Number 4: The staff of this church works hard to keep things going. But we haven't had a raise for two years."

Poe shook his head. "That has nothing to do with this endeavor. I think we can move to the next question."

Deacon Crump stood up. "Again if the question was asked, I think it deserves an answer. This is a business meeting. And that certainly is church business."

Poe was furious. "Look, Deacon Crump. We are here to talk about a monumental undertaking to help battered women. We don't have time to go running down every little rabbit trail."

Crump scowled. "I ain't here to chase rabbits either. But I know when one is trying to get away."

Pastor Fordham stood up. "Brothers, brothers. Let's stay on track, here. If this question is going to be a distraction, let's answer it and move forward."

Crump shook his head. "That's all I'm asking, Pastor."

Poe's head was bobbing like a fishing cork in a fast-moving Gulf Stream. It did that whenever he became extremely angry.

"Okay I'll answer it," he relented. "We are not in a position financially to give raises. In fact, some staff members are already making too much for the work they actually do?"

Anita was still sitting at the organ when she raised her hand. "What do you mean by that?"

Poe flashed a disarming smile. "I wasn't talking about you, Anita."

"But you could've been, since I haven't gotten a raise either." She fired back.

Someone yelled from behind the smoked glass partition enclosing the upstairs sound room. "Amen to that!"

Pastor Fordham intervened. "Why don't you explain to them what you've based your statement on?"

Like a little boy, forced to spit out his chewing gum before reciting his Easter speech, Poe continued.

"Twice a year we get a benchmark study from the National Baptist Association. It shows what other churches are spending for services and staff. Where most churches our size spend 40% of their budget on salaries, we're spending 62%. Where most churches our size have one choir director, we've got three. Now do you all get the picture?"

"Oh, yeah," said Big Mildred, who was being paid a small salary as Coordinator of Medical Services. "I get the picture every time I open up my check."

The whole church burst into laughter.

"What can we do about it?" asked Pastor Fordham.

"Nothing this year, Pastor," explained Deacon Poe. "Besides spending an arm and a leg to replace some portions of the roof, every extra penny has been plowed into security. We now have bars on every window and every door. We've got cameras and sensors back, front and center. We've sealed up every hole on the street side, but we still have some major wood problems and foundation cracks on the west side. All of that costs. I shouldn't have to lay out the whole plan tonight. We've already talked about this."

Deacon Crump stood up. "Then, git off the security. I'd like to make a motion right here and now that we give our church staff first priority during the next budget cycle."

The whole church started to applaud.

"I second that motion," added Deacon Grubbs, cutting his eyes toward the choir stand.

Anita flashed a gracious smile.

Deacon Crump started smiling too, the same kind of hero

smile that Deacon Poe usually displayed when he received credit for something he didn't deserve. It was exhilarating to see Poe get a taste of his own medicine.

I thought: *What a blessing! Having old cussing Crump on the Deacon Board might not be such a bad idea after all.*

Finally, we got to question 5, the one that Cora Williams had stuck into the box for me.

"Question 5: Who chose the contractor and how was the decision made?"

Womack and his attorney looked at each other, then glared back at Poe. Poe walked over to remove the card from Deacon Grubb's hand. He studied it a while as if trying to detect any clue that would identify its author.

Finally, he spoke. "There were many factors that went into our decision. First, we wanted somebody who could do the job. Secondly, we needed somebody who had the connections in Austin and Washington, DC. When you're dealing with government money, you need to know where all the bodies are buried."

Womack waved his hand in the air. "Amen to that brother!"

Attorney Westgate shook his head, vigorously, instructing Womack to refrain from any incriminating outbursts.

Poe continued, "We also wanted to use one of our own; somebody in the community who would help generate employment for our people. Too often the money flows out of our community and into the hands of the fat cats in Memorial and River Oaks. We wanted to get away from that same old tired scenario. And Mr. Womack's company fit the bill in every respect."

Pastor Fordham stood up and glanced at his watch. "Does that answer the question? If so, I think we can vote on this proposal and get the ball rolling."

I flipped the switch on my newly installed light bulb.

Pastor Fordham smile. "Well, Sister Kizzy. I see you're putting your new hardware to good use. Do you have a question?"

I smiled back. "Yes, Pastor. Seems like I'm full of questions these days."

"Go ahead," he instructed.

"Somebody asked about the selection process. I guess my question is along those lines."

"We're listening," said Poe in a condescending voice.

"I would like to know more about your process of elimination. I take it some companies were included while others were excluded. Which companies made it to the short list? I'm just curious."

Poe glared at me for a while. "I can't really remember all that, Sister Kizzy. Besides, it's somewhat irrelevant now, since the Board has already made its selection. Where are you going with this?"

"I just want to make sure we have the best company and our money will be secure. I know that Brown Construction is the biggest minority-owned construction company in Houston. They've done twenty-six different projects in the last two years where government money was involved. GRACIE Contracting is both black and woman-owned. She's just finishing up her third contract with the Department of Education. There is also Sawyer Bauman's company. His uncle works for Housing and Urban Development. He's done over fifteen buildings in Texas and two in Louisiana. Then there's-"

Poe interrupted. "I get your point."

"I guess my question is which of these companies made the short list and how did they get eliminated?"

Womack jumped up. "Let me tell you something, lady. There wasn't no short list. You know why? Because none of them companies you mentioned give a damn about you or your church.

I'm the one that brought this deal to y'all. Not GRACIE, not Sawyer. I did."

Pastor Fordham got up. "Brother Womack, I know this project is dear to your heart. But this church is dear to my heart. I'm going to ask you to conduct yourself with that in mind. We're in the house of the Lord."

Womack took a deep breath. "Sorry, Pastor. But people who don't know about this business ought to stay out of this business."

He sat down again.

Poe's head was still bobbing. "Okay, okay, I hope we're ready to ratify this document and move forward."

I turned my light bulb back on.

"Yes, what is it now, Sister Kizzy?" Poe barked, impatiently.

"Well, I know I'm getting on up there in age and sometimes I miss things. But if I'm not mistaken, you didn't answer my question."

Poe began to perspire. He took out a handkerchief and wiped his forehead. "Mr. Womack answered your question, Sister Kizzy. There was no short list."

"Is that the same as no competitive bid?" I asked. "Because I know how Southwestern Bell treats you when it comes to phone service. They don't have any completion so they treat you any kind of way."

Womack tried to get back up, but his lawyer restrained him.

Big Mildred walked over and stood next to my platform. She winked her eye, then whispered, "Keep your roll going, Sister. I'm just praying he's foolish enough to come back here."

Poe painted his face with a sarcastic smirk. "So you're afraid Mr. Womack's company is going to treat us any kind of way?"

"This document certainly gives him the opportunity."

"Where do you see that, because I don't see anything in this document that says: Mr. Womack, you can treat us any kind of way?"

I straightened by fancy glasses and flipped a few pages. "If you look at section 21 under disbursements, you'll see the proposed schedule of funding transfers. Approximately $125,000 is being transferred from the church's account to Mr. Womack's account. At that point, no work has started, no materials bought, no employees hired. At that point, Mr. Womack is in a position to treat us any kind of way."

Poe shook his head with disgust. "Sister Kizzy, if you knew anything about this business, you'd understand that this is an honest money disbursement to get the ball rolling. This is standard procedure for all projects of this magnitude."

"Did you say ALL, because I know of several projects that use a surety bond to guarantee payment rather than transferring cash in advance before the contractor demonstrates the ability to perform the work?"

A hush fell over the crowd. Everyone was combing through the disbursements section, trying to see if there were any other surprises waiting for them. This was the moment for which I had hoped. The members of the church were now fully engaged.

"Look. The man can't take a surety bond to the grocery store. He can't pay his utilities and office rent with a piece of paper. He and his people have to operate just like everybody else," defended Deacon Poe.

Deacon Crump stood up. "Why is his grocery bill our business? I mean, Sister Kizzy has a good point. We're the client. Shouldn't we be doing what's best for the church?"

"Amen, amen." The congregation moaned a muffled affirmation.

"This document is what's best for the church," Poe insisted. "It gets us to exactly where we need to be."

"Is that a quote from your I-KNOW-IT-ALL Bible? Because I

ain't buying it." Crump challenged him, harshly.

Womack stood up again. "Who in the hell are you, anyway? Deacon Poe is the one been working this here deal."

Crump whirled his blubbery frame around and started walking toward Womack. "Who am I? Who am I? I'm your worst nightmare if you wanna take it there."

Womack started toward Crump. "Brang it, baby!"

Big Mildred looked up at me with a girlish sparkle in her eye. "Oooooh yeah! The chickens done come home to roost." Then, she hurried toward the front.

In math, there are numerical hypotheses dealing with two freight trains leaving the station at the same time and traveling in opposite directions. The answer, however, is never good when they're traveling in the same direction and on the same track. It's even worse when your pastor decides to establish himself as a human buffer zone to minimize railway damages. The problem evolves from one of measuring motion and distance to one of calculating the lift coefficient necessary to get the pastor off the floor.

Pastor Fordham was tired of *fighting* demons invading his church. A few seconds before Womack and Crump collided, he stepped between them.

"No, no, Brothers! We can't have this!" That was the last we heard from him before they carted him off to his study in the back. It would take a full dose of Big Mildred's smelling sauce to bring him around. But by the time he regained his senses, most everyone had gone home.

Four deacons, two ushers, one associate minister and two technicians from the sound room finally managed to separate Womack and Crump; but not before they exchanged a black eye for a bloody nose. I really didn't think it was necessary for Big Mildred to hit Womack in the back of the head with a stack of heavy brass collection plates. But the Lord tells us in his word that we shouldn't judge.

Crump had ripped a gaping hole in Womack's fancy, gold suite. In return, Womack had snatched off Crump's wavy toupee. It reminded me of the old Thanksgiving Classic football games where local arch rival Jack Yates High won on the field, but Phillis Wheatley High won in the parking lot after the game. It was a primitive equilibrium of bragging rights. But no one went away empty handed.

Reverend Abernathy, the only associate minister present, tried to close us out in prayer. But the most he could push out of his stuttering mouth was, "Oh, God, uh, uh, uh, uh...."

After about twenty uh's, somebody in the back of the church shouted *Amen* and the congregation flooded through the exits.

Before Ububee could unlock my wheels and back me down the ramp to the floor, Deacon Poe stormed over to my bird nest. He was fuming mad. "So this is the way you show your appreciation?"

I responded with an unflinching stare. "Beg your pardon?"

"You call yourself a Christian woman. But you don't understand the meaning of give and take."

"What did I give and what did I take?" I asked him, candidly.

He looked at my bird nest and all the fancy upgrades. "It's seems to be us doing all the giving. We've tried to accommodate you in every way."

And then it hit me that Deacon Poe had orchestrated my special day. It was his way of creating a sense of obligation that would ultimately gain my support of their project. Unfortunately, I was too old and senile to make the connection.

"Deacon Poe, I appreciate all that you've done."

"Do you?" He reprimanded me. "Because, standing down there, trying to move this church into the 21st century, I really couldn't tell."

Ububee, who stood behind my chair, turned to Poe with a hard expression. "Deacon, I wish to stay out of dis. But I cannot allow you to talk to my mother-in-law in dis tone."

"Oh, don't worry I'm finished. But understand, if your mother-in-law wants to play hardball, then that's what will play."

He stormed off, down the aisle.

Ububee examined me with his big white eyes. "Are you feeling the best, Mama Kizzy?"

"I'm fine," I assured him. But deep down inside I felt quite guilty. To Poe and the other deacons, I was a cog in the wheel, an expert saboteur who blocked their march toward progress. I wondered how many others in the congregation felt the same way.

To me it was a simple proposition. We needed the shelter for battered women. What we didn't need were the crooks that came along with the package.

As we rolled toward the front door, I asked Ububee a question. "Do you think God is pleased with what happened here tonight?"

He thought about it for a long time. "I don't think he is pleased with us, period! That is why he sent his Son, so he don't have to look at us so hard. Instead he see de blood."

I smiled to myself. *Maybe Lizzy didn't do so bad after all.*

Once outside, I noticed a figure standing under the tall willow trees, his foot resting upon one of the wrought iron picnic benches. To my surprise, it was Pastor Fordham, puffing on an orange-tipped cigarette. His puckered lips sent white plumes of smoke into the moonlit sky.

I glanced back at Ububee. "Go ahead and unlock the van. I'll be along shortly.

Tightly gripping my oversized rubber wheels, I rolled down the red brick walkway, toward the picnic grounds.

I parked my wheelchair adjacent to the bench, just so I could get a full view of his beleaguered face. Then, I waited until the serenity of the night's summer breeze and the moonlight, shining through the trees, dampened my intrusion into his tangled world.

A few crickets chirped from the garden behind us. An old frog croaked from the bayou nearby. Finally, I broke the ice.

"I'd ask if you're okay, but I think I already know the answer."

He inspected the smoldering cigarette stub, glued between his long fingers. "I stopped smoking twelve years ago. But I guess desperate times call for desperate measures."

"I hope you're not beating yourself up for what happened back there?"

"No, I think the brothers took care of that already. I'm just wondering where God's protective angels are when you need them."

I chuckled, lightly. "Pastor, I don't think they do freight trains."

He tried to smile, then grabbed his right jaw, the one that had taken on Deacon Crump's elbow. "Wise angels. Wise angels, indeed. Maybe next time I'll follow their lead."

"I know it looks bad now. But you'll get through this, just like before."

"Maybe. It's just that this time, I feel different. I feel like I brought this on myself. I compromised when I didn't have to."

I continued to comfort him. "Just remember. God chastises those whom he loves. Besides, Olivia is not your average temptation."

He frowned. "Who?"

"Olivia ... Olivia Boudreaux? Remember you told me about the trip to Hawaii?"

"I don't understand. What does this Olivia have to do with my trip?"

"I ...aah, well ... I guess I'm a little mixed up. It happens at my age. Can you tell me about your trip again?"

He sucked in a deep breath from the humid, night air.

"Brother Crump and his wife went to Hawaii a few months back. They were having trouble with their marriage, so I suggested they get away, spend some quality time together. Marriage is one of God's most precious institutions. Of, course, you already know that. You and Deacon Myles were married, what, thirty years?"

"Forty-one years, six months."

"You, see. You've already experienced the power of God's sacred union."

I nodded, knowingly.

"Anyway, while they were there, they won a free return trip, all expenses paid. When they got back, Brother Crump offered the package to me."

"There's nothing wrong with that," I said. "We all love you, Pastor. We want to bless you whenever we can."

"I do appreciate that, Sister Kizzy. But this one, I should've turned down."

Pastor Fordham went on to explain that Crump had asked several times to become a deacon. Knowing he was not ready, Pastor Fordham had turned him down.

"Once I accepted the free trip to Hawaii, I felt a certain obligation. I said yes when I really should've said no. I put myself in a compromised position. And tonight, you saw the results."

Suddenly, everything was crystal clear. I was seeing heads and tails at the same time. And that was just fine with me. My lying meter had been correct all along. The flaw resided in my limited comprehension of the truth.

Like the NASA Shuttle on a glorious mission to the stars, I catapulted myself out of my chair to give Pastor Fordham a great big hug. My Pastor was still my Pastor, righteous enough to live on another day.

As he observed the joy in my eyes, he seemed a bit confused. "Have you been listening to all the mistakes I've made?"

"I have. And, as far as I'm concerned, they don't amount to a hill of beans."

"Pastor!" A raspy voice cried out from behind us.

We both turned to see Deacon Grubbs, standing on the steps.

"We need to see you before we lock up," he explained.

"Pastor Fordham waved, acknowledgingly. "I'm on my way." Then, he turned to me. "Sister Kizzy, we've got to stop meeting like this. People are going to talk."

I smiled with renewed confidence. "Don't worry. I know exactly what to tell them."

Inside the van, Ububee and Lizzy were already sitting, waiting, and finalizing the details for the trip to the airport the next day. Once Ububee had loaded my chair, we headed toward the freeway.

I reached into a brown paper bag and pulled out the brightly colored sweater.

"Ububee, you're leaving tomorrow. You're going to need this." I placed the sweater on the armrest beside him."

He grinned, widely. "I knew you ladies wouldn't let me down."

Lizzy snatched the sweater away. "It wasn't we ladies. It was that-"

"That friend of yours, Lizzy. That very special friend of yours." I shelved an imaginary foot into her big mouth. "I just talked to Pastor Fordham. And everything she said was true."

Lizzy's whole face lit up like a Christmas tree. "Everything?!"

"EVERY...THING," I said it slowly so she would understand.

"What things?" Ububee inquired.

"Girl stuff," Lizzy reported. "Now take your sweater and wear it with distinction, like Tarzan would."

She placed it back on the armrest.

A few miles down the freeway, Lizzy turned back again. "Can you believe that Deacon Crump? What do you think about him?"

Before I could answer, Ububee weighed in. "He's a mad man."

"He *is*." Lizzy agreed. "He's no different from the hustlers on the street. He shouldn't be on the Board, should he, Mama?"

I smiled, coyly. "Crump has his place."

Her eyes widened. "As a deacon?"

"As an instrument," I clarified.

"I don't get it," she grumbled. "All that profanity and stuff. He's a disgrace to the church and to the kingdom. People like that should just stay away."

I couldn't help thinking how naïve her perspective had been. It was typical of her generation, the tendency to embrace the reality in front of them without having a clue about the big picture.

Crump had played a vital role in circumventing Poe's plan. Because of Crump's carnality, Womack had walked away empty-handed. More importantly, Pastor Fordham had found his way back into our good graces.

Like Judas Icarius who betrayed Jesus or Cyrus the Great who attacked Babylonia and freed the Jews, Deacon Crump had done his job. Of course, Lizzy and Ububee would never understand such a complex balance between good and evil. And so I didn't bother to explain. Instead, I admonished them to remember one thing. "God can do whatever he wants to do, with whoever he wants to do it with, Amen?"

Chapter Thirteen

Thursday, June 10th was a day of fours. At 4:44 am my alarm clock went off for no apparent reason. I wanted to blame the nerve-shattering cowbells on my tinkering with the knobs or setting the wrong time. But since my retirement way back in '88, I hadn't set the alarm at all ... well, there was that one time in 1991, after months of indigestion and stomach discomfort, I had to go to the hospital for a colonoscopy. I set the clock for 5:30 am in the morning. But other than that, the old nickel-plated, twin-bell Westclox just sat on my nightstand and ticked my life away.

After six decades on God's green earth, I had come to realize that nothing happens by chance. Everything in the universe is somehow, connected. Newton's Third Law states that for every action there is an equal and opposite reaction, even if the original action takes place a million miles away.

What Newton couldn't measure, however, was the push factor of evil, rippling through the invisible world. A critical, irresponsible word out of the mouth of a parent, though invisible, could kill a young child's dream for life. A vicious lie, spread by enough people, could ruin a person's reputation. A sinister plot from the belly of hell, hatched by Satan and his Imps, could fill the cosmos with waves of impending doom.

Sometimes the waves were so strong they created supernatural events in the natural world; like the time the picture frame holding Charlotte Lueese's photograph fell off the wall and burst into a million pieces. It was the same week she went to that hair convention in Portland. It was the same day she came up missing.

There were other frames on the wall right next to hers. But only hers fell to the floor. Most people would call it a coincidence, a random occurrence that could happen any time, any place. But deep in my heart I knew better. Whatever happened in Portland, happened the day that frame fell off the wall.

Christians, in general, had a problem with the supernatural. They would pray for a miracle. But when it happened, they'd spend an inordinate amount of time trying to tie it to a natural cause: "The man had a heart attack but he didn't die. That's because the paramedics arrived early with a special machine. The car went head-on with an eighteen-wheeler and nobody got hurt. That's because of the angle of the crash and the new safety bumpers. The house note was overdue, but the mortgage company lost the papers for eight months. That's because they were installing a new computer system at the home office and things got mixed up. Jesus fed the 5,000 with two fish and five barley loaves of bread. That's because the bread was crumbly and the fish were giant tunas that had beached themselves along the Sea of Genneseret."

I had no trouble with the supernatural. I had seen a miracle or two in my lifetime and realized that faith was actually believing in things we couldn't explain. God said he spoke the world into existence. How could I explain that to a rational minded evolutionist? I couldn't even explain the smell of cigarette smoke coming from Mr. Myles' favorite bench or the over-heated walking cane in my hallway closet. How was I going to explain a triune God, reaching into his vocabulary and calling into existence the sun and moon and the sea?

Though I couldn't explain supernatural events, I couldn't ignore them either. When the alarm clock went off at 4:44 am, I got up and girded myself with prayer and a few scriptures from the big print Bible I kept on the nightstand next to the bed. If evil was rippling in my direction, I wanted to be prepared.

I had been reading about forty minutes when I heard a loud crash from the back of my house. I stumbled to my kitchen door just in time to see a blurred, darkened figure, leaping over my back cyclone fence.

Suddenly, I felt something cold under my bare feet. The frosty sensation reminded me of a stray ice chip from daddy's old hand-cranked ice cream maker back in Hattiesburg. When I turned on the light, I realized it wasn't an ice chip at all, but a long shim of broken glass, sticking out of my big toe. The blood had already begun trickling along the edges of my white medallion tiles. And slowly, but surely, the pain worked its way up to my brain.

I stood there, frozen in terror. The window between the refrigerator and the back door had been smashed. A trail of shattered glass led to a jagged concrete rock, partially wrapped in crinkled paper, resting, ominously, in the middle of the floor. I could see there was writing on the paper. But I was too petrified to pick it up.

I found myself thinking about Mr. Myles and how I wished, so desperately, he was still here. That's when I recalled the solemn instructions he had given to me long ago.

If ever I'm gone and somebody breaks in on you, remember your worst enemy is not the person breaking in, but the fear that keeps you from thinking, and doing what you need to do.

I wasn't thinking. I was just standing there, wild-eyed,

trembling, and trying my best to bleed to death.

I took a few wobbly steps back to my dining room table and flopped down in one of the end chairs. I grabbed one of the decorative blue cloth napkins off the table and slowly removed the sheet of glass from my toe. I took a few deep breathes. And then I began to reason with myself, not silently or fearfully or discretely like a defeated old woman would do, but boldly and loudly like a determined adversary. I needed to hear the words, undergirding my spirit and speaking victory to my heart. I needed to remind myself of the source of my strength and my help.

I will lift up mine eyes to the hills from which cometh my help. My help cometh from the Lord.

And so, I reasoned:

If someone was going to break in on me, they would already be inside. Instead, I saw the coward jumping the fence.

I took a deep breath.

If God is my protector, then whom shall I fear?

I took another deep breath.

God woke me up so I would be ready. He did his part. Now what is mine?

I didn't need another breath. I mustered all the strength left in my frail bones and hobbled back to the bedroom. I reached up on the top shelf of my closet, found Mr. Myles' old lunch kit and dumped the assorted contents on the bed. I plunged my trembling hand into the pile and pulled out his pearl-handled 38 revolver. Then, I hobbled back to my chair in the dining room and took up my solemn watch. I prayed no more rocks came through my window because, if they did, somebody was going to reap a harvest of lead.

For what seemed to be an eternity, I sat in that chair, watching and waiting for my adversary to return. I told myself I was a great sentinel, sitting on the wall of Jerusalem; not the frightened old lady, reflected in my dining room mirror. God did not give us the spirit of fear. God gave us a pearl-handled 38.

As the morning light slowly crept through my thick blue curtains, I felt a sense of relief. The reflection in the mirror didn't look so vulnerable any more. The worst was over and the people of God were still standing ... well ... sitting ... aching. I poured a bottle of peroxide into a big cooking pot, then stuck my whole foot inside. I pulled the phone from the counter and began to dial.

It shouldn't have surprised me that Lizzy's answering machine came on. If everything had gone according to schedule, she was already at the airport, putting Ububee on the plane. No doubt, she had the big white death phone with her. But I felt guilty giving her a reason to jam it against her brain. Those mobile phones were eventually going to kill a bunch of people. I didn't want her to be in that number.

In years past, I would've called Charlotte Lueese. She was my best friend. She would've known what to do. But Charlotte Lueese was somewhere fighting her own battles, if she was still able to fight at all. I needed someone who could come right away.

I called my baby sister, Estelle. Her answering machine came on as well. I suspected she had spent the night at the good Bishop's house ... reading the Bible and praying for the children of Africa, of course.

Finally, I called Cora Williams. On the fourth ring she picked up. "Kizzy?" She wanted to let me know she had that new caller-ID box.

"Somebody tried to break in." I informed her in an artificially calm voice.

"Are you alright?"

I looked down at the big pot that contained my bloody toe. "More or less."

"Did you call the police?"

"Not yet?"

"Why not?" She scolded me.

I hesitated a long while. Since the infamous reign of Police Chief Herman Short, I had lost confidence in the Houston Police Department. Back in '71, he had released the blue-badge dogs on the black community, using indiscriminate raids, traffic stops and arrest to bolster his "tough-on-crime" image.

Back then, President Richard M. Nixon and Vice President Spiro T. Agnew were in office. It was popular to be tough on crime, even if you were a criminal, yourself. Police Chief Short used illegal tactics on certain targeted groups. They had even stopped, detained and threatened Mr. Myles on his way home from work ... threatened him for no reason at all.

Lee Brown had come in from Atlanta and tried to turn things around. But, as far as I was concerned, the core of racism and double dealing was still deeply embedded in the force. It wouldn't have surprised me one bit if they had come over to my house, pulled my King Arthur Flour can out of my cupboard, took it to their infamous crime lab and declared the contents to be white cocaine.

I finally told Cora, "I don't want them to get involved."

An hour later, Cora's 1961 black Chrysler DeSoto lumbered into the driveway. She kept it as a backup to her Chevy Impala which stayed in the shop. Like Mr. Myles' lunch kit, the old DeSoto held great sentimental value. It was the last car her husband, Malcolm, had bought before he got killed in Viet Nam.

Not knowing exactly what she would encounter, she left her

two daughters and a visiting niece in the car. Clad in baggy jeans and flat black Sears Roebuck sneakers, she entered the house with big, suspicious eyes and a baseball bat in her hand. Unlike her altercation with Big Mildred, this affair was destined to go her way.

She gave the whole house a once-over, then, opened the back door. She looked at me with a grim expression. "You need to see this, Kizzy. You need to see it right now."

With the help of my slightly heated, wood grain walking cane, I hobbled over to the door.

Even before I reached the door, I smelled the stint of diesel fuel coming through the screen. Diesel, the lethal combination of kerosene, ether and amyl nitrate, was what the coward had used to spray my beautiful red roses and my fig trees and my tomato plants and my honeydews vines. The whole garden had already begun to wither with a yellow-brown sickness. The culprit had even left his murder weapon, lying in the dirt.

Cora pointed to the rusty can and spray pump at the edge of the fence. "There may be finger prints on that cylinder."

"How many years do you think they'll give him for spraying an old woman's garden?" I turned around and went back into the house.

Cora followed me into the kitchen and picked up the concrete rock. She removed the rubber band and held the crinkled paper up to the light. "You read this?"

"Not yet."

She finally handed the note to me. "I'll give you one guess."

It read:

THE WORLD IS A DANGEROUS PLACE FOR A
STUBBORN OLD WOMEN LIVING ALONE.

I shook my head in disgust. "This is Poe, isn't it?"

"Who else would do something this stupid?"

"So this is what he means by hardball."

No," she declared. "Hardball is when I accidentally run over his ass in the parking lot this Sunday."

"Cora, don't even talk that way," I reprimanded.

She didn't hear me. She was still staring up at the ceiling, her eyes half closed. "I could run over him, then back over Mildred. Two for the price of one, if you know what I mean."

"Listen, Cora. We're not into violence. You know better than that. It's not the Lord's way."

She fixed her eyes on the pearl-handled revolver, fully loaded and resting, handily on the dining room table. "Explain to me again what we not into."

I put my hand over my mouth and began to sniggle ... and then laugh ... and then cry, uncontrollably. I let it all out on Cora's comforting shoulder.

"Poe's right," I whispered, softly. "We're too old for this."

She stroked my back, reassuringly, allowing all of the pent up fear and anguish to drain out. "You can't give up, Kizzy. I'll tell you what my old Pastor use to tell us back in South Carolina."

"What's that?"

"Only the dead have done enough."

I started laughing again, a laugh I needed deep down in my soul. Then, warned her. "Don't you tell a soul about this, Cora. You hear me?"

"Are you kidding? This is a wonderful funeral story. Only thing I can say is don't die before me or the cat's out of the bag."

She was still laughing when I grabbed the revolver, hobbled into my bedroom and placed it back into Mr. Myles' lunch kit. As I gathered the other odds and ends that I had dumped onto the bed, I came across an envelope with a letter inside. It was addressed to Mr. Harry Wilcox, Monsanto Chemical.

It was Mr. Myles' resignation letter. I remembered because I had helped him to write it. It was short and to the point:

BECAUSE OF RECENT DEVELOPMENTS I CAN NO LONGER CONTINUE AT MONSANTO CHEMICAL. YOU HAVE BEEN A GOOD SUPERVISOR. BUT THE IRRESPONSIBLE CONDUCT OF OTHERS HAS BE- COME TOO MUCH. BE ADVISED MY LAST DAY IS AUGUST 23, 1964.

Four lines, that's all. But they represented four years of pure agony. Being the first black in an all-white, low-skilled, hick-infested plant in the heart of the KKK's playground, Pasadena, Texas, meant being subjected to every petty indignity in the book. There were racial slurs, lewd jokes, bad work assignments and constant isolation waiting for him each time he entered the gate. They broke into his locker so many times, he finally took the lock off. It wasn't that they were stealing from him. Rather, they were leaving him little gifts like dead rats, monkey bread and photos of Little Black Sambo.

I tried to remember the final straw that had prompted him to write the letter. And then it came to me.

He had worked a double shift to make sure the trucks got loaded for a big job in Dallas. They were shorthanded, so he did most of the work. The next day at the safety meeting, his supervisor, Harry Wilcox, recognized him publicly for his long hours and hard work.

I remember him coming home that night, feeling proud and appreciated. It was all we talked about at the dinner table. He went to bed with a smile on his face.

The next day when he got off from work and walked to the

parking lot, he found his truck covered in cow manure and the doors, painted with the ominous title: NIGGER SHOWOFF. That's when he came home and wrote the letter.

"I could understand if I was lazy and missing days," he confided. "But I'm doing the work. I'm there every day. And they're still not satisfied. I got enough of this #s*#*h!"

He took the letter with him the next day, but never turned it in. When he arrived at work, he found that Harry Wilcox had hired two more blacks. They were younger than Mr. Myles and visibly shaken by all of the hard, threatening, hateful stares. They had immediately come to him, seeking advice.

"No way they're going make it if I leave." That's what he had told me that afternoon when he got home.

And so he stayed there, not for his sake, but for theirs. One of those young men eventually became the first black plant superintendent, all because Mr. Myles didn't quit.

I didn't know what Poe was going to do next. I just knew I couldn't quit. People were counting on me, just like they had counted on Mr. Myles. If he could've spoken to me from heaven, he would've told me, "Hang in there, Kizzy Marie."

That's what he would've told me. And that's what I was going to do.

****

That afternoon, the phone rang at exactly 4:00 p.m. I knew because I had just finished watching the weather report on Channel 2. Though, with all of the banging and sawing, it was hard to hear the announcer, I found out a weak tropical wave had been detected over the Caribbean Sea in Central America and was headed our way. A tropical wave was the baby stage for a hurricane, especially in that part of the world. The National Hurricane Center had promised to give North American viewers an update every few hours.

I hobbled over to the counter and grabbed the receiver. It was Lizzy on the line, cruising down the freeway, calling me on her death phone.

"What's that noise?" she immediately inquired.

Hector had just cranked up his electric saw.

"That's Cora William's handyman. He's doing some work for me," I explained.

"What kind of work?"

"He's replacing a window, that's all."

"What happen to your window?"

"You're asking me all of these questions. Don't you have your own house to take care of?"

I didn't want to tell her about the early morning break-in. She would've gone into a state of panic, recited some kind of crime statistic and then insisted on me staying at her house. I wanted to stay at my own house. She'd find out about the break-in soon enough.

"I have to keep up with you, Mama. Otherwise, you'll get into trouble."

"I can handle my business without you butting in, thank you. I was doing it long before you were born."

I couldn't hear her response. Hector and his assistant started arguing in Spanish, then proceeded to hammer away.

When the noise finally died down, I ask Lizzy about Ububee's departure.

"Oh, Mama, you wouldn't believe this day."

"Did Ububee catch his flight?"

"Yes, finally, after a four hour delay. But in a way it was good. It gave us a chance to talk."

"About what?"

"Actually, I don't really know. He was trying to tell me something. He kept saying just in case this, and just in case that. And why did he need to keep telling me he loved me? I think he was nervous about the flight. He was definitely nervous about something."

"So have you heard anything yet? Has his plane landed?"

"Yes, he made it to London. He won't leave for Nigeria until tomorrow. I told him he'd be fine, just fine." She seemed intent on convincing the both of us.

She went on to explain that she had talked to Olivia Boudreaux.

"We had lunch at that new café downtown, the one on Fannin Street where all the bougie Negroes walk around with their noses in the air."

"Everything alright with you and her?"

"Never better, Mama. But did you know that sorry bum still hadn't made a firm commitment to her?"

I hesitated a moment. "I don't know what you mean. That's a mighty big engagement ring on her finger."

"She's been wearing that ring forever," Lizzy grumbled. "It was time for him to get down to brass tacks."

"Well, there's nothing you can do."

"Oh, yeah," she insisted. "There was something I could do, and I did it."

Lizzy had gone over to Councilman Anthony's office and demanded to see him. She had given him both barrels and a bazooka to boot.

"I told him by some fluke in nature, he was engaged to the most beautiful woman in Texas. Did he really think he could do better? He would be a fool to let her get away, which I hinted, he was about to do. I told him she was getting ready to move to Austin. Someone in the governor's office had made her a very attractive offer."

"What was his response?"

"His eyes almost bulged out of his little coconut head," said Lizzy. "He kept saying 'Employment, right? This is about a job, right?' He was trying to make sure it was a legitimate job and not another meal ticket arrangement where the going bid was over his head. I just smiled at him and said ... you could call it that."

"That is so shameful and treacherous of you. Did it work?"

As soon as I left his office, he got on the phone. He called Olivia and set a wedding date right there over the phone. You hear me?"

"Did Olivia know you were going over there?"

"No," she declared. "And she still doesn't. I told Anthony if he ever mentioned my little visit, I would call the local newspapers and give them some secrets that would make his head swim."

"What kind of secrets?"

"Bedroom secrets, Mama. His little weird fetishes. You don't want to know."

"Uuuh." I cringed.

Lizzy continued. "Anyway, Olivia and I are driving up to the Dallas Fashion Market in the morning. We're going to find her a wedding dress."

"That's wonderful, Lizzy. Your big mouth finally paid off."

"It did, Mama. Now, do you need anything before I leave? Because we won't be back until Sunday afternoon."

"I'm fine, child. You girls go on up there and enjoy yourself. Put a big hole in the Councilman's wallet for him dragging his feet."

"We plan to do just that."

There was a long pause before she spoke again. "One more thing before I go."

"Yes."

"I dreamed about daddy last night. It was kind of strange."

"What happened?" I prodded.

"He brought you four red roses. It wasn't your birthday or anniversary. He just came into the house and handed them to you."

My heart began to pound. "That is strange."

"You know me, Mama. In the dream I asked him why he was being so cheap. Why didn't he bring you a full dozen?"

"What did he say?"

"He looked kind of sad. He said those four were the only ones left."

She waited for me to respond. But I was too choked up.

She finally asked, "Does any of that make sense to you?"

I... ah ... I'll have to think about it." I forced out a meager reply.

"Okay, Mama. I've got to go. I left my charger at home and my battery is dying on the spot. I'll call you when we get to Dallas."

She hung up the phone.

For some reason I couldn't hang up, not right away. I kept holding on, waiting for more words to come through the receiver, words that would reveal the true meaning of Lizzy's odd concoction. It took Hector's light tap on my shoulder to bring me around.

"Sorry to problem you, Senora. We have finished the work."

I finally released the phone and turned toward the back door.

I was astonished by their expert craftsmanship. The new window was immaculate, an exact match to the existing wood, but with fancy trimming around the glass panes.

"It's beautiful. Much better than the old one."

The compliment extorted a hearty smile from both of them. The assistant began carting tools to the truck. He stopped on the sidewalk to talk to my neighbor, Joe Martinez, a top notched mechanic who lived directly across the street.

Meanwhile, Hector employed a big cotton cloth and some Windex to give the glass its final sparkle. Cora Williams had brought her girls in earlier to clean up the original mess. But Hector and his crew had created an entirely new episode.

Still, the new clutter was worth it. Except for the sawdust, wood chips and a few silver nails, scattered across the white tile, my house was back to normal. My knees were percolating and my injured toe was feeling much better. With the help of my electric broom and a damp mop, the evidence of Poe's cowardly attack would soon be swept into oblivion.

Hector finally presented me with the bill: $370. I asked him how much he would charge to have his assistant trim the fig tree limbs, fatally drooping from the diesel attack.

"Whatever, you think, Senora. If it help you, we do it for free," he offered.

"Not for free," I insisted.

Too often, Christians held their hands high to the heavens on Sunday, then used those same hands to pickpocket their co-laborers on Monday. I thought about my *Scholium of Numeric Prediction* and made the check out for $444.

Soon Hector and his crew were gone. The house was quiet again and the day's new light that had brought me so much comfort was fading into dusk. I should've been worried; frightened by the new horrors the darkness would bring. Instead, I found myself preoccupied by a single thought.

What did the four roses in Lizzy's dream represent?

There was so much about the universe I didn't understand:

the precise relationship between time and space, energy and matter, or how the spiritual world consistently tampered with our physical absolutes. What I did understand was that everything was somehow connected, no matter how small the event or insignificant the visible ties seemed to be.

I was thinking about roses because my prize bushes had been destroyed. But why was Lizzy thinking about roses?

And then it dawned on me that she wasn't thinking about roses. It was Mr. Myles who was thinking about them. He had brought me four roses because they were the only ones left.

But there were no roses left ... *or were there?*

I got up from the table, grabbed my walking cane and opened the back door. I hobbled down the steps, along the crimson brick walkway and into the garden.

The tragic effects of the diesel had multiplied. The yellow-brown sickness had slowly transformed into a modern-day Black Plague. A terse sorrow filled the air.

That's when I spotted it.

In the corner, near the edge of the house was a single, elegant bourbon rose bush, erect and undefiled, glistening in the twilight. I counted its four beautiful lush red blossoms, slowly and methodically, the way you would count precious diamonds in a royal solitaire. The tally gave my knees a chance to stop shaking and kept my heart from running away.

I gathered my pruning shears from a nearby work bench and snipped the delicate stems, one-by-one. All along, I was mesmerized by the sweet, innocent fragrance of four little roses and how their blissful aroma overpowered a garden contaminated by death.

As the fullness of night covered the garden, I stepped back inside and locked the door. I put the four roses into a lightly tinted vase, filled it with water and set it on the dining room table.

I sat there for a long time, staring at the roses. And then, I decided to say what was on my mind.

"Thank you, Mr. Myles. I love the roses. And I love you."

There! I had said it. I had finally crossed the line. I was a senile old woman, living all alone, spending her nights, talking to her dead husband. If anybody had a problem with that, they could take it up with my new pearl-handled friend.

Amen?

Chapter Fourteen

O n Sunday morning, June 12th, I awakened refreshed and a bit relieved. Two nights had passed without a single bizarre night-invasion on the old woman living alone. I didn't know whether Poe was trying to lull me to sleep or whether he felt his one-rock garden assault was enough to drive me away. Whatever the reason, I relished the peace and quiet that cradled my little world.

While relaxing from the grueling task of cleaning out my garden, I had spent a good part of my time tracking the baby hurricane in the Yucatán Peninsula. After three days, it was no longer a baby, but a raging tropical storm that had already killed twenty people in El Salvador. The National Hurricane Center had predicted that it would interact with an upper level low band of pressure, and by Sunday afternoon, be upgraded to a full-fledged hurricane. They had already given it a name: Arlene.

I often wondered why they endowed powerful, destructive storms with the names of women. It seemed hypocritical that men who coveted power and who went out of their way to associate themselves with raw strength and potential destruction would slap a woman's name on a natural phenomenon that epitomized them in every way. I even had one of my science classes to write letters to the Hurricane Center to suggest the naming process begin to reflect the diversity of the population. There were men, women, blacks, browns, whites, Asians, you name it. Didn't it make sense for the perception of destructiveness to be spread around?

I guess they finally got it. The storm that had gone through Florida the year before and killed over 200 hundred people had been named Hurricane Andrew. Now the world knew that not only Carla and Alicia were merciless killers, but Andrew was too.

With Ububee in Africa and Lizzy in Dallas, I asked Cora Williams to pick me up for church. But a few hours before it was time to go, she called to say Bayboy had had a bad reaction to some new medication the night before. Plus, her Impala was still in the shop and her old DeSoto was acting up.

"I think the Lord is trying to protect Deacon Poe," she said. "How can I run over somebody if I'm walking? Me and the girls might as well stay home."

I didn't want to stay home. I wanted Poe to see me, alive and well, in spite of his monkey shine. I called for the church van.

An hour later, the church's dilapidated gray and black Ford van pulled up in front of my house. The windows were tinted, but I could see a few heads, peering through the glass. Deacon Moore jumped out, retrieved my wheelchair from the front porch and buckled me into the first seat behind him.

"I've got the last one." He reported back to the church office on a handheld walkie-talkie. "We're on our way in."

I noticed a human lump beneath a black tarpaulin on the seat across from me. White sneakers peeped out from the edges, but did not move. I presumed, after an overactive night in the honky-tonks, someone was getting a last minute nap in before the word of God shoveled a load of fire and brimstone down their unclean temple.

I waited until Deacon Moore had pulled away from the curb, then, chuckled. "So you're the designated driver these days?"

He shook his head with disgust. "Kizzy, you do what you gotta do. The Brotherhood swore up and down they could handle this job. But where are they?"

"Is it like this every Sunday?"

"Just about. I mean, they all can quote scripture just fine. But when it comes to service and getting their hands dirty, now that's a different ball of wax."

"I remember when you and Mr. Myles were in the Brotherhood."

"Yeah. That was a long time ago when the Brotherhood, which, by the way, I hear they're renaming *Men's Ministry*, was doing something worthwhile. We might paint the whole church in a week or feed a hundred senior citizens in a day." He shook his head with repugnance. "These guys? We can't even get them to do little stuff, like clean out the church basement. We set three dates and everybody had excuses. We eventually had to hire somebody."

I reminded him of Pastor Fordham's words. "You can't make people do what they don't have a mind to do. God's work is a volunteer business."

"I don't think these cream puff college boys know what the word volunteer really means."

When Deacon Moore said *"means"*, the black tarpaulin flew back and Frogman leaped up from his seat. "Boooh!!"

He was too far away to startle me, but I grabbed my heart anyway. "Oh my God!"

He sat back down, the smile of accomplishment, plastered across his ashy face.

Deacon Moore whispered under his breath. "He wanted to

scare you. I was supposed to give the signal. But, hell, we got to talking and I forgot the magic word."

I looked across the aisle. "What was the magic word, Frogman?"

"*Jeans!* Because I got a new pair this weekend." He rubbed both blue denim legs with the palms of his hands.

"Those are really nice jeans, Frogman. Really nice," I said.

"You wanna know how I got 'em?"

I nodded. "Yes. How did you get them?"

He flashed an even wider grin. "I cleaned out the church basement. It was fun down there. And now I know a lot of secrets."

"What secrets do you know, Frogman?"

This time he flashed the widest grin of all, but said nothing. Instead, he unwrapped a piece of green Wrigley's Spearmint gum and tossed it into his mouth.

Deacon Moore looked back at me. "Told you we had to pay somebody. Might as well be somebody we know."

I was so preoccupied with Frogman's jeans, I almost overlooked the other passengers on the van. There were only three. Another lady in her late twenties sat a few seats behind me, fixing the pink bows in her daughter's hair. I admired the little girl for a long while. She reminded me of Lizzy in the first grade, when she lost her front teeth.

My attention, however, was quickly drawn to the last passenger at the back of the van. It was Larry "GeeNet" Willis, a former student of mine and drug head extraordinaire. The last time I had run across him was at Buster's funeral, doing flunky work for Reedy & Sons. Though I was saddened to see so much potential going to waste, his mere presence on the church van, headed for the house of the Lord, filled my heart with a ray of hope.

As teachers, we're supposed to release our students, push

them to the next rung on the great ladder of learning and hope the next caretaker does the same. But most of us never truly release. Once the invisible bond between teacher and student is established, only death is strong enough to sever the ties.

I made sure he saw me, then, waved, enthusiastically. He responded with a callous nod. Maybe the Lord would fix it so I'd get a chance to talk to him. Maybe there was something I could say to help him turn his life around.

A few miles from the church, Frogman slid over into the seat next to me. "Mama Kizzy, do you want my autograph?"

Deacon Moore's baritone voice echoed from the driver's seat. "Now, Frogman, we talked about that."

"No, no, Deacon Moore, He's fine." I gazed into Frogman's innocent eyes. "Yes. I would like that very much."

"Do you have fifty cents?" he inquired.

"Well, let me see." I looked into my purse but couldn't find any change. The smallest denomination I had was a five dollar bill. "Do you have change?"

He reached into the pockets of his new jeans and pulled out five silver dollars. "I have this."

I gave him the five dollar bill, took four silver dollars from him and then winked my eye. "Don't worry about the rest."

He whipped out a white index card from a pouch lying on the seat next to him. He signed it on the front and again on the back. He winked his eye. "The Bible say owe no man."

I was startled by his ingenuous application of scripture. If you looked at it in the literal sense, he was right. Two signatures at fifty cents each was one dollar. I couldn't help but chuckle. The Frogman had struck again.

Deacon Moore pulled up in front of the church and slid open

the middle door. Everyone bailed out but me. I waited until he had set up my wheelchair, just like Ububee would've done. I looked forward to cruising up my newly constructed ramp, recently dedicated in my name, on my day.

It didn't take long to realize there would be no ramp ride today. As we rolled up to the church steps, I spotted the big orange cones, blocking the entrance to the ramp. The hand rail was draped in construction tape, with two dreadful signs hanging on the side. The first signs read: RESTRICTED AREA. The second one read: UNSAFE FOR USAGE.

"What's this?" I asked Deacon Moore.

He stuttered, "I ... I don't know. I went to the Farmers Market yesterday to pick up some watermelons. When I came in this morning, I noticed some changes."

"Changes?"

"Yeah, but not this one."

"Then what changes are you talking about?" I pressed.

He shook his head again. "You'll see."

Deacon Moore looked up toward the top of the steps to find two younger deacons talking. "Excuse me, men. Can you give me a hand? We need to lift this wheelchair up to the door."

One of them came down the steps and whispered into Deacon Moore's ear. He, then, retreated to the top of the steps, completed his conversation and went inside.

Deacon Moore grunted, loudly. "Well, if that don't beat all...."

He explained that Poe had instructed the deacons not to help me up the steps. It seemed that carrying my chair created a potential liability for the church.

"They've never had a problem with it before," I reminded him.

"Yeah, I know."

I was steaming. I wanted to walk. But after working in the garden all week, my knees were shot.

I thought, *What a deplorable way to be greeted at God's house.*

At that moment Big Mildred stuck her head out of the door. "Good morning, Mama Kizzy."

"No, Mildred. It's not a good morning at all."

Deacon Moore had barely explained the situation to her when I felt my chair rising. With him on one side and her only other, we reached the top step faster than ever before.

Inside the foyer, Mildred turned to me. "Mama Kizzy, I don't know who's playing these games. But if you run into any other problems just let me know."

She headed down the hallway.

When Deacon Moore pushed me inside the sanctuary I was still unaware of what he had meant by "changes". It wasn't until we reached my bird nest in the sky that I thoroughly understood.

What bird nest in the sky?

There was no bird nest in the sky. The entire platform had been dismantled and flattened to the floor. What remained was a piece of five foot long plywood to cover the carpet stains. They had packed my box of Kleenex and accompanying accessories into a little cabinet the size of a water cooler and set it on the board. They had placed two strips of red tape on the board to show where my wheels should go.

Before I could say anything, a youth usher walked up and handed me a piece of paper. "Deacon Poe asked me to give this to you."

The paper was an official citation from the City of Houston stating that the ramp outside and the smaller ramp that led up to my platform inside did not meet building specifications. Just as I finished reading the last line, Deacon Poe walked up. "Good morning,

Sister Kizzy."

I took a deep breath then mustered one of his patented fake smiles. "Good morning, Deacon Poe. How are you today?"

"Excellent," he reported, then glanced at the paper in my hand. "I see you got a copy. I wanted you to know what happened."

I nodded, politely. "I think I understand what happened."

"You never know when these city inspectors are going to pop in."

"You never know," I concurred. "But I am curious."

"Yes."

"You all built this platform six years ago as a memorial to my husband. You said it would be a fitting tribute to him to accommodate his widow in this way?"

"Yes."

"Are you saying that during that six-year period not a single city inspector came by?"

"Not a single one," he confirmed.

"Why do you think they suddenly decided to come by now?" I asked.

"That's something you'd have to ask them. I believe their number is on there." He pointed to the citation.

"I wonder if this is also the number you'd use to report pollution, like the smell of diesel fumes?"

"Diesel fumes?" He tried to keep a straight face. "I'm no expert on the City's fuel policies. It's enough to try to keep up with the business of this church, which by the way, I need to take care of. Have a blessed day."

He sashayed off, down the aisle.

Deacon Moore looked at me. "He's lying through his teeth. We've had plenty of inspectors out here."

"I understand. I understand everything."

I even understood why the people kept staring at me. They had been so accustomed to me sitting high and looking low, of speaking from the clouds, of having the whole church answer my every beckoning call. And now it seemed as though I had been demoted. I HAD been demoted. I was an enemy of the State now. And the State was Deacon Poe.

The service was long and drawn out. A guess minister from one of the revival churches in Kansas City preached for forty-five minutes with nothing to say. I did, however, like his closing remarks.

He said: "Those of you who think that evil should play fair, or take a day off or skip your house altogether are missing the point. Evil will flee only when you force it to flee using the principles of God's word."

I was guilty. I had tried to repel evil with my pearl-handled 38. The coward had jumped over my back fence. But there was no guarantee evil, in some form or fashion, would stay away. I needed a spiritual covering to keep evil out of my house, permanently.

At the end of the service, I rolled up to the front and ask Pastor Fordham for special prayer. That's when something very strange happened.

He prayed a powerful prayer for protective angels to descend all around me with the explicit purpose of keeping me from all hurt, harm and danger. When he finished, I opened my eyes to find fifteen or twenty people standing behind me. They had left their pews to show their support, touching and agreeing on my behalf. They didn't know exactly what I was asking for. Yet, they stood there, blindly petitioning Heaven to hear my faithful cry.

That's when it happened. That's when the plasticity of my brain exploded to some distant horizon and the trusted intersections between time and space melted away. The people were still behind me, but their continence had changed. They were suddenly terrified.

Their clothes were soaking wet, as if they had wandered through a giant car wash. Their sluggish movement was bizarre and out of step with my sense of reality. It were as if they were zombies, caught in a slow motion reel.

I clamped down my eyelids, tightly, desperately, as though I were trying to push new holes into my sockets. When I opened my eyes again, everything was back to normal.

Katherine Baker handed me a Kleenex to wipe my tear-drenched face. "Don't let them get to you, Kizzy. People are with you one hundred percent."

****

On the way back home, I leaned over to whisper into Deacon Moore's ear. "Did you see anything strange at the end of service?"

"Yeah, I saw some men from the Brotherhood helping to put up those folding chairs."

"No. I mean while Pastor Fordham was praying for me."

He thought about it for a while. "No, not really. Did you see something?"

I didn't know exactly what to tell him. Aunt Twigg use to say the line between sanity and insanity is so thin, you could push it though the eye of a needle and sew a nice quilt. Perhaps, the battle with Deacon Poe and his cronies have chipped away at my sanity. Perhaps, the stress was getting to me more than I realized.

Watered down church members didn't make sense to me, unless God was exposing the quality of their righteousness. Then, he'd have to water down the whole world.

I decided not to answer.

When the van pulled up in front of my house I didn't get off right away. Instead, I made my way to the back seat and sat down next to GeeNet.

"It's good to see you again, Larry. How have you been?"

"I'm okay," he replied, unconvincingly.

"I'm sorry Pastor Fordham didn't preach today. If you come back next week, I'm sure he'll have a good word for you."

"Maybe so." He refused to look me in the eye.

"Listen. I know the rest of the people are trying to get home, so I won't hold them up. But you know where I live now. If ever you feel like talking-"

"Ain't nothing to talk about," he snapped. "What good will talking do?"

I paused a brief moment, allowing his anger to settle. "Do you remember talking me into giving you a seventy so you could play in the district championship game?"

He managed a reluctant grin. "Mrs. Myles, you didn't give me a seventy. You made me come back after school for two months straight doing makeup assignments."

"Yes, but you had to talk me into trusting you, didn't you?"

"I suppose."

"And what about the game before you went to State? I went to see you. What did you score, thirty?"

"Thirty-one." He corrected me.

"You know what I remember most about that game?"

"What?"

"The way you talked to your teammates. You kept yelling, screen and press and rabbit and blue and a lot of other stuff I didn't understand."

"That's code, once you read the floor and see what you're up against," he eagerly explained.

"The point is talking got you through."

Deacon Moore yelled from the front. "Sorry, Kizzy, but we gonna have to roll."

"Rock and roll!" Frogman embellished.

"Okay, I'm coming right now." I got up from my seat, then placed my hand on his shoulder "It's never too late to talk, Larry. Sometimes a few words can make the difference between victory and defeat."

He listened, but kept his head down, saying nothing.

Once inside my house, I flipped on the television to get an update on the storm. Arlene was a full-fledged hurricane and headed our way.

I walk over to the dining room table to fill my nostrils with the titillating fragrance of Mr. Myles' special bouquet. Then I told him, "I'm going to watch all three channels. Depending on how worried these white folks look, I'm gonna run like hell."

Chapter Fifteen

On Monday, it rained all day. The last thing we needed was the ground to be soaked with water before a hurricane came in. But who was going to tell God he had pulled the wrong lever? Certainly not a senile old widow woman like me.

Lizzy got off from work and came straight over to my house. She flopped on my sofa, took off her black patent leather pumps and started massaging her feet. "This has been a horrible day."

What happened?" I asked

"I took a vacation day last Thursday to make sure U got to the airport on time. I'm off on Friday anyway. So Olivia and I went to Dallas. I mean, what I do with my Fridays is my business, right?"

I nodded, "Right."

"I get to work this morning and my supervisor has the nerve to ask me if I was serious about my job. She said she was concerned about a future pattern of absenteeism."

"Absenteeism?"

"You heard me," Lizzy confirmed. "Now, Mama, exactly, when was I absent? In five years I've missed one day. And that was when I got sick trying to eat that Congo Groundnut Stew that U brought home."

"It's probably something else on her mind."

"I know it's something else. It's those hags I work with. They're jealous because I get Fridays off."

"You didn't say that to your supervisor, did you?"

"No, not yet."

"What did you tell her?" I asked.

"I suggested she read the hospital's policy manual to get a better understanding of what absenteeism meant. Then I reminded her that when I was hired, long before she got there, my package deal included Fridays off."

I shook my head, thinking of my younger days and my trigger-happy mouth. "Lizzy, Lizzy, Lizzy."

"What?"

"Why didn't you just come out and call the woman a dumb bell? Because that's the way you made her feel."

"I told her the truth."

"But look how you did it. She's going to come back on you, I guarantee."

She paused a moment. "Like the deacons did you?"

"Huh?" She caught me off guard.

"Oh yeah, I heard about what happened Sunday. And don't think I'm not going to Pastor Fordham on those scumbags. But first I wanted to hear your side of the story."

"I don't have a side. Everything's okay. I don't want you going to Pastor Fordham or anybody else."

"Why? You know what they did was wrong."

"You mean canceling my right to sit above the crowd and be catered to?"

"Mama, are you feeling guilty about the special honor they

gave you and daddy for your long years of service at the church?"

"No, I'm just facing facts. Privilege is not forever. Even Jesus lost his cozy spot in heaven for thirty-three years so he could complete his mission."

She looked over at the scattered piles of construction papers and building permits, strewn across my kitchen counter. "Are you on a mission like Jesus?"

I thought about all the things that had happened since the idea of a battered women's center reared its ugly head. Ridiculous, unpredictable, inexplicable circumstances had pulled me deeper and deeper into the fray. I didn't know whether I was on something or in something or being trampled by something too big for a retired old widow woman, who spent her time looking at watered-down Christians and talking to her dead husband, to endure.

My face succumbed to a blanket of naiveté. "Maybe, it is a mission, Lizzy. For now I'm going to call it a foolish old woman's journey. We'll have to wait to see if God upgrades the title later on."

****

By Tuesday morning, Hurricane Arlene had received her upgrade. She was a Category 4 storm, with winds gusting to a 150 mph. Because of her slow movement across the Caribbean, the center of the storm had intensified, dramatically. The National Weather Service predicted that within forty-eight hours, the storm would enter the Gulf of Mexico. From there, not even the experts could predict where she would go.

About 10:30 am, as new tracking information danced across

the bottom of my screen, Cora Williams called with a question. "Where does Poe work?"

"Humble Oil, downtown." I couldn't remember the company's new name. "Why do you want to know?"

"Girl, I saw this movie last night. This hit woman parked outside this lawyer's job and waited for him to go to lunch. When he crossed the street to get to his car, BAMB!!! She ran him over like a pancake."

I fought back my laughter for a more serious, non-supportive tone. "Did they show the part where she fried in the electric chair up in Austin?"

"No, the police killed her before that. But she died in a very nice black leather jumpsuit with a slightly dented Maserati parked outside. The show ended with Poe ... I mean, the lawyer ... taking a chilly nap inside the city morgue. Don't you just love happy endings?"

"You need to quit, Cora."

"It's the best ending I could come up with after hearing how he treated you on Sunday."

"I'm okay, really I am."

"Well, I'm not," she declared. "When I see him at that meeting on Wednesday night, I'm giving him a piece of my mind."

That's when it occurred to me Cora had missed church on Sunday. She had also missed the announcement moving the business meeting to Friday night. Pastor Fordham had been invited to some big race relations conference at the Eagles Nest megachurch in Dallas and was scheduled be out of town Wednesday and Thursday.

"Ummh, Friday night," she moaned. "That's not going to work."

"Why not?"

"That storm will be in here by then."

216

"Maybe. But then, again, maybe not. The National Weather Service is tracking the storm right now. But nobody knows exactly where it's coming in."

"Let me tell you something, Kizzy. My big toe started throbbing last night. The last time my toe throbbed like this was when Hurricane Carla tore this place up in 1961."

"Okay, why don't I call the National Weather Service and tell them to shut down all their fancy monitoring equipment and stop flying their sophisticated airplanes into the eye of the storm. There's no reason to put their people in danger. Your big toe has already spoken."

"Make fun if you want. But I'm picking you up in the morning and we're going to load up on candles, flashlight batteries, bottle water, can goods, and toilet paper. You'll thank me when it's over. You'll see."

****

On Wednesday morning Cora Williams neither called nor came by. When I rang her house around noon, a woman with a heavy smoker's voice answered the phone. After a bit of prodding, she introduced herself as Grace, a cousin from East Texas ... *probably one of the ones that had beat the tar out of young Reedy.*

"I guess you hadn't heard," she surmised. "Bayboy passed away last night at the hospital."

My heart dropped to the floor.

Cora had spent everything she had on his perpetual treatments. There was Didanosine and Stavudine and Lamivudine and Emtricitabine; medications with names that burst through the stratosphere like encrypted profanity from another world, obliterating our medical vocabularies and leaving us with unfulfilled hopes and dreams.

In the end, the long names and high price tags were just not enough. AIDS was too vigilant, too all-consuming to tuck its tail and run from a few experimental cocktails that, at best, offered marginal results. In 1993, gay men in the black community were dropping like flies. But as fast as one died, another would come out of the closet.

I often wondered if it were possible for God to accidentally overload a little boy fetus with too many female chromosomes. Could there have been a biological mistake made in the womb? The small question kept leading to a larger, more profound question the Bible had already answered: *Could God do anything, accidentally? Could God make a mistake?*

As a young boy, Cora had allowed Bayboy to wear dresses and play with Chatty Kathy dolls because it pleased him so. But why did it please him so? Why didn't a Power Ranger uniform and a Tonka truck please him instead?

The universe had its quirks and Bayboy had been one of them. But now it was over. All of the rashes and warts and fevers and vomiting and $300 pills were behind her now. Cora could get on with her life, that is, if there really was a life for a parent after losing a child.

I watched one day as the neighbor's cat climbed a tree and pull a little helpless chick from a blue bird's nest. The cat ate the chick on my side of the fence. Despite the mother bluebird squawking and flapping; despite her swooping down and pummeling the cat's head, he still ate the little chick and walked away.

For weeks, the mother sat on the fence, just above the spot where the attack had taken place. She never chirped or flapped or changed the direction in which she faced. She just perched there for hours, watching the ground. Finally, one day she didn't come back. That was the day she got on with her life.

I knew Cora. One day she would get on with her life. It was going to take some time. But, if for no other reason than for the sake of her teenage daughters, she would eventually go on. I made a promise to myself to be there every step of the way.

****

On Thursday morning the universe designated my house as Grand Central Station.

At 8:30 am, I had just finished boiling me a big pot of harmony grits, when Lizzy called.

"My supervisor is out today. You think I need to write her a note about absenteeism?"

"I think you need to leave well enough alone," I advised.

"I'm kidding, Mama. I called you for another reason. It's about U."

As it turned out, Ububee had called her the night before. He was concerned about the big storm sitting out in the Gulf of Mexico and wanted to know if she had made preparations. He gave her a list of things to do.

The conversation had gone well until Lizzy began to ask questions about the family reunion.

"He seemed evasive, Mama. He told me they were winding everything down and he would be leaving Lesotho on Sunday."

"So, what's wrong with that?" I asked.

"What's wrong is the number he left on my caller-ID was not in Lesotho. It was in Johannesburg."

"South Africa?"

"Yes, he was calling from South Africa."

Technology, I thought.

"You, see. That's why I didn't let you order me one of those ID boxes. They cause too many problems."

"Mama, what is U doing in South Africa? You think he's got another wife or some children there?"

Months earlier, I would've jumped on the speculation train and rode it all the way into the station. Christians do that, you know. It comes with the territory. But I had come to know Ububee as an honorable man. He loved Lizzy with all of his Sarengette Lion/Blue Wildebeest heart.

I told her, "Relax, you're making something out of nothing. If my geography serves me well, South Africa is right on the border. It would be the same if we took a trip to Louisiana to see Thelma Mason lose her money at the horse races."

"You think?" Her whiny voice purred with relief.

"I think," I reassured her. "Now go back to work so I can eat my breakfast."

"One more thing, Mama. Don't worry about buying a bunch of supplies for the storm. I've got all of that at my house and I'm coming to get you tomorrow."

"Fine, fine. Now go make your boss proud." I hung up.

I had just turned my delicious Earl Campbell smoked sausages over in the skillet and sliced into a juicy grapefruit when the phone rang again. This time it was Estelle. "Kizzy, are you alright?"

"Yes, why do you ask?"

"With this storm coming in, Bishop and I thought it might be best for you to come stay with us."

"*Us?* Are you Holiness people living together now?"

"No, no of course not," she quickly denied. "But with a

220

Category 4 hurricane, anything can happen. He felt like his house would be the safest place. We've already claimed the covering of the Lord."

I suspected more than that. A few weeks earlier, when her washing machine went out, she had come to my house to do a few loads. I spotted a big ugly pair of red and yellow striped boxer shorts in one of the baskets, which she claimed was an old dust rag she used around the house. If she was washing the man's drawers, there was a good chance a lot of other things were going on.

I finally responded. "Thanks, but Lizzy is picking me up tomorrow. I hope there's enough covering left for her house too."

"Okay. If anything changes, let me know because, Praise God, we have already cast down the strongholds of the Devil and rebuked any ill winds this demon storm might blow in. Oh zuskesrter, seuzeeha, melika, oh mighty one-"

I hung up the phone. Speaking in tongues was one thing. Hot Earl Campbell sausages *on* my tongue was another.

I flipped my eggs over for a few seconds, then, while they were still good and runny, dumped them into my plate. I quickly partnered them with five heaping spoonfuls of hot grit, drowning in butter. I set the tantalizing, artery-clogging platter on the dining room table, next to the slices of fresh grapefruit. Then, after blistering through a race-car prayer, I dug in. That's when the phone rang again.

The words that formed on my lips would not have been pleasing to the Lord. So I substituted Estelle's heavenly variety: "zuskesrter, seuzeeha, melika...."

Finally, I answered the phone. To my surprise, Deacon Crump was on the line. "I hope you don't mind me calling you. I got your number out of the church directory."

"No problem," I said.

Hearing his voice, I suddenly imagined myself in one of his

XXX-rated thrillers, taking off my big girdle and brassier, letting some young suitor rub me down in Bengay liniment.

He explained. "I called to give you some information. I think we have the same objective in mind."

To get the latest pornography as the lowest possible price? Right?

Though my mind continued to race, I posed a more sensible question. "What objective is that?"

To stop Deacon Poe from ramrodding this battered woman's thing down our throats."

"Go on."

"Deacon Poe was out on Womack's boat earlier this year. They cut some kind of deal."

"Are you sure about this?"

"I'm telling you. It came from a damn reliable source."

I paused. "Deacon Crumb, sometimes I compromise on things. But respect is not one of those things. I want you to respect me up until the time my casket hits the bottom of that hole. After that, you can talk to me any way you want."

Saa-Sorry about that, Sister Kizzy. Old habits die hard."

"I'm curious. When did it get to be a habit?"

He laughed, amusedly. "You heard the saying: Cuss like a sailor?"

"I have."

"My father was a merchant marine. My mother ran a set-up club near the waterfront in Port Arthur, Texas. I got it both ways."

Suddenly, an odd possibility stirred in my head. "You know what? They say Mama Kizzy is always sticking her nose into something. But so be it. I'm going to send you to someone who can break that generational curse. He holds classes every Thursday night and when

222

you're through with him, you'll have a heavenly vocabulary. Amen?"

Crump's voice perked up. "Is he a minister?"

"He's a Holiness Bishop leading a congregation of fanatics. But he's a good man. He specializes in cases like this."

I took down Crump's number.

"Now, what about this deal?"

"I don't have all the details. I just know they agreed to scratch each other's backs. The man who told me was fixing an engine on Womack's boat. He could only hear so much. But I can tell you this. They're both looking for a big payoff."

"You plan to bring this up on Friday night?" I asked.

"I can't go Friday night. I've been suspended from the church for 90 days. You know, the fight and all...."

"Yeah, and knocking the Pastor out and all...."

"I'm really sorry about that," he confessed.

"Look, Deacon Crump. I could bring this up. But all Poe's going to do is deny it."

"Okay, let me do some more digging. If I find out anything else, I'll hit you back. By the way, Sister Kizzy, I love you. You're one tough bitch." He hung up the phone.

Somehow, coming from the son of a merchant marine, it didn't seem so bad. It didn't seem bad at all.

I headed back to the dining room table. My delicious breakfast was cold as ice. I didn't like using my microwave for the same reason I didn't like using a mobile phone. But what choice did I have? I slid my plate into the microwave and set it to REHEAT. That's when the doorbell rang.

It was that nosy postal woman. She had a certified letter for which I needed to sign. It was some kind of proxy from Mr. Myles' investment portfolio. Before he died, he had accumulated a tidy sum.

As I signed the slip, she cut her eyes toward the FOR SALE sign two houses down.

"Know anything about that house?" she poked.

"I know it's for sale," I responded, nonchalantly.

"I hear the couple is divorcing."

"Really, where did you hear that?"

"Legal documents. Attorney fees. The mail has a way of telling the whole story."

Including the one about you sticking your big nose into everybody's business.

"Not a bad house, huh? I mean seems like they've taken care of it. Wonder what they're asking?" she inquired.

I cringed at the thought of her being my neighbor. For the sake of every law abiding citizen who cherished their right to privacy, I had to send her on her way.

I shook my head, ominously. "You don't want that house, not with those termites."

"Oh God no!" She recoiled. "And not to mention all these junky cars parked on the other side of the street?"

I played the race card. "Mexican family, you know what I mean."

Actually, as a top-notched mechanic, Joe Martinez and his family grossed over $300,000 a year. I knew because we used the same tax man. If Joe had ever stopped sending money back to Mexico, he could've bought the whole neighborhood.

She retreated down the steps. "Okay then, I think I'll keep looking."

Yeah. Maybe in another state.

I closed the door and breathed a sigh of relief before heading to the microwave.

To my surprise, it was still going. It had somehow turned REHEAT into overcook. I opened the oven door to find my delicious breakfast parched to the heavens.

What a fitting reward for my deceitful termite presentation. God was still on the throne, handing out liars their just due. I took the plate and set it on the table just to make sure the rubbery eggs and dried up sausage wouldn't miraculously come back to life. That's when the phone rang again.

"What!!!" I answered in a hungry rage.

A voice responded with obvious timidity. "Is this 713-227-0887?"

"Yes."

"Can you tell me who you are?"

"Can you tell me who you are?" I fired back.

"Yes, I'm with the Pacific State Medical Facility."

Telemarketers! I thought.

"I already have medical insurance, thank you." I was about to hang up.

"No, please. I'm not selling insurance."

"What then?" My stomach was still growling.

"A lady gave me your number."

"What lady?"

"I-ah, I don't know for sure. But she said it twice before she drifted off again."

I was growing impatient. "I don't mean to be rude. But you're not making sense."

"Listen, I'm a nurse here. I could lose my job for giving out confidential information. But this lady has been in a coma for such a long time. She finally woke up last night on my shift. She repeated this number. And then she said she was feeling dizzy. She drifted off again. Can you tell us anything, anything at all?"

For what seemed to be an eternity, I pressed the receiver to my ear, lapping in the full possibility of her revelation. My heart lodged in my throat. My body trembled with disbelief. My eyes unleashed a torrent of pent up tears. Could this be some kind of tormented dream? Would I wake up to find the twilight of reality, creeping through my bedroom window?

Or was this the call I had been waiting on for fourteen years?

I finally mustered the strength to speak. "Are you sure she said she was feeling dizzy? Or did she say *Kizzy*?"

The nurse thought about it for a long time. "Now that you mention it ... it could've been Kizzy?"

"Is her name Charlotte Lueese Cooper?"

"That's the thing. We don't know her name. We don't know anything about her."

Suddenly, I could hear other voices in the background. Her tone shifted into high gear. "It's my floor supervisor. I'll have to call you back."

"When?" I pleaded. "When will you call me back?"

"Tomorrow. Maybe tomorrow." She rushed off the phone.

"But where are you calling...." She was already gone.

Stubborn me. At that moment, I would've given my life for one of those caller-ID boxes. I should've listened to Lizzy. I should've followed the fickle indulgence of the new generation. I could've traced the call right away.

I wasn't hungry any more. I sat down in the nearest chair to soak it all in. Charlotte Lueese, in a coma since 1979; It didn't seem possible. And yet, I could hear Mr. Myles' voice ... *As long as she's not officially dead, she's officially alive.*

But was she?

I tried desperately to think of the name of the hospital from which the nurse had called. *Pacific Life* ... no, that was insurance. *Pacific Medical Center* ... maybe that was it.

I called the Portland Police Department. "Can you connect me with the officer in charge of missing persons?"

The man sounded as if he had swallowed a hundred frogs. "We've got four officers assigned to missing persons. Which one do you want?"

"I don't know. Which one would most likely handle an old case from Texas?"

"None," he said, flatly. "We've got enough new cases to keep the whole force busy."

I spoke to a nice young man last time. His name was ... *Oh God help me to remember, please* ... Heffron, Heparin, Hellerman ...."

"That's Helfelman. He's out sick today. Jumped into a cold lake to save a dog. Now he's sick as one. You want his voicemail?"

"No, I need to ask a question. Have you ever heard of Pacific Medical Center?"

"I don't recognize that name, Ma'am. You need to look in the Yellow Pages."

"I don't have a Portland Yellow Pages in Texas."

I could hear the other lines beeping.

"You'll have to work it out on your end, Ma'am. If these phones roll over to the sergeant's desk and he finds out I'm helping somebody in Texas look through the phone book ... Sorry, Ma'am."

He went to another call.

In desperation, I called Katherine Baker's daughter at the Houston Post Newspaper. "I've got one more favor to ask."

"For you, Mama Kizzy, I'll do it right now."

A few minutes later, she came back on the line. "Pacific Medical is not in our system. I even looked in the National

White Pages."

"Thanks for your help." I hung up.

The only way I was going to find out anything was to go to Portland, myself.

I called Lizzy at her job. "Find out how much it costs to fly to Portland, Oregon. I want to leave tomorrow."

She sniggled. "You're kidding, right?"

"I'm not kidding. Somebody just called about Charlotte Lueese. She needs my help."

When I told Lizzy what had happened, she responded, slowly, cautiously, as though she were walking along the edge of a steep cliff.

"Now, Mama. I need you to settle down and listen to me good. I know you've waited a long time for this call to come in. Maybe it is the call. But maybe it's not. Maybe, the person in that coma is someone else. Are you prepared for that reality?"

"It's got to be her," I insisted. "Who else would have this number?"

She waited a while. "Mama, you didn't answer my question. You didn't answer it because you're not prepared."

"I-ah ... I'm aware that, ah ...." I babbled along like an idiot, resisting her unthinkable reality, trying desperately not to boo-hoo from the potential disappointment lurking beneath the surface. After all these years, why would God lift me up just to slam me back down again? It had to be Charlotte Lueese. It just had to. No other reality made sense.

Lizzy continued to reason with me. "Even if it is her, Mama. There's no way you're going to get a plane out of here tomorrow. With that hurricane coming in, all of the airports are going to shut down."

My mind wouldn't stop racing. "What if I left tonight?"

"Is God telling you to leave tonight, Mama? Is he telling you to get on a plane by yourself, fly into an unfamiliar airport, catch a cab in the middle of the night to a strange hotel and then rumble about the city like some kind of black Miss Marple, trying to find a medical center nobody's heard of?"

"I-ah, I thought, maybe you'd go with me."

"You bet I'm going with you," she declared. "But it also means I'll have to call my supervisor and tell her I can't work on Friday."

"Aren't you off on Fridays?"

"She asked me if I would come in to help her baton down the office in case the storm comes in. You know it's just a stupid test."

"Yes. It's a stupid test you need to pass though. No need of messing up a good job to go on a wild goose chase."

"I'm not worried about the job, Mama. I'm worried about you."

At that instant, my heart melted. I thought about all of the lonely souls who had lost their children, or whose children never came around, or who dare not put down their purse or credit card for fear their child would buy another smoke or drink or vile of cocaine. Here I was, arguing with my daughter about whose well-being came first.

God hadn't told me to do anything. I had heard the voice of possibility and stampeded out of the barn like an old mare with blinders on. In my mind, I was already in Oregon, standing over Charlotte Lueese's bed, coaxing her back to consciousness.

But Lizzy was right. It didn't have to be Charlotte Lueese in that bed at all.

"Didn't the lady say she would call you back tomorrow?" asked Lizzy.

"Maybe."

"Then why not give her a chance?"

I thought about it. I had waited this long. One more day wasn't going to kill me. Even if it did, Jesus was waiting on the other side. He could tell me whether or not it was Charlotte Lueese. And then, I would persuade him to send an angel down to whisper in her ear. *"Rise Charlotte Lueese. Take up thy bed and walk."*

The rest of the day seemed to drag along, slowly and torturously. Surely, the old hourglass in heaven realized it was standing in the way of destiny. Tomorrow was the day of promise, where miracles could unfold and kindred spirits could reunite. One phone call could wipe out fourteen years of mystery and agony and desolation. One nurse's voice could cleanse my weary soul.

Where was Superman when you needed him most? I had watched him fly around the earth and reverse time. Now I needed him to come back around and take this day with him. Surely, there was a nearby phone booth where he could change. Surely, fourteen years of kryptonite wouldn't be too much for him to overcome.

At bedtime, I took one last look out of my window. Dark clouds danced across the horizon like billowed ghosts on parade. An uneasy breeze whistled through my window screen, perhaps, an ominous prediction of things to come.

A monster hurricane lingered out in the Gulf, waiting for a signal from heaven or hell. But to me it was small potatoes, compared to the news I hoped to receive. Until Charlotte Lueese was officially dead, she was officially alive. Tomorrow, I'd know for sure.

Chapter Sixteen

Friday morning I awakened just before dawn. My knees were percolating quite well and my mind was crystal clear. After a hot bath and a little Oat Bran Cereal with lots of fiber, I turned on the television and sat by the phone.

I remembered telling my students, "*Stop spending so much time in front of the idiot box*" and "*Get off the phone with that useless teenage chatter and do your homework*". Now I was leading the pack of chattering idiots with no intentions of reforming my ways.

The midday news anchor looked worried, and with good reason. Hurricane Arlene had stalled out in the Gulf of Mexico just long enough to intensify to a Category 5. Now it was headed directly toward the Galveston coastline packing 180 mph winds and a 30 foot storm surge.

"Arlene should make landfall about 11:30 pm tonight." He predicted. "But as erratic as this storm has been, I wouldn't bet my life savings on it."

In 1961, Dan Rather had gone down to the Galveston and waited for hurricane Carla to come in. That's how he had gotten the national anchor job with CBS News. These modern-day, soft-shoe desk jockeys, however, didn't feel that reporting the weather justified a suicide run down Highway 45. There were enough Accuweather satellites and Dopler computer gadgetry to tell the story as distressingly as it needed to be told.

A hurricane is a well organized tropical system with a low pressure center packed into a hodgepodge of fierce thunderstorms and powerful winds. The winds rotate counterclockwise in the Northern Hemisphere and feed off of heat released by large bodies of water. As long as Arlene sat out in the Gulf, she was only going to get stronger. The stronger she got, the more damage she was going to cause.

I watched the continuous weather updates until 11:00 am. That's when the first call came in.

Deacon Poe's "Sky Witch" wife greeted me in her typical proper tone. "Sister Mylesssss?"

"This is she."

"I am calling to inform you that, due to the inclement weather, the business meeting for First Reunion Baptist Church has been can-cillled."

"Thank you for letting me know."

She hung up the phone without a goodbye. Any enemy of her husband was an enemy of hers.

I was about to go into the bedroom and gather a few things for my trip to Lizzy's house, when Hector and his crew pulled up into the driveway. They jumped out with two large sheets of plywood and began boarding up the two front windows.

"Ms Cora sent us over. She say to take care of you for the storm. She will pay."

"Nonsense. I will pay," I insisted.

"No, no, she got good money now; come in quick. How you say, the polsee." I finally realized he was talking about Bayboy's insurance policy.

I nodded. "Okay, she pay."

Sometimes we can use our independence to slap people in the face. I had the money. But she needed to pay. It was her small blessing to me.

As they backed out of the driveway the phone rang again. I thought, *Oh God, let it be that nurse from Portland.*

It was Deacon Crump instead. "I think I've got something."

"On Poe and Womack?"

"Even better." He went on to explain that the receipt for the City of Houston tax lien release had been made out to First Reunion Baptist Church. It took a full history lesson to make me understand.

The Silver Dollar Hotel had originally belonged to the millionaire oilman, Jim West. In 1958, after his death, some business men from Saudi Arabia had bought it, but never did anything with it. The City had eventual slapped a tax lien on it and then set it aside to become a historical site. The taxes and interest had accrued to $1.3 million.

Womack had negotiated a deal to buy the property for ten cents on the dollar. But, at that price, the City would sell only to a nonprofit organization. That's when First Reunion used its 501C3 nonprofit status to buy the property for $130,000.

I almost gagged. "Are you telling me that our church owns the Silver Dollar Hotel?"

"Daaaa-darn straight," he confirmed. "This whole thing about having the church vote is just a dog-and-pony show."

"Why would Poe deceive the congregation like this?"

"Sister Kizzy, it's something about that hotel; something that Deacon Poe knows that we don't know."

"Well, this should blow the lid off the pot," I said. "Just bring me a copy of that receipt next week."

"Next week? Hea-hea-heck, you need this tonight!"

"They cancelled the meeting because of the storm. I guess nobody called you."

"I guess they got no reason to," he sadly acknowledged.

"Don't worry. Ninety days is not that long. You'll be back before you know it." I tried to offer a word of encouragement.

"Guess you're right. I'll bring this tax receipt to you next week. Love you, Sister Kizzy." He hung up.

I had just finished packing my clothes for the trip to Lizzy's house when the phone rang again. It was a nurse, but the wrong one. Lizzy was calling from the mechanic shop. "I'm off from work, but I can't get to you, Mama. My radiator overheated."

"You need me to call somebody to come and get you?" I asked.

"No, they're working on it right now. I should be out of here in about an hour."

"No rush. I'm not going anywhere." *Not Portland, not anywhere.*

"You see how dark it looks. And the wind is really blowing over here." She said something to the mechanic then came back on the line. "Did the call from Portland come in?"

I sighed. "Not yet."

"It's only 2:00 pm. There's still plenty of time."

By 4:00 pm, the call still hadn't come in. The wind had picked up another fifteen or twenty knots, blowing someone's plastic garbage can onto my front porch. When I went outside to remove it, I was surprised to find late afternoon almost totally cloaked in darkness. Four o'clock looked like seven o'clock. The runaway clouds had cast an eerie gray veil over the earth and tiny droplets of rain peppered the angry breeze.

There was something else.

Across the street, just behind Joe Martinez's familiar line of parked cars, underneath the swaying limbs of a giant oak tree, loomed a shadowy figure. He reminded me of the coward that had ransacked my garden, only taller and stronger. Although I couldn't see his eyes, I knew he was looking my way.

I went back inside and locked the door. With both windows boarded up, I couldn't see whether the culprit, having been exposed, decided to move on. It didn't take long to realize he hadn't moved on. He was now pounding on my front door.

My first thought was to seek refuge behind the barrel of Mr. Myles' 38 revolver. And then I realize that was no longer an option for me. Through a special prayer, Pastor Fordham had placed a spiritual covering over my house, one that didn't require the carnal services of my pearl-handled friend.

In the Bible, Peter took out a sword and cut off a man's ear. Jesus picked up the ear and pasted it back on. The short-term solution the sword offered was not the long term spiritual solution Jesus was after. He wanted us to have faith beyond the sword ... and the revolver.

And so I answered. I answered without seeking the help of my pearl-handled friend.

"Yes, who is it?"

"It's ... Larry."

I opened the door to find Larry "GeeNet" Willis, standing on the porch.

"Larry?" I had to remind myself that he was my student, not some desperate drug addict looking to take advantage of an old woman living alone. I had invited him to come over and talk to me. And now, here he was.

"Is this a bad time?" He asked in a muted voice.

"Oh, no. Come in, Larry. Come in."

I offered him a soda and a few knickknacks, which he

gladly accepted.

Sitting at the dining room table, looking through his old class photos in one of my many scrapbooks, he finally opened up.

"You always shot straight with me, Mrs. Myles. I can't say that about many people."

I smiled. "I'll take that as a compliment."

He eyed me, grimly. "Why wuzz that, Mrs. Myles? Why were you willing to tell me all the things I didn't want to hear?"

"Because I wanted to prepare you for a cold, hard, predatory world, that's why. You know by now it's not the fairyland you expected it to be. There are disappointments and hard knocks that have nothing to do with you putting a ball through the nets."

He grunted, painfully. "I guess I found that out the hard way."

"You're not alone, Larry. We all eventually find out. The sticker shock of human cruelty has a way of getting us off track. But the key is finding our way back."

He shook his head. "Me? Finding *my* way back ... You talking about a long shot, Mrs. Myles. A half court shot with your eyes closed and one hand tied behind your back."

"Yes. But if anybody can make that shot, Larry, you can."

His eyes slowly filled with tears. "I guess that's why I'm here. I'm tired of who I am. I'm tired of what I've been doing. I want to make that shot, Mrs. Myles. I want to make it right now."

An eerie gust of wind shook the entire house.

He reached into his pocket and pulled out a shiny diamond ring. I recognized it as the Tuskegee Airmen ring the crack head had stolen at Buster's funeral. He handed it to me.

"You know where this came from ... a dead man. Never got a chance to pawn it. He OD'd that night after the wake. No reason I shouldna' gone down with him."

"But you didn't, Larry. You didn't go down with him. God has something in store for you," I predicted.

"That's what the preacher used to say when I was growing up. God has something in store for you."

He slowly rolled up his sleeve to reveal a jagged line of needle marks in his arm. "You think this is what he meant?"

I paused for a long while, searching my inner guts for a deserving answer. Larry had chosen the garish roar of the crowd and soothing sizzle of a drug-infested high. These were the enduring scares that came along with his choices.

I rubbed my age-old fingers across his arm with a confident stroke. "These needle tracks will save a soul one day. Someone will realize that if you found your way back, they can too."

I was no longer predicting. I was prophesying.

"I don't want to be a hypocrite, Mrs. Myles, not like the people I've seen at so many different churches."

"Then, you'll never find your way back."

He frowned. "I don't understand."

I explained in a slow, caring voice. "Christian means Christ-like. The moment you don't do what Christ would've done, you're in violation of the code. You're a hypocrite."

"Come on, Mrs. Myles. Nobody's perfect."

"Precisely. The church is full of hypocrites. I'm a hypocrite. The preachers and deacons are hypocrites. You'll be one too."

"So what is the point of it all?"

"The point is we believe in a Savior whose blood exempts us from punishment for being hypocrites. You could say we're hypocrites with a free hall pass, on our way to heaven, while the rest of the world goes to another place. Only, the pass is not free, Larry. It comes with a high price ... a price that Jesus has already paid for those who accept him."

He looked at me with the eyes of a young child. "You think it's too late for me to be a hypocrite?"

"It's never too late, Larry. As long as you have breath."

"You really think I can find my way back?"

"I'm going to see to it," I promised. "As soon as this storm blows through, we're going to get you some help."

He walked to the door, then turned back to look at me. "One more thing."

"Yes?"

"Promise me you won't go to that meeting tonight."

"You mean the church business meeting? It's been cancelled."

"Are you sure?" he persisted.

"Yes, I got a call this morning. Why do you ask?"

"I-ah ... I took that bus to church last Sunday because Mr. Reedy asked me to check things out."

"What do you mean?"

"He wanted information like how many security guards, how many exits, you know." Larry shook his head, a gleam of sarcasm in his eyes. "Mr. Reedy never really got over the way they beat him down in front of his people. I think he's got something planned."

"Like what?"

"I don't know. I already quit working there. Like I told you, I'm looking for a fresh start."

"You're making the right decision, Larry. Come see me next week."

I gave him a big hug.

As soon as he left, I called Deacon Moore. "Did they cancel the business meeting?"

"Not to my knowledge. But with this hurricane coming in,

only a fool would be out there."

"Or a slick-headed devil." I hung up and called Cora Williams.

She sighed, apologetically. "I've been meaning to call you. Just been so busy taking care of funeral arrangements. With the storm coming in, we had to move everything to next week."

"I'm so sorry about Bayboy. If there's anything I can do-"

"I'm fine, Kizzy. We knew it was coming. And now it's here. The Lord knows what's best."

I paused a long while, not wanting to stampede through her pain. "Did you get a call today from Nora Poe?"

"No, did you?"

"Yes, she told me the business meeting had been cancelled."

"I doubt that," said Cora. "My daughter saw Deacon Grubbs up at that Kinko's by the church making copies for tonight."

Finally, it dawned on me why Nora Poe, rather than the church secretary, had called. Deacon Poe wanted to make sure I didn't come.

"He's trying to pull a fast one," I told Cora. "He's counting on nobody showing up so he and his cronies can push this thing through."

"Don't they have to have x-amount of people at the meeting for it to be official?"

"Twelve." I informed her. "They need a quorum of twelve. It's in the church's bylaws."

"Poe will get that easy," she predicted.

"No doubt. He will."

"That jackass," she scoffed. "You should've let me run over him when we had the chance."

"Well, it's too late now."

"What do you mean, too late? It's 6:30 pm now. The meeting doesn't start until 7:30 pm."

"Have you lost your mind? How are we supposed to get to the

church in this weather?" I asked. "It's already flooding on the East side. And they're closing down freeways as we speak."

"Look, Kizzy. I know we're both old and tired and maybe a little scared inside. But we're too far out here to turn around now. If they can get to that church, then we can too. You put on your fightin' clothes, girl. I'm on my way."

Chapter Seventeen

At 7:05 pm, Cora's big black DeSoto rumbled into the driveway. The desperation with which she flashed her lights and pounded on her horn reminded me of an old movie I had watched where a woman fled her house because the killers were on the way.

There were no killers on the way; just Lizzy who had called a few minutes earlier and forbade me to leave the house.

"Under no circumstances are you to go to that church, Mama. It's too dangerous out here. I'm picking you up, we're going to my house and that's that."

With the rain beating down on my yellow hooded slicker, and the wind, thrashing my old bones from side to side, my daring escape to Cora's getaway vehicle seemed less like the action-packed thriller I had seen on TV and more like the retake of a senior citizens' slow motion horror film. I'd walk a few steps forward, only to have a ferocious gust of wind blow me back. What in the hell was Dan Rather thinking?

It didn't help that I lugged my huge briefcase purse, loaded down with construction documents and church voting procedures. I had even thrown in my precious bottle of holy water, just in case things escalated into an Armageddon showdown.

There was no time to load my clunky wheelchair. I needed to travel lean and mean. The only survivors that made it to the getaway vehicle were me, my big purse and my trusty wood grain walking cane.

Before I could slam the passenger door, Cora's foot was on the gas. She backed out of the driveway and into one of Joe Martinez's junk cars. There was no time for apologies and oopsy daisies. If anything, Joe needed to apologize for having those clunkers out on the street. Cora floored the accelerator and never looked back.

"It's bad out here, Kizzy. Lot worse than I thought." She swerved to miss a flying tree branch and ran over some kid's three-wheeled scooter. "If you've got a mind to turn around, you need to speak it right now."

"I ... I'm in." My foolish voice trembled out a final commitment. "It's like you said. It's too late to turn back now."

She smiled. "That's all I needed to hear."

Good friends are not made in heaven. They're made on the battlefields of life, when the hour is dark and the future is fading away. Cora Williams should've been at home, mourning the death of her only son. Instead, she was plowing down a rain-soaked highway, trying to complete a mission that neither one of us was sure we had been assigned.

She powered through one red light after another, not caring that the red was on our side of the street. On a good day red meant stop and wait. But Arlene and Poe had made sure this wasn't a good day.

The closer we got to the church, the more our thoughts merged on one impossible feat: getting through the underpass on Almeda Road. The sunken highway beneath the old train tressel flooded all the time, even without the help of a hurricane. We were petrified to imagine how it would look on this unbelievable, terrifying night.

The detour around the underpass would've taken thirty-five minutes. And that was assuming those low-lying, pothole-infested West Orem wagon trails weren't already flooded. If we were going to get to the church in time, we had to go beneath the train tressel. That meant crossing through the fine print in the back of our minds, that trivial, unpretentious disclosure clause that stated neither one of us knew how to swim.

With the windshield wipers, flapping at full speed and the old defroster, grinding through another feeble attempt to defog the misty glass, Cora revealed an eerie secret about her late husband.

"Malcolm went over a bridge in this car. He said it didn't sink and the motor never stopped running."

My eyes bulged with disbelief. "You're saying this car can float on water?"

She tightened her lips and stared ahead. "We'll know in a minute."

When we reach the underpass, it looked like a small lake. A couple of stalled cars had already succumbed to the rising current, sinking slowly beneath the surface like metal bars of soap. Cora never stopped to consider the consequences of our decision, never allowed our good common sense to intervene. She plowed into the dark waters like a speedboat on Labor Day weekend. The next thing we knew, we were gliding beneath the tressel to the other side.

A wrecker truck plunged in behind us, but stalled out about half way though. The tidal wave it created was just enough to give our back tires some traction. Cora gunned the sputtering engine and sent us on our way.

There were all kinds of red lights blinking on the dashboard, warning us that what we had done was totally unacceptable, that all the old DeSoto engineers were turning over in their graves. But we had ignored red lights the entire evening. There was no need to start paying attention to them now.

When we pulled into the church parking lot, we spotted seven vehicles. Deacon Poe's shiny black SUV was parked right up front. When Cora saw it, she stomped the accelerator. She rammed her old DeSoto into his driver-side door.

Our heads jerked forward and then back again. The engine coughed out a billow of white smoke, then trembled into silence.

She looked over at me, a proud expression on her face. "He did say hardball, didn't he?"

I glanced at the gaping hole in Deacon Poe's wounded vehicle, then, flashed a reciprocal smile. "He did, indeed. Now, let's go in here and finish the job."

Chapter Eighteen

When we entered the church, a small group of deacons were huddled down front. Deacon Poe's wife and Deacon Grubbs' wife sat together on the second pew, casually dressed in golf shirts and slacks. Horace Womack sat on the far end of the third pew in a maroon suite spotted with rain drops. No doubt he had only recently arrived.

The church's janitor, an older man with hunched shoulders and graying hair, sat on the fourth pew, a visible scowl on his face. I found out later Deacon Poe had strong-armed him into hanging around just in case the quorum of twelve didn't materialize. I don't know how Poe figured he was going to get away with it. The janitor wasn't even a member of our church.

When the foyer doors flew open, everybody turned around. Cora and I strolled into the sanctuary like notorious gunslingers entering a wild-west saloon. I wanted us to look more menacing. But the water that had seeped into the floorboard of Cora's car made my old loafers squish each time I took a step.

Still, the sight of us coming down the aisle gave Deacon Poe a sense of rage that even his fake smiles and polished expressions couldn't conceal. He whispered something to one of the deacons who went over to the janitor and told him that he could leave.

The first person I spoke to was Nora Poe. I nodded my head and gave her a smile that Dr. DeBakey could've used to slice arteries during open heart surgery. Then, I turned to Deacon Poe.

"Can you believe this weather?" I asked the question as we took a seat directly behind Nora Poe. "You think we're going to have enough for a quorum?"

I had already counted seven people. Cora and I brought the total to nine.

Deacon Poe cleared his throat, as though one of the little demons inside of him was trying to get out. "I'm not concerned. Lord willing, we'll have enough."

At that moment, Deacon Grubbs came down the steps from the back offices with a stack of papers. That made ten. We were still two members short.

With a worried look on his face, Deacon Poe walked over to the edge of the sanctuary and got on his big mobile phone. I suspected he was calling a few of his comrades, missing in action.

Suddenly, the foyer doors flung open and Frogman walked in. He was soaking wet, carrying his saxophone in a big plastic bag. He flaunted his usual chest cat grin, then, dropped onto the first pew. He looked back at me. "You got any crackers, Mama Kizzy? Cause these hamburger people done gave up the ghost."

I didn't want to feed him. I wanted to slap him like Sally Howard had done. What in God's name was he doing there? Didn't he know he was a full-fledged member? Didn't he know he had just upped the count?

I slowly gathered my thoughts. He *was* a full-fledged member. He had every right to be there, the same as me. Who was I to say that God hadn't sent him? Who was I to say he wasn't on a mission too?

I pointed to the little igloo water cooler where my bird nest in the sky used to be. "There may be some crackers in there. You're welcome to look."

He came back with a package of saltines and a bottle of water. He held up the water so I could see it. "Thank you, Mama Kizzy. This here will give me the strength I need to play my horn."

"No playing, tonight," declared Deacon Poe. "We got business to take care of."

Still grinning, Frogman took his horn out of the wet plastic bag and held it up so I could see it. "We all got business. Don't we, Mama Kizzy?"

At that moment, I didn't know whether Frogman was being defiant or naive. What I did know was that everything in the universe was connected. If Frogman came out, there had to be a reason why.

At 7:55 pm we sat there, quietly, listening to the rain beat against the rooftop. We all flinched with growing anxiety as the old building creaked and swayed in the wind. Time was running out on Poe's little game of cat and mouse. The bylaws allowed only thirty minutes for a quorum to be established or the meeting would have to be rescheduled.

I looked at the back of my hand as a though I were wearing a fancy precision wrist watch. "Is Pastor Fordham coming?"

"We don't expect him," replied Deacon Grubbs.

"Then, I say we call it a night before Arlene calls it for us. Amen?"

Poe appeared dejected. Womack dropped his head. That's when my big mouth daughter, Lizzy, stumbled through the door.

I frowned at her, then, discreetly motioned to her to go back outside. But she was sopping wet and hopping mad and had seemingly perfected her own frown.

Deacon Poe smiled, widely. "Well, well, well. Sister Lizzy, you are a sight for sore eyes."

Deacon Grubbs shouted. "Amen to that!"

"Come on in. Have a seat. We're about to get started." Poe paused a moment to give me a callous stare. "As I was telling your mother, if the Lord is willing and the creek don't rise, we'll get this business done tonight."

****

Deacon Grubbs uttered a short, useless prayer, then immediately passed out revised copies of the proposal. He gave everybody five minutes to look it over and then he called for a limited discussion.

"By limited I mean fifteen minutes total. Like Sister Kizzy said earlier, we need to call it a night before Arlene calls it for us."

I raised my hand. "I don't think anyone has the right to arbitrarily limit the discussion to fifteen minutes, especially if there are some lingering issues."

"Then, let's don't make it arbitrary," said Poe. "I will entertain a motion for the fifteen minute cut off."

Deacon Grubbs made the motion and Nora Poe seconded it. The motion passed by a vote of nine to three. I don't know why Frogman voted with them. I think he was supporting whoever held up the most hands.

In the new document, there was a clause requiring a separate vote on the project management company. There was only one company listed ... Womack's company. A statement at the bottom of the page in small print indicated that nominations were not limited to companies listed on the page.

Poe cleared his throat again. "I will now entertain nominations for a company or companies to serve as project manager for this proposed undertaking."

Deacon Grubbs stood up again. "I nominate Womack & Partners, LLC for this distinguished honor and responsibility."

This time Deacon Grubbs' wife seconded the motion. There were no other nominations. The vote carried nine to three.

Horace Womack stood up and took a big stretch. "Hallelujah!" They all chuckled as he sat back down.

Poe continued. "Now we are ready to vote on the proposal, itself. Is there any discussion?"

With time running out, I went straight to the heart of the matter. "Yes, I would like to discuss the Silver Dollar Hotel."

Poe rolled his eyes at Womack, but kept a straight face. "What about the hotel, Sister Kizzy?"

"Are there any tax liens against the property that might prevent us from going forward?"

He smiled, confidently. "Of course not. All of that was taken care of in the front."

"Who took care of it?" I asked.

"Mr. Womack's company took care of it."

Womack looked back at me. "Like I told you. Them other companies don't care diddly-squat about this church. I'm the one that negotiated this deal. I'm the one that brought it to you on a silver platter."

"Were you the one who paid for it? I mean, somebody had to pay for the back taxes on the hotel?"

Not knowing exactly how to answer, Womack turned to Poe. "You want to deal with her? Cause my patience done run out."

Poe grimaced. "Sister Kizzy I believe I told you that all of that was taken care of in the front."

"Yes, I know what you told me. But I'm still waiting for you to answer my question. Who paid the back taxes on the hotel?"

"Let's just say it was a collaborative effort." He squirmed, uncomfortably, careful to avoid a direct answer.

"Who collaborated?" I pressed.

"Sister Kizzy, I believe you're wasting our time again with all these ridiculous questions. This is a done deal. Let's move on."

I continued to press. "Since you won't tell me who collaborated, let me tell you. First Reunion Baptist Church collaborated. The problem is they collaborated without knowing."

Deacon Grubbs stood up and looked at his watch. "The fifteen minutes is up. Let's vote and get out of here!"

"Not before he admits what he did. He spent the church's money without any kind of consent from the congregation or the Pastor or anybody. Didn't you, Deacon Poe? Tell the truth for once in your life."

His face bristled up, into a big angry ball. "Truth?! Truth?! Let me give you some truth, Sister Kizzy."

But that was as far as he got. Before he could answer, five men wearing black ski masks burst from the darkened foyer, into the sanctuary. They ran down the aisles waving pistols and one shotgun.

The stocky one with the biggest pistol fired several shots into the air. "I've got your truth, people, right here in my hand."

They shouted for us to get down on the floor. But there was no way my knees were going to cooperate. I slid my elbows and face down on the seat, as if I were praying. But I wasn't praying. I was watching Lizzy, underneath the pew, dialing the police on her death phone.

I heard her say First Reunion Baptist Church, before sliding it back into her purse. Now it was a matter of waiting to see if they got it right. My guess was the squad cars would end up at New Reunion or First Union or Union Baptist down the street. With Arlene's ferocious winds tearing up the city, there was a good chance they wouldn't end up anywhere at all.

The stocky spokesman continued. "Okay people. Let's make some ground rules here." And then he added a sinister chuckle. "You know what? I think I'm going to call them holy rules, since we're in this building and since if you don't listen to me you gonna end up with holes ... yeah that's a good one, holy rules."

The short robber with the shotgun laughed the loudest. "Yeah, boss man, that's a good one, holy rules."

"Rule number one: I'm in charge. No more voting. The voting booth is closed. Do what I say and stay alive. You got it?"

Nobody said a word.

The stocky spokesman fired off another round. "I said, you got it?!!"

Muffled voices rose from beneath the pews in terrified harmony. "Yes, we got it."

"Rule number two: I'm going to let you sit in your seats, mainly because I want to see your faces while I'm taking all of your money." He paused a long second, then shouted, "Wow! I've only been in here a few minutes and already I'm thinking small and narrow-minded like you people. What I meant to say was taking all of your money, credit cards, rings, necklaces, bracelets, maybe even the gold in your teeth if it's not too cheap."

The one with the shotgun laughed again. "Can we throw in some of these Gucci loafers and alligator belts I see the good deacons styling?"

"Yeah, yeah we'll do that too," he agreed. "Now sit up in your seats like good little children. Any false moves and you're going back down on the floor. And next time I'll get my friend, Mr. Shotgun, to blow off your heads."

Everybody slid into their seats, except Deacon Poe. He was so frightened, he stayed crunched up in a knot on the floor by the offering table. And then I realized it wasn't fear that was keeping him down. It was pain that was keeping him down. One of the bullets had apparently ricocheted off the pipes in the ceiling and lodged in his right shoulder. Dark splotches of blood soaked through his starched white shirt.

I thought, *God was still on the throne, handing out liars their just due.*

When Nora Poe saw the blood dripping from her husband's shoulder, she screamed, "Oh my God! He's been shot!"

Don't you mean heeeezzz been shoytttt? My panic-stricken minded tried to humor itself away from the growing sense of terror.

She attempted to get up, but one of the robbers shoved her back down into her seat.

The spokesman with the big pistol walked over to Poe. "My, my. You must really be on God's bad side."

"You got that right!" Cora blabbed out.

I hunched her in the side to quiet down.

The big pistol spokesman continued. "Since I wasn't aiming at you ... yet ... I'm thinking maybe the man upstairs is saying your time has run out. Thing is, you've got a little piece of information that I need before you head through the pearly gates. After all, you are the head honcho around here, aren't you?"

Poe could barely speak through the excruciating pain. "Wha– What do you want?"

"Well, Mister??? ... what is your name?"

"Poe," he grimaced.

"Yeah, yeah. I think they told me that," he recalled. "Well, Mr. Poe. We live in modern times where every church dome size or toilet size gotta a safe. Mr. Poe, somewhere in this church you gotta a safe. And since you're the head man, there's a real good chance you know the combination."

Poe shook his head. "I don't know what you're talking about."

He leaned over the offering table to grab a white tithe envelope and pencil. Like throwing a dog some scraps, he tossed the items on the floor next to Poe's blood droppings. "I believe you know. What I need you to do is write down the combination, just in case the man upstairs got you on speed-dial."

Pope propped himself up against the leg of the table, blood oozing from his arm, and tears streaming down his face. He was helpless like a baby chick, ready to be eaten by the cat on my side of the fence.

I should've been happy to see him in his moment of misery. After all, he was finally getting what he deserved. But there was another flaw in the Christian system. God had injected his people with a troublesome dose of compassion and mercies.

And so I spoke up because ... well ... I couldn't keep quiet. I couldn't let him die on my side of the fence.

"Wait a minute, Deacon Poe." I shouted from my third row pew. "Isn't it worth something?"

The spokesman with the big pistol stepped away from the table and in my direction. "What? Did I hear a death wish from the peanut gallery?"

I continued anyway. "I'm just asking a question. Isn't that combination worth something? I mean, if he doesn't give it to you, you're going to kill him, right?"

"Right, right," he confirmed. "You seem to have a grasp of this situation. So I'll let you continue."

"If he does give it to you, you're going to let him bleed to death. So what is his incentive for giving it to you? I'm just saying, isn't it were something ... to a dying man?"

He used the barrel of the gun to scratch his head. "What do you propose, Madame Negotiator?"

"Why not give you the combination and the location to the safe. In return, you give him a fighting chance. My daughter here is a nurse. Maybe she can help him."

Lizzy grumbled beneath her breath. "Oh sweet Jesus. Throwing her own daughter to the wolves...."

He thought about it for a while. "I'm not an unreasonable man, although it'd be a lot more fun to pistol-whip this fallen angel into a confession. But I *am* on a tight schedule with Arlene and all. Let's do it your way."

As Deacon Poe wrote down the combination, I whispered into Lizzy's ear. "See what you can do, baby. If possible, figure out a way to get me up there with you."

"But Mama?"

"Just do what I say, okay?"

Lizzy made her way to the front of the church to examine Poe's wound. She removed some cushions from the pulpit seats and placed them under his head. Then she pointed to the big green and white first aid kit on the back wall. "I'm going to need that."

Frogman jumped up. "I'll get it."

The short robber used the butt of his shotgun to push Frogman back down. "Don't even think about it, fool."

One of the other robbers, wearing a bright yellow shirt, went to the back and snatched the kit off the wall. If only Big Mildred would've been there to see him tearing up church property.

Returning to the front, he went over and whispered something into the spokesman's ear.

"Damn!" He swore. "Go back there and lock those doors and make sure none of them five-O pigs haven't already slipped in."

He looked at me. "Well, well, Madame Negotiator. We got a parking lot full of pigs out there. You know anything about that?"

Before I could answer, Lizzy's phone started to ring from inside her purse.

"Whose phone is that?" he asked.

"It ... It's mine." I declared in a shaky voice.

He nodded his head. "Why don't you answer it?"

Me, answer that death phone?

"And put it on speaker," he added. "Let's all listen in."

I slowly removed the phone from Lizzy's purse and surveyed all of the confusing buttons. I didn't know which one to push. If I couldn't answer the phone that supposedly belonged to me, it was a sure giveaway that it wasn't my phone at all. Then how could I protect Lizzy if the stupid police said the wrong thing?

Cora snatched it from me and pressed the green button. Then she pressed another button to put it on speaker. Handing it back to me she remarked, "Every time you buy a new phone it takes you forever to learn how to work it."

A brash, demanding voice came on the line. "This is the Houston Police Department. We know you're in there. All we want to do is get you out, safely. There isn't much time. The bayou in the back of the church is coming in on you right now. Please, unlock the doors and come out."

The spokesman growled, "They're full of *#!*t. Hang it up. Hang it up right now! I ain't walking into nobody's trap."

As it turned out, it wasn't a trap at all.

Braes Bayou was a major tributary of Buffalo Bayou, the

largest waterway flowing through Houston. Whenever a hurricane blew in from the Gulf, Buffalo Bayou flooded. Whenever Buffalo Bayou flooded, Braes Bayou flooded too. The problem with Braes Bayou was that it meandered deep into the residential neighborhoods of Houston's Third Ward. Seeking to capture the serenity of the water, the old Synagogue had been erected only a few hundred yards away from the stream.

That night, when the bayou finally left its banks, it took only ten minutes to reach the church. Another thirty minutes and the sanctuary was ankle deep in muddy water.

We were astounded. The bayou had flooded many times before. But the water had never come into the church. Because of the budget shortfall, Deacon Grubbs had commissioned the workers to seal up the holes and cracks on the street side of the church. It was completely waterproof. On the west side, however, no work had been done. Termites had eaten most of the wood, leaving gaping holes in the half-century old foundation. The resulting scenario was an artificial dam. A torrent of bayou water had flowed in on the west side, but couldn't flow out on the street side.

As the cold, dirty water continued flooding through the rotten crack and crevices, the wind rocked the old building with 100 mph gales. The lights flickered on and off, and little by little, we all became aware of a faint but familiar scent.

Cora gazed at me with a stern expression, her nostrils, cocked high in the air. "You smell that? That's natural gas, isn't it?"

I nodded, reluctantly, with an asterisk in the back of my mind.

Actually, natural gas, in its true form, is colorless, odorless and tasteless. During its early years of usage, it had killed so many people, the government had mandated gas refineries to include a man-made chemical called mercaptan so people would know when the deadly gas was escaping. We were smelling mercaptan. In Texas, mercaptan was the smell of death.

Like children in a drainage ditch after a heavy rain, the spokesman and his crew sloshed up and down the middle aisle. He consulted with them in low whispers, hashing out their next move. Thanks to Lizzy's death phone, the police were waiting out front. Thanks to the many years of neglect, the sanctuary had become an overflowing bathtub, filled with chocolate water. Thanks to the janitor's preparation for the storm, the back exit was completely boarded up. And now, thanks to an apparent stray bullet in the ceiling, gas fumes were slowly consuming the air.

I waited until the spokesman sloshed back to the front of the church. "Don't you think it makes sense to quit while you're ahead?"

He rolled his secluded eyes at me. "Ahead? You think I'm ahead? Explain that Chinese checker logic to me."

"So far, you haven't done anything. You haven't robbed or killed or maimed anybody. What can the police do about a gun, accidentally going off and wounding a bystander?"

"Thatahh was no accident!" Nora Poe spewed out the verdict from her proper lips. "He shot my husbaaand in the act of committing a crime and he's guueing to pay!"

He shook his head, pitifully. "Well, Madame Negotiator. Looks like your amnesty bill just died in committee."

At that moment, Lizzy cried out in panic. "He's losing too much blood. We've got to get him to a doctor!"

With so much water flooding in, the deacons had moved Poe off the floor and onto the first row pew. Now, the water was lapping over the pew onto his shoulder.

Poe shouted in agony as they tried to relocate him to the choir stand.

"Yerr're hurting him!" protested Nora Poe. "Why don't you

imbeciles watch what yerr're doing?"

The deacons finally relocated him to the elevated seats in the choir stand and stretched him out across several chairs.

That's when Horace Womack stood up. "Look! I'm not with these holy rollers. I just came to close a deal and git the hell outta here."

"Well, now. All we need is the rooster to crow three times and we got ourselves a modern-day Bible story," said the spokesman.

The robber in the yellow shirt chuckled, scornfully.

The spokesman spat with disdain into the rising current. "You know what? You church people make me sick of the stomach. You're nothing but a bunch of hypocrites. Not a single one of you done tried to pray your way out this mess. Isn't that supposed to be your God-all-mighty silver bullet for tight spots like this?"

"We opened this meeting with prayer," defended Deacon Grubbs.

You mean your last deposit to the big trash compost, I thought to myself.

The spokesman continued, "All these Bibles 'bout to float down the drain pipes to hell. Seem to me you holy rollers would be thumbing through the pages trying to find the magic chant Moses used to open up the Red Sea. But nawh, nawh, this ain't Sunday morning. The TBN TV cameras ain't rolling. So you out here in a storm with your real faces on, bickering and backbiting and doing a hocus-pocus with the funds. The big boy here is now telling me this God thang ain't his thang at all. Hell, that ain't news. I can see that for myself."

Womack reached inside his coat pocket and pulled out a stack of business cards. "Like I told you, I'm a businessman. Look, here's my card. You'll probably recognize my company."

The spokesman smiled. "I tell you. I might not recognize your company. But I do recognize that $8,000 Montres Rolex you got on your wrist. As a businessman, myself, I think our little compensation package for this hazardous storm duty should start with you. Hand it over."

Womack shook his head, defiantly. "I ain't giving up my watch."

"Well, I guess we could just take it off your dead body."

Lord knows he's had plenty of practice, I thought to myself.

He signaled to the man with the shotgun. Slowly and methodically, he waded toward the outside aisle.

"Wait a minute!" My voice swelled, frantically. "If you shoot that gun, you're going to blow us all up."

The spokesman stopped in his watery tracks. "What do you mean?"

"Natural gas. Can't you smell it?"

He pushed his head up toward the ceiling. "I don't smell nothing. But just to be on the safe side and treat you onlookers to the kind of entertainment you're used to, why don't we just beat him to death?"

The man with the shotgun smiled. "A business to business trans-action, up close and personal. I feel that. I feel that a lot, boss man!"

The spokesman yelled to another robber who had been watching the front doors from the foyer windows. "Cat! Give us a hand with this Chapter 13 liquidation."

The lookout man trudged up the side aisle where the water was already waist deep. The three men closed in on Womack like ferocious jungle cats, stalking their prey.

I looked at Cora. "We can't just sit here. We've got to think of something before Reedy kills us all."

She blinked. "Reedy? Did you say Reedy?"

"That's who's behind the mask. He's trying to get even with the church for making him look like a fool."

"I should be the one getting even, the way he did my

brother. Can't tell you how many times I've thought about poor Buster, spread out all over the floor."

"Please, Cora. Try not to dwell on that. What's done is done. We need to concentrate on getting out of this mess."

That's when the drama intensified.

Determined not to give up his precious watch, Womack kicked Cat in the groin and retreated in a wild, splashing frenzy to the north rear wall. He knew. We all knew. It was nothing more than a delaying tactic. Sooner or later, Reedy was going to get tired of the little cat-and-mouse game and pull the trigger.

Cora pondered. "Maybe that heathen is right, you know? We're supposed to be God's children. But nobody's praying for help."

I thought about it. Prayer was no silver bullet. I had prayed for so much and gotten back so little. Mr. Myles had kept on smoking. Lizzy was still without a child. Charlotte Lueese was still ... *wait a minute.*

Charlotte Lueese was still alive. The nurse hadn't called back. But I knew it was Charlotte Lueese in that bed. I knew it in my heart. Never mind God taking fourteen years to let me know. He had the right to answer when he got good and ready. It came with the territory.

One thing was certain. With the water rising higher each second and the natural gas fumes clogging our throats, none of us would be around to hear another answer fourteen years in the making. It had to be now.

I grabbed Cora's hand. "Dear Lord. Here we are, two old warriors, trying to fight a battle that's way over our heads. We think you sent us out here, but we don't know that either. All we know is we need your help and we need it right now. Please come get us out of this mess we've gotten ourselves into. Please show us your mighty power before it's too late."

Cora hollered, "In the name of Jesus!"

That's when we heard the sound. That's when time seemed to

stand still.

Chapter Nineteen

We didn't know the bulk of the storm had taken a last-minute turn away from Galveston, slid down the coastline and gone inland at the southeastern marina town of Padre Island. We didn't know the police had been ordered to pull back from the area because a tornado had been spotted a few miles away. All we knew was that we sat paralyzed in a drowning pool, pleading for the Lord to intervene. And now the ominous sound of a freight train was coming our way.

On the Gulf Coast, everybody knew one of the most deadly consequences of a hurricane was not the hurricane, but the killer tornadoes it spawned. Tornadoes were like giant ten-story buildings generating hundreds of millions of volts of electricity and highly pressurized walls of wind. The wind rotated at unbelievable speeds and gobbled up everything in its path. A tornado could pick up a brick building or a Mack truck or drive a toothpick through a person's throat. Unlike hurricanes, tornadoes didn't give much warning. They swooped down from the clouds, wreaked havoc on an unsuspecting world, and then funneled back up into obscurity. If you heard the freight train, you had your warning. Death was on the way.

A few tormenting seconds passed before the swirling winds

slammed against the old building. Immediately, the lights went out, casting us into a hellish, epileptic darkness. Then, to our amazement, the whole bell tower over the foyer came crashing down.

We had envisioned ourselves, escaping the rising tide, marching out of the front doors, down the steep steps and into the waiting arms of the police. But now that vision had crumbled into a hopeless nightmare.

Nora Poe screamed to the top of her voice. The gas fumes drifted, relentlessly, from the ceiling, like an invisible cloak of death. And though we couldn't see it, we could feel the water rising faster than before.

I heard Lizzy cry out. "Mama! Mama, are you alright?"

I wasn't alright. Cora and I were standing on the third row pew, watching horrible silhouettes of the robbers and Horace Womack, kicking and flailing as the powerful funnel sucked them through the jagged opening where the bell tower used to be.

That's when we heard it, the glorious sound of Frogman's horn. We couldn't see him. But we knew he was there. And, as if delivering a personalized message from heaven to me, he blew a tune familiar to my heart. It was the same tune that Mr. Myles used to sing while sitting on his favorite white bench outside the front door:

Oh when the saints
Go marching in
Oh when the saints go marching in
Yes Lord I want to be in that number
Oh when the saints go marching in

I stood next to Cora, clutching my big purse and wood grain walking cane. That's when she touched me on the shoulder.

"Look at your walking stick, Kizzy. It's ... glowing."

It was glowing, indeed, softly, quietly, like a lethargic firefly on a summer's night. I hadn't told anybody. But the cane had never gone back to room temperature since the day Bishop Ebenezer delivered it. Ububee had described it as wood left next to a cooking fire. It were as though that fire had never gone out.

Like a gigantic floating turbine spitting fire and debris, the swirling wind and blinding flashes of lightning gradually moved on. The angry waters, however, continued to rush in, taunting our ears with a gurgling sound of death.

"Where is he? Do you see him?" Cora bellowed.

As Frogman's saxophone faded in the distance, our hearts saddened, quite certain he was being swallowed up by the rising tide.

"There!" With my outstretched cane, I point through the darkness, up the steps, toward the door leading to the Pastor's study. A brilliant blue light burst out of the metal tip. It was as though I were shining a powerful flashlight across the dark, swirling water. The entire area illuminated with ethereal shades of indigo and green.

"Kizzy, are you seeing what I'm seeing?" asked Cora.

Sometimes, in a terrible crisis, the mind can play tricks on you. It can stretch beyond the limits of plasticity and conjure up realities that are not actually there. But if my feeble mind had stretched too far across the valley of plasticity, then so had everyone else's. They were all gazing in blissful awe at the outstretched cane.

As a scientist, familiar with chemoluminescence, I realized I didn't need to have a battery or be plugged into a socket in the wall. The combination of certain chemicals such as cyalume and hydrogen peroxide could create light independent of any other source. But who was mixing the chemicals inside my old cane? And why did this light look like no other light I had ever seen?

And then it all began to fall into place.

When I saw the hallway door wide open, and heard the sound

of the horn fading away, I realized Frogman was not just playing a melodious tune to amuse us. He was trying to lead us out.

"That's the way!" I shouted to everyone. "That's the way out!"

I could see a few watery figures slowly moving toward the door. They trudged up the split-level steps, down the hallway, and finally, down the wooden staircase leading to the basement. I held the light steady as Cora and I joined Kizzy up in the choir stand. With Deacon Poe stretched out on a string of folding chair, she was still hovering over him, nursing his bloody wound.

Her eyes were filled with tears. "I was the best in my class, Mama. I know all these procedures inside and out. But he won't stop bleeding. And if we move him, Mama, he's just going to get worse."

My heart pounded with compassion, more for her than him. "You've done your best, child. Now you and Cora go on. Let me figure this out."

"You can forget it, Kizzy," Cora growled.

"Yeah, Mama. We're not leaving you behind."

Poe grunted. "Your stubborn ways is what's got us out here in the first place. Get out of here, Kizzy. Get out of here while you still got time."

"I will. But first there's something I need to do."

I told Lizzy to hold the light. Then I reached into my purse and pulled out the bottle of holy water. If God had his miracle engine in high gear, maybe I could bring Poe along for the ride.

I opened the bottle and held it over the wound.

"No, Mama!" Lizzy shouted. "You'll end up thinning his blood."

"Listen, child. You've got to forget about all your medical training. We're in a different kind of hospital now. You understand?"

She nodded, silently.

I looked at Poe. "There's healing in the name of Jesus. Do you remember him at all?"

"I'm not the devil you've made me out to be," he defended. "I still believe in the Lord."

"Let's hope he still believes in you." I poured half the bottle into the bloody wound.

Like dropping Alka-Seltzer tablets into a glass of water, the whole abrasion started to fizz. Poe closed his eyes and clenched his teeth. A gritty, foam-like substance ran down his arm. His shoulder turned a bruised dark blue, then back to his normal brown skin tone.

Cora's eyes squinted in the dim light. "Is it working, Kizzy? Or did you send this heathen off to hell?"

"I-ah, I don't know?"

Lizzy's mouth flew open. "Look. He stopped bleeding."

Deacon Poe opened his eyes and stared at us in bewilderment.

"How do you feel?" I finally inquired.

He shook his head. "I would ask who was driving that bus. But I already know."

Cora lifted her head high into the air. "You smell that? It's getting worse. We got to go."

"One more thing," I insisted.

I poured the rest of the holy water into the palm of my hand. Then, I ordered Lizzy to open her blouse.

She looked at Poe as if reminding me of his presence. "Mama???"

"Just do it," I repeated.

She slowly complied.

I rubbed the glistening liquid across Lizzy's stomach. "In the name of the Father, Son and Holy Spirit."

The whole building shook in the restless wind. And then I

whispered into her ear, "While the miracle engine is still running ... You understand?"

She nodded again, a torrent of tears, sliding down her cheeks. "Okay, let's go."

Lizzy handed the cane to me. Then Poe draped his good arm across Cora's shoulder. Lizzy grabbed him around the waist. I shined the light toward the hallway door as we all hobbled through.

We made our way to the end of the hallway and down the rickety wooden stairs to the basement. Three deacons, plus Deacon Grubbs and his wife were huddled in a corner. Nora Poe had passed out in an old swivel chair against the wall. Somehow, all of the rising water had washed away the memory of her marriage vows, especially the one to stay by her husband's side.

As it turned out, the small band of survivors had found themselves caught in the middle of nowhere. I had the cane with the light upstairs and Frogman's horn had fallen into silence.

"We didn't know which way to go," admitted Deacon Grubbs.

I didn't either, until I shined the light on an old mahogany bookcase in the north corner of the room. Loaded down with old Bibles and Sunday school books, the case had been jarred from the wall.

When Deacon Grubbs swiveled the case around, we discovered an opening the size of a mini refrigerator. A five-foot high tunnel stretched as far as our eyes could see.

Deacon Grubbs shook his head. "This was never in the blueprints, I guarantee."

Lizzy gawked with fascination. "Where does it go?"

"Away from this death hole," said Cora. "That's all that matters."

The muddy water had already begun streaming down the basement steps; a menacing revelation that our Egypt was under water, and there was no turning back.

One by one we stooped and slithered through the hole in the wall, only to reassemble in the dark, sewer-like tunnel on the other side.

A single brown wood rat scampered in the distance. A string of ghostly spider webs drooped from the old wooden beams. There was no glorious pathway, paved with gold, leading us to the Promise Land. There was only the rustle of anger waters behind us and the eerie cloak of darkness ahead.

We began our trek like tattered soldiers, lost behind enemy lines, trying to find our way back home. The only thing that kept us from being swallowed up by the damp walls and the thick darkness was the perpetual glow of one little wood grain walking cane.

"God told me to bless it for you." Bishop Ebenezer, former street thug turned oddball fanatic for Jesus Christ, had stoutly proclaimed. And bless it, he had.

God can do whatever he wants to do, with whoever he wants to do it with, Amen?

****

Ten minutes into the tunnel we reached a heart shaped storage area about twenty feet wide. It reminded me of a museum from the 1950's, where life had suddenly stopped in time and captured a static reality that no longer had meaning to the rest of the world.

Cobwebs covered a single metal desk surrounded by several workbenches and mildewed boxes of paper supplies. Metal containers filled with antiquated construction tools rested like rusty tombs against the concrete walls. Blue overalls covered in mud, remained neatly stacked on a small wooden counter.

"What is this place?" asked Lizzy.

"Maybe a good place to catch our breath," said Deacon Poe. Observing his weakened steps and heavy breathing, Cora lowered him, gingerly, onto one of the dusty workbenches.

"Don't get too comfortable," she warned. "Gas fumes love these kinds of hell holes."

Deacon Grubbs speculated on Lizzy's question. "I bet it was for the workers who built the tunnel."

"But who would want a tunnel leading to the church?" Lizzy pressed.

Deacon Grubbs walked over to the metal desk to pick up a piece of paper. "This work order is dated 1956. Who wanted a tunnel down here 40 years ago is anybody's guess."

"Not really," said Poe. "Back then there was only one man who had the money and political connections to pull this off: Silver Dollar Jim West."

"The hotel's original owner?" I asked.

He nodded. "One in the same."

"You knew about this tunnel?"

"No. But from what I do know, it's the only thing that makes sense," said Poe.

"I think it's time you told us what you *do* know," I scolded him. "You've been lying to us, stealing church funds and cutting deals on the side. I think it's time we knew the truth."

He shook his head. "It's a long story."

"We don't need no long stories down here," said Cora.

"No, no. Tomorrow is not promised. We deserve to know

right now."

He took a deep breath. "First of all, I want you to know I've never stolen a dime from the church. If anything, I've put my own money in at different times, just to keep things going."

"Now thaattah is the painful truth," Nora Poe attested.

I frowned with lingering suspicion. "That's hard to believe."

"Think about it. I know your husband didn't like me. But in all of his years on the Deacon Board, did he ever accuse me of stealing?"

I paused. "No. He never did."

"That's because I never did."

"Then what about the $130,000 for the back taxes on the hotel?"

"I'll get to that," Poe promised.

His story began two years earlier, on his job at Humble Oil, which he reminded me was now Exxon USA. His boss had given him a special project which involved going to Dallas to clear out an old warehouse the company had bought. While going through the records, he had found a box containing the possessions of an eccentric treasure hunter named Wilbur Hump. Before his death, Hump had been credited with finding a sunken ship off the coast of Florida carrying $10 million in gold. In Arizona, he had helped to find a Wells Fargo money box buried by the infamous Red Jack gang.

Buried deep in Hump's unpublished memoirs was a copy of a letter to his partner suggesting he was on to a new treasure.

Through meticulous research, Hump had discovered that in 1957, several months before the oil baron died, Silver Dollar Jim had withdrawn a large sum of money from his bank. At least a quarter of a million was in silver dollars. Rumor had it he had planned to run away to a foreign country with a mystery woman with whom he had fallen in love.

Hump suspected Silver Dollar Jim West had planned to leave the country because of the potential ridicule to which he'd be subjected by his rich, socialite friends. In the letter, dated August 15, 1960, Hump had asked his partner, a Mr. Red Vargo, to look into the activities of a Negro woman in Houston named Mildred Yates.

Poe recalled, fondly, "I remembered that name because when my daddy and the other trustees bought the Synagogue from the Jews, I saw her picture hanging on the wall. She was the only black face on the wall."

"Was she some kind of woman rabbi?" Lizzy asked.

"Not hardly. She was the woman who cleaned the church for seven years. At least, that was how it started out."

Poe went on to explain that one night while she was cleaning the Synagogue, one of the priests heard her humming a tune. She had a beautiful voice. So he convinced her to sing at one of their Friday night services. The people liked her so much they asked her to come back again. And again; and again. Pretty soon she was a regular part of the Friday worship service.

"Somehow, Silver Dollar Jim heard her sing. Treasure hunter Hump believed that's how the romance got started."

"Was Silver Dollar Jim, Jewish?" asked one of the younger deacons.

"Absolutely not," said Poe. "He hated Jews. In fact, he built the hotel in the heart of the Jewish community to spite them."

"So how did he find out about this Yates woman?" I asked.

"Red Vargo strongly believed that, somehow, Silver Dollar Jim had access to the Synagogue. Now you can see why this tunnel makes sense."

Lizzy frowned. "I don't get it. He built this tunnel so he could slip over to the Synagogue to hear the Yates woman sing?"

"Not at first," Poe explained. "You have to understand that

Jim was a strange bird, born with a silver spoon in his mouth. His daddy was a successful oil man and lumber dealer. Jim grew up with people bowing down to him. It didn't set well when somebody said no to him."

Poe speculated that when the Jews at the Shamrock Hilton Hotel turned him away, it triggered a deep sense of rage. It wasn't enough just to build the hotel in their back yard. Silver Dollar Jim needed to prove to himself he had control over their most precious domain: the Jewish Synagogue. He could come and go as he pleased and nobody could stop him.

In the notes, Red Vargo had talked to a priest who told him, occasionally, they would find a silver dollar on the organ or at the prayer table or next to the Sabbath bread. No one could explain how these coins had gotten there. But everyone knew that was Silver Dollar Jim's calling card.

Hump believed Mildred Yates had discovered Silver Dollar Jim in the church one night. Or maybe, while she was singing and cleaning, he became infatuated with her voice. Either way, the unlikely couple began their precarious romantic journey.

In another letter, Hump's partner had written:

I SPOKE TO MR. WEST'S FORMER NEGRO DRIVER WHO FONDLY GOES BY THE NAME OF BLACK JIM. THE LITTLE PRIVATE TALK COST ME A HUN-DRED DOLLARS AND A BOTTLE OF GORDON'S GIN. BUT IT WAS WELL WORTHWHILE. IN THE MONTHS BEFORE MR. WEST EXPIRED, HE HAD ASKED BLACK JIM AN INORDINATE AMOUNT OF QUESTIONS ABOUT "COLORED GIRLS"; THEIR LIKES AND DISLIKES. I DO BELIEVE SOMETHING WAS AFOOT BETWEEN HIM AND THE NEGRO WOMAN, MILDRED YATES.

In his final letter to Hump, before Hump died in '62, Red Vargo wrote:

I HAVE CONFIRMED THE THREE DELIVERIES TO THE HOTEL. MR. WEST PERSONALLY ACCOMPA-NIED ALL THREE. THE FIRST WAS FEBRUARY 12, 1957. THE SECOND AND THIRD WERE IN MARCH OF THE SAME YEAR. ESTATE RECORDS SHOW THE FIRST WAS HIS PRIZE PISTOLS COLLECTION. THE SECOND WAS HIS FAMILY HEIRLOOMS. THERE IS NO ACCOUNTING FOR THE THIRD DELIVERY. IF IT IS THE TREASURE, IT IS MOST LIKELY STILL HIDDEN SOMEWHERE IN THE HOTEL.

"What did he mean by treasure?" asked Lizzy.

"He meant the $250,000 in silver dollars that Jim had taken out of the bank in preparation for his trip," explained Poe. "The money is still hidden somewhere in the hotel."

Deacon Grubbs' big eyes shifted back and forth "Do you know how much $250,000 in silver coins is worth today?"

"At least four million," declared Poe. "That's why I bought the hotel."

"You didn't buy the hotel. The church did." I reminded him. "They did it without knowing."

Poe looked at me. "What do you think would've happened if I had announced to the congregation there was four million dollars in silver coins across the street in an abandoned hotel?"

Deacon Grubbs flashed an amused smile. "Silver Rush '93!"

"It doesn't matter. You can't justify lying to the congregation about their money," I said.

"Now that's where we differ, Kizzy. You see, when the congregation gives the money to the church, it no longer belongs to the congregation. The book of First Timothy calls for chosen men of integrity to make those decisions."

"You think a man of integrity would make Horace Womack his partner?"

"True, Womack is a bottom crawler. But he was the only one in a position to negotiate the deal with the City."

"If the Devil is the only one in a position to help you, do you really want help?" I continued to question his distorted sense of morality.

"God uses the Devil all the time," said Poe.

It was a rare Biblical precept I couldn't deny. And since we were the children of God, following His example, my impending spiritual algorithm would end up in conflict with God, Himself.

Deacon Grubbs surveyed the room. "By the way, what happened to Womack and the others?"

"They got raptured through the bell tower, straight to hell," Cora grimly reported.

I glared at Poe. "I guess that means you get to keep his cut too?"

"He never knew about the treasure. I couldn't trust him with that kind of information. He was just working for the fee."

"It appears there were otheeerrsss who couldn't be trusted, including your own wife," declared Nora Poe.

No one bothered to respond. The consensus of silence was enough to validate his decision.

I shook my head with disdain. "My God, Poe. You were going to keep it all, weren't you?"

"Like I told you, Kizzy, I've never stolen a dime from the church and I never will. That money was going to be used to fix up all the things that needed fixing. You know why it was so easy for that flood water to come in on us this time ... termites, millions of them. They had eaten up 90% of the back side walls. You know why those gas pipes started leaking ... because they're 30 years old. We only had money to replace one section, the very worst section, on the front side of the building. You know why we didn't get a new bell for the bell tower and patch up the leaks ... because that whole column was rotten to the core and needed to be reinforced. The extra classrooms you wanted couldn't be built because the boiler was leaking and the foundation under the utility area next to the proposed classrooms had cracks from front to back."

"So I guess I'm the villain. I was wrong for going against your secret plan to save the church. Is that what you're telling me?" I asked.

Poe took another deep breath. "You did everything you were supposed to do."

Cora's mouth flew open. "Come again!"

"What if I wasn't on the up and up? What if I was trying to take the church for a ride? What if everybody just sat there and let it happen? How would you feel then?" he asked.

"Pretty bad, I guess."

"Real bad, Kizzy. You would've felt real bad," he proclaimed. "You would've kicked yourself over and over again, especially since God has given you the good common sense to smell a rat."

"I suppose."

"Don't get me wrong. I didn't like what you did. But it was the right thing to do. You love the church and I do too. We just show it in different ways. I guess it'll always be that way."

"I guess it will, Deacon Poe." I took a deep breath, as the years of resentment slowly melted away in my heart.

Cora intervened. "So can we go now? Or do we need to give

those fumes a little more time to catch up?"

"Settle down, Cora." I tried to calm her jittery nerves. "God has gotten us this far. Everything's going to be fine."

That's when we heard the tremendous explosion. That's when we felt the tunnel caving in.

We didn't know it, but we were already beneath the hotel. We scurried through a rusty metal door on the other side of the storage area, up an iron stairwell, through a utility room and into the main lobby.

We could hear the deafening roar of the liquid fireball, blazing through the tunnel. We could feel the old building trembling like a condemned prisoner, marked for death.

For years, the hotel had been an eyesore, a big white elephant, crumbling to its knees. But now inside, I saw it in a different light ... a cocoon of high Texas grandeur, dripping with old secrets and glorious intrigue. Despite the thickening smoke and slithering streaks of fire, leaping up through the floor, the old spinster of a structure fought back with original beauty that flames could not conceal.

Though the carpet was stained and most of the furniture, gone, the vaulted ceiling, spiral staircase and exquisitely paneled walls preserved the structure's elegance and style. If you listened long enough you could hear the ghostly echoes of senator and governors and oil barons, polishing off their deals. A Dixie band played in the lavish bar as, young girls in skimpy dresses frolicked along the marble steps.

They didn't frolic for long, however. The gas inflated fireball roared through the tunnel, knocked down the metal door and set the whole bottom floor of the hotel ablaze.

"Told y'all! Didn't I tell y'all?" Cora kept scolding us as we scrambled for the hotel entrance.

The doors were tightly boarded. For a brief instance, it

appeared we were doomed. But Deacon Grubbs found an old rusty bed rail and transformed a small wooden crack into a gaping hole. We raced out of the smoky death trap like spooked cattle. Nora Poe led the way, trampling over crack head mattresses, grocery carts and smelly piles of trash.

Surrounded by the flickering flames and distorted light, I couldn't be sure. But looking back into a distant corner, I caught a glimpse of several Schepps Dairy milk cartons, sitting in a wheel barrel; the same kind of cartons Frogman used to collect tips during his Main Street serenades.

In an instant we were standing on the sidewalk half a block away. We watched as both buildings burned to the ground. The misting rain trickled down our smoke covered faces as Fannie Grubbs pushed her chin into Deacon Grubbs' chest and began to cry. The heavy winds were gone now. Only the sounds of crackling wood and approaching sirens filled the night air.

I don't know exactly when the light in my walking cane went out or the precise moment Poe mentioned his shoulder no longer throbbed with pain. The only thing I was certain of was the deep sense of gratitude, stirring in all of our hearts.

A string of mighty miracles had guided us to safety; nothing the world would believe. But at that moment, who cared about the world? We knew the truth. It was a powerful, enduring truth that would brand our hearts forever.

I watched Poe as he studied the hotel flames with sad intensity. He finally asked, "You think silver dollars can withstand that kind of heat?"

"I hope so. Otherwise, the church is going to end up with a big silver bracelet too heavy for any of us to wear."

We both chuckled, still somewhat reluctant to let our guard down.

I finally asked, "What if the treasure isn't there, Poe? Will it be a total loss for the church?"

"Loss?" His head cocked back. "There's no loss here. The church owns a piece of property appraised at $870,000 for an investment of $130,000. With this new urban renewal coming in, the price of the land will probably double in three years."

"I guess you've got everything figured out."

"Not everything," he admitted. "I still haven't figured out why you didn't leave me behind."

"Why?"

I thought about it a long time. Why did foolish Christian compassion keep getting in the way of heavenly recompense? There was a flaw in the system. That was the reason why. God's mercy was holding back the reins of justice, even for the slick head devils of the world.

"I guess I went soft on you, Poe," I shamefully confessed.

Cora, who had been listening from a distance, stepped up behind him. "But don't you get too comfortable. Next time we might have some decent holy water and send you straight to hell."

Chapter Twenty

It took almost four months for the insurance company to pay off on the church's comprehensive fire and flooding policies. Claims adjusters kept calling, asking me questions I couldn't answer, at least not with the truth.

Who could blame them for being suspicious about a glowing cane or a self-healing wound or secret tunnel leading to an old broken down hotel? Surely, the City of Houston knew what was under their public streets? Surely, a freak tornado wouldn't pick up only robbers and sleazy real estate developers and leave church members behind?

I was too embarrassed to explain why God's people had come out in a storm in the first place, fighting each other like cats and dogs. What message would that send to the heathens of the world who already poked fun at the high profile blunders of television evangelists, fake healers and preachers with too many wives?

And then there were the questions about Frogman. No one had seen him since his melodious horn led us to safety. No one ever saw him again.

But I had a sneaking suspicion where Silver Dollar Jim's treasure had gone. One night, while rummaging through my purse, I found the four silver dollars that Frogman had given to me for change. They were all dated prior to 1957. What was the likelihood of that?

Had Wilbur Hump and his treasure-hunting partner, Red Vargo, still been alive, I could've told them where to find him. All they needed to do was look wherever there was a gathering of kindred hearts in need of a sassy horn and a pumpkin smile.

Two days before Thanksgiving, Deacon Poe called me to help resolve what he referred to as "a critical church matter".

The call didn't come as a total surprise. In the ensuing months after the fire, he had called me a lot. As a member of the relocation committee, I had contacted Benjamin Weingarten of Weingarten's Realty to secure the old vacant Safeway store. He and Deacon Poe had negotiated a ten year lease which covered the three years we needed to rebuild the church and another seven years to provide an initial home for the Reunion Battered Woman's Shelter. I pressured Deacon Poe and Attorney Grits Macklin to include Eddie Maye Lewis in the grant money as the shelter's full-time cook. No high school diploma required.

It was a wonderful arrangement. We took a dried up lake and refilled it with living water. The resilience of First Reunion Baptist Church echoed throughout the city, and we believed, in heaven above.

When Deacon Poe called just before Thanksgiving, he tried to sound very official. But I detected some boyish trickery in his voice.

"Sister Kizzy, we're going to need your assistance. We can't decide which of our two banks to deposit the $28.5 million. Maybe with all of your great wisdom, you can help us out."

It was Poe's way of letting me know, after months of haggling, he had finally received the insurance check.

I told him I thought the best solution would be to deposit the money into my account until a decision could be reached. And then we both began to laugh.

We laughed a lot after the fire. Even Cora warmed up to Poe. Occasionally, after church, she'd threaten him with an old perfume bottle she'd filled with drinking water, her homemade holy water, just as a reminder that she was in control of his eternal destination.

We laughed in celebration of Olivia Boudreaux's gigantic September wedding. At their Hyatt Regency reception, City Councilman Anthony got drunk and tried to do the moonwalk atop one of the long food and beverage tables. His boyish antics and slapstick fall almost cost him the election.

We laughed at Reverend Larry "GeeNet" Willis' first sermon in October. I paid for his three-month drug rehabilitation program. When he came out, he had "found the Lord". Furthermore, he had a calling upon his life to "preach the gospel".

When you looked into his eyes to see the renewed radiance of life, there was no doubt he was a new creature in Christ. But he was a baby Christian. There was no way Pastor Fordham should've put him into the pulpit during prime time morning service. I felt he needed more training, more time to find his voice.

When Pastor Fordham called his name to preach, he was petrified. The first thing he did was throw up a long, slimy blubber into the big silver pan used by the Mission sisters to wash feet. When he finally got his sermon rolling, he had the Father, drawing up a play, the Holy Ghost bringing the ball down the court, and Jesus, weaving and bobbing, and making a spin move to the goal. The Devil had to call time out because he and his Imps couldn't break heaven's full court press.

We old timers laughed with joy and amazement. But that day, eight young women and men gave their lives to Christ. It was obvious that some of them had drug problems. But I wasn't worried. Reverend GeeNet had an arm full of needle tracks to turn their fragile lives around.

The only time we didn't laugh was the third week in July. That was the week we brought Charlotte Lueese's body home.

The Portland nurse never called me back. But a few days after the fire, I launched a phone campaign that would've made most bill collectors salivate at the mouth. I called everyone who owed me a favor and gave them the number to the Portland Police Department. I told them to ask for Officer Helfelman.

By the time they'd finished bombarding him with questions about Charlotte Lueese, a three man task force began working the case. Finally, on July 13, 1993, at 3:30 pm, Officer Helfelman called me back.

He began in a somber tone. "I'm afraid I have some bad news. Charlotte Lueese Cooper is deceased."

Mr. Myles used to say, "as long as she's not officially dead, she's officially alive." Now, the hopeful meaning embodied in those precious words had finally slipped away.

Charlotte Lueese had been an early victim of the infamous Green River Killer. Dressed in a police uniform, a smooth talking serial killer named Gary Ridgway had lured her away from the hotel and strangled her to death ... at least he thought she was dead. When they found her in a remote area outside of Portland, partially nude and severely beaten, she was barely breathing.

"The doctors didn't give her much of a chance," reported Officer Helfelman. "But she was a fighter. I think it was her sheer will to bring the perpetrator to justice that kept her hanging on."

The trauma had pushed her into a deep coma for fourteen years. Some of her records had been lost. No one knew her identity or her connection to the sixty other women who, ultimately, fell victim to Ridgway's deadly seduction.

"It took us a while to put all the pieces together," admitted Officer Helfelman. "But your friend was a big help."

Charlotte Lueese had scribbled a partial license plate number in the mud, in her own blood, next to her body. The information had led police to Ridgway's rental car, which he claimed had been stolen. He was subsequently questioned and released.

"The scumbag passed a polygraph test. Can you believe that?" Helfelman grumbled. "The officers working the case back then had no choice but to let him go. Luckily, they grabbed a couple of DNA samples. Those samples, along with updated forensics, led us back to Ridgway."

"Did she suffer much?" I had asked, not really wanting to know the answer.

He paused a long time. "He beat her pretty bad, probably because he got frustrated?"

"Frustrated?" I asked.

"Mrs. Myles, you have to understand. He was trying to have ... relations with her. But she fought him off to the very end. She denied him the physical and psychological reward he was looking for."

That's my Charlotte Lueese, I thought to myself.

Helfelman continued. "I'm not a doctor. But I do know the body has its ways of dealing with pain. Sometimes it just shuts down. It just goes into a trance until things get better, or worse."

Worse was what the doctors had reported in those final days before her death. Somehow, she had willed herself into a few seconds of consciousness to give the nurse my number. She wasn't feeling *dizzy*. She was trying to call out to *Kizzy*, her best friend, the one to whom she needed to say goodbye.

The nurse didn't call back because Charlotte Lueese Cooper, unidentified patent #97937, had died the next day.

We laid Charlotte Lueese to rest in one of the two gravesites she and I had bought together at Paradise Cemetery on the north side of town. One day, I would join my best friend next to the big white mausoleum, under the cool of the oak trees. We would smell the sweat wild flowers and listen to the wind call our names. Maybe then, she would tell me the whole story.

****

On Christmas Day, sitting next to the fireplace, oblivious to the frosty northern ice glaze that covered the ground, we laughed again. Among the many gifts stacked under Lizzy's huge ten foot tree was a small shoe box wrapped in radiant oranges, reds and greens. When I opened it, I found a t-shirt and a diaper. The t-shirt read: PROUD GRANDMA.

"De diaper," Ububee explained, "is to get you some practice in changing his wet behind."

"Her wet behind," corrected Lizzy, who was three months pregnant. They had agreed to wait until the child was born to find out whether it was a girl or boy.

I finally stopped crying long enough to change into my new t-shirt. I didn't want another moment to pass without spreading the good news.

Afterwards, we jumped into Ububee's van and rode over to Estelle's house. She stuffed us with more turkey, dressing, mincemeat pie and eggnog before baiting us into helping her pack. This was her last Christmas at her Sunnyside home. She and Bishop Ebenezer had a special New Years Eve wedding ceremony planned. They had made a vow before God to enter the new year as husband and wife.

The next morning at breakfast, Ububee complained about misplacing his wallet. With all the gift bags, scattered boxes and strips of wrapping paper covering the floor, we didn't know where to start.

It wasn't until later that afternoon, when they brought me back home, that I found his wallet in one of my gift bags. The contents had spilled out, covering my new pink house shoes with money, credit cards, and assorted pictures of Lizzy, me, his African reunion family, and of course, his two renegade uncles.

There was something else.

Folded neatly between a stack of old receipts was a short article from a South African Newspaper. It read:

LAST WEEK, A PROMINENT SOUTH AFRICAN BUSINESSMAN WAS GUNNED DOWN OUTSIDE HIS ESTATE IN THE KWAZULU HOMELAND. AUTHORITIES SAID THAT Y. HOTTA GOWON, A DIAMOND TRADER AND FORMER NIGERIAN COUNTRYMAN WAS FOUND DEAD AT THE WHEEL OF HIS MERCEDES, WITH THE MOTOR STILL RUNNING. BECAUSE NO PERSONAL EFFECTS WERE TAKEN, AUTHORITIES HAVE RULED OUT ROBBERY AS A MOTIVE. WITH NO SUSPECTS IN CUSTODY, SPOKESPERSONS FOR THE AFRICAN NATIONAL CONGRESS ATTRIBUTE THE INCIDENT TO A LAST MINUTE EFFORT BY THE AFRIKAAN RULING NATIONAL PARTY TO SABOTAGE THE DISMANTLING OF APARTHEID. THE PARTY HAS DENIED ALL CLAIMS OF INVOLVEMENT....

There it was in black and white ... his mystery trip to Johannesburg.

For a long time I sat there, gripping the article in my hand. It was like holding a stick of dynamite with the fuse already lit. How was I going to tell Lizzy that her husband, the father of my grandchild -to-be, was a murderer? Even if he didn't pull the trigger, he was involved. He was just as guilty.

I thought about Moses, fleeing from Egypt after he had killed a man with his bare hands. And then there was King David who murdered Bathsheba's husband by sending him to the front lines. Eventually, I remembered my own, quiet, unassuming sweet-as-pie grandfather. Before Aunt Twigg died, she told me he had killed a white man and buried him in the woods.

"Why would grandpa do something like that?" I had asked.

"Because the man raped your oldest sister, Mattie," she had revealed. "He raped her and laughed about it."

Still, it wasn't right. Murder wasn't right no matter how you looked at it. I wanted to condemn Moses and David and Grandpa and now Ububee. I wanted to send them off to hell with one fell swoop. But as I caught a glimpse of Charlotte Lueese's glass picture frame, hanging on the wall, I realized if I sent them, I would have to go too.

In those early weeks after Charlotte Lueese's funeral, I ached for a chance to meet this Green River killer face-to-face. I would've told him how much Charlotte Lueese meant to me and described, in painstaking detail, the fourteen years of untold agony he had caused. And then I would've introduced him to my pearl-handled friend. I would've emptied every ounce of poisonous lead into to his wretched soul. And then I would've walked away.

I realized this kind of Christian thinking did not come with the territory. But the thought of her innocent blood, spilling into a muddy ditch alongside a dark, abandoned highway overpowered my fragile obligation to righteousness. I wanted him to receive his just recompense, not only in hell where he was surely headed, but on earth where the rest of mankind could see. In my heart, I was a murderer too.

... Outwardly you appear righteous unto men, but inwardly you are full of hypocrisy.

Pastor Fordham had been right. Even if I chose to ignore him, the heathens of the world wouldn't let me rest. They berated our double standard of righteousness and called our religion a sham. And who could blame them.

At that very moment, Christians all over the world were doing what I was doing. They were putting on their holy face, condemning everyone else's sins and justifying their own. I had a right to kill Gary Ridgway. But Ububee needed to go to hell. That was my distorted reasoning. That would've been my flimsy defense before God's throne.

At that moment the phone rang. Lizzy was on the other end. "Mama, have you had a chance to look for U's wallet. This man is about to drive me insane."

"It was in a shoe box," I informed her.

She immediately yelled to him in the other room.

She continued. "I hope you weren't offended because I waited this long to tell you about the baby? I just wanted to wait until the time was right." And then her voice dropped to a whisper. "I'm going to let you in on a little secret. At my last check up, I overheard the doctor talking to the nurse. I'm having triplets, Mama. Three for the price of one."

"My God, Lizzy. That's unbelievable!"

Still whispering, she reported, "I'm not telling U just yet. I don't want him to freak out at all the responsibility coming his way."

"Afraid he'll join Martha Marie's husband over at the Road Runner Inn?"

We both laughed, hysterically.

"That's the least of my worries, Mama. U is a wonderful husband. He's not perfect. But then, who is?"

I looked into the dining room mirror to gaze at the brittle image of the old would-be murderer, sitting at the table, hiding her callous brand of larceny, deep inside her heart. I had tried to assemble my own high court of righteousness. But in the end, there was no one worthy to serve as judge.

Slowly, I took my free hand and slid the article, photos and credit cards back into Ububee wallet. And then I confessed with comfort and relief. "Perfection left and went to heaven. But don't you worry, he'll be back one day."

"That's beautiful, Mama. I love you. Merry Christmas."

"I love you too, Lizzy, loud mouth and all. Merry Christmas."

We both held on, silently cherishing the tenderness of our lifelong bond. Finally, we hung up the phone.

We ended 1993 laughing. A small group of friends and well-wishers gathered at Greater Pilgrim Holiness Tabernacle for Estelle's New Year's Eve wedding. Toward the end of the ceremony, Bishop Ebenezer dropped the ring. When he bent over to pick it up, he split his white trousers right down the crouch.

I couldn't resist the opportunity. The moment I spotted those ugly red and yellow boxer drawers, I stood up in denominational scorn and bellowed, "Dust rag, huh? Oh zuskesrter, seuzeeha, melika, kuros!" That was to let Estelle know that God had pulled the covers off the Holiness crowd and given favor to the Baptists.

The whole building roared with laughter. And then the starry-eyed couple finished with, "I DO".

With a long, slobbery kiss, they became man and wife.

It was at that moment we heard the horn's melodious sound. A lone saxophone screamed for the parking lot outside. Ububee got up from his seat to investigate. But I waved him off. There was no need to interrupt a beautiful serenade, streaming in from the cold, starlit night.

And so, we sat there, quietly, reminiscently, soaking in the last minutes of an extraordinary year gone by. And then, just as unpredictably as it had begun, the soothing melody tapered off and faded into the night.

**************THE END**************

FEEDBACK

One of my personal joys in writing is the opportunity to hear directly from readers and fans. My driving philosophy is simple: "Satisfy your readers and everything else will fall into place." I am eternally grateful to know that I am achieving this goal, or that you care enough to tell me when I fall short.

Contact him at: adgrogan@groganbooks.com

This is important: If you enjoyed this book, please, please leave a review. This helps future readers to make an initial decision about the book's quality, and supports my effort to provide you with the extraordinary reading experience you deserve.

BOOKS BY LEANDER JACKIE GROGAN

Orange FingerTips

Exorcism At Midnight

Baby, Put That Gun Down

Layoff Skullduggery: The Official Humor Guide

King Juba's Chest [Not yet released]

Black Church Blues

Help! The Bible Gobbled Up My Big Sister [Not yet released]

What's Wrong With Your Small Business Team [Nonfiction Bestseller]

CPSIA information can be obtained
at www.ICGtesting.com
Printed in the USA
BVOW03s1310171017
497906BV00001B/10/P